THE
ANNIVERSARY

THE ANNIVERSARY
COLE BAXTER

bookouture

Published by Bookouture in 2024

An imprint of Storyfire Ltd.
Carmelite House
50 Victoria Embankment
London EC4Y 0DZ

www.bookouture.com

ISBN: 978-1-83525-235-2
eBook ISBN: 978-1-83525-234-5

ONE

"Tom." Catherine's voice faltered slightly. "Could you maybe slow down a bit? I'm feeling a little dizzy." Her words came out softly and slightly slurred to her ears.

By the way Tom was driving, Catherine knew he was attempting to shave off a few extra minutes from their journey. She glanced at him nervously as the rhythmic whoosh of passing scenery enveloped them. His salt and pepper hair was swept back from his forehead in an elegant cut and his narrow blue eyes were focused on the road with determination. He was in his element behind the wheel. At least Catherine imagined he felt that way. Tom did everything with determination.

Her husband's brow wrinkled in concern as his icy blue gaze turned toward her. "It must be the mix of the champagne and your medication." He continued to look at her instead of the road, which caused her even more anxiety. "You really shouldn't have had any," he murmured with a slight smile touching his slender lips, "but don't worry, dear. I know these roads like the back of my hand. Besides, the interstate is nearly empty at this hour. I'll get you home fast so you can settle down." He turned his gaze back to the road as he added, "I would offer an antacid, but they're all at home. Just hang on."

Her heartbeat picked up as Tom's foot pressed against the accelerator, the car surging forward. The speedometer climbed steadily, the numbers blurring together. Catherine's fright grew, her brows furrowing as she realized they were going significantly faster than the posted limit of seventy. The needle was wavering between ninety-five and a hundred, and this set her teeth on edge. Catherine's initial sense of elation at the evening out waned. The expensive champagne, which had initially added to the festivities, now swirled within her stomach like an unpredictable storm. She shifted in her seat, her fingers gripping the armrest, as there was nothing else to hold on to.

The city lights streaked past them in a blur, creating a disorienting tapestry of colors. Catherine forced a smile, attempting to appear unaffected even though he probably wouldn't notice in the darkened car, but her grip on the armrest tightened. She'd only had the one small glass of champagne to please him. He had gone to so much trouble to celebrate their fifth anniversary.

"I will, but slowing down still might help. Or maybe pull over? I think I need some fresh air."

Tom's thin smile didn't leave his lips as he gently patted her hand. "Trust me, we'll be home in no time. You're in the most capable hands. Just hang on for an hour."

That was a bit worrying in itself. Eldon, the town they lived in, was nearly two hours from Cincinnati where they were coming from. It was a tiny little rural town in southern Ohio with a population of about six hundred people. A town in which Tom, a lawyer, was one of the most prominent and well-respected leaders. Everyone deferred to him, trusted him.

The moonlit trees and shadowy fields out the window created a surreal tableau that offered her a momentary distraction from her discomfort in the passenger seat. Catherine forced

another smile, though her apprehension and slight feeling of
fright remained. She leaned back in her seat, her eyes fixed on
the road ahead. The wind whispered through the now partially
open window, as she tried to take in as much fresh air as
possible.

Tom merged the car onto the road that would take them to
Eldon. His foot pressed down harder on the accelerator, the car
responding with another surge of energy. The speedometer
needle climbed once more. Catherine's heart raced in tandem
with the car's speed, her fingers gripping the seat as if trying to
anchor herself. It was one thing to be going nearly a hundred on
the interstate and something different to be going that fast on a
narrow two-lane road.

"Tom!" Her voice was a mixture of urgency and concern.
"Please, can you slow down a bit?"

Tom's gaze remained fixed on the road, his grip on the
steering wheel unwavering. "Catherine, we're fine. I've got
complete control. Can you just shut up? I can't think straight
with you blabbing in my ear."

Catherine's anxiety grew, her next words a desperate plea.
"I know you're a skilled driver, Tom, but this is just—" her
sentence shifted into a gasp of surprise as she realized the
approaching danger.

But Tom didn't seem to notice the stop sign. Oblivious, he
continued driving, turning his head to stare at her.

"Tom, *stop!*"

Tom's eyes snapped to the road. He slammed on the
brakes, the tires screeching against the asphalt. The Camaro
skidded, the world beyond a blur of motion and panic. Time
seemed to stretch, a split second that held the weight of an
eternity.

The sickening sound of metal meeting metal shattered the
silence as the front of the Camaro collided with another vehicle
that had the right of way. Catherine's scream echoed in her ears.

"Catherine!" Tom shouted; his voice laced with desperation.

She couldn't answer as she slumped against the passenger door, and her normally wide eyes fluttered as pain shot through her. Smoke billowed from the wreckage, and there was shattered glass everywhere. As her eyes drifted closed, she wondered what had happened to the airbag and why it hadn't engaged.

"Catherine, wake up!"

TWO

Earlier that evening...

The warm hues of the setting sun painted the sky in shades of vibrant orange and dark pink as Tom and Catherine strolled away from the two-seater Camaro down the bustling Cincinnati streets, hand in hand. It was a momentous occasion—their wedding anniversary—a milestone that marked five years of shared laughter, tears, and endless love. Tom had decided they would celebrate it in style at the renowned Subito—a luxurious restaurant known for being a culinary haven with a charming ambiance and unique character.

As they approached the grand entrance of the restaurant, Catherine's heart swelled with anticipation. She had never been to any place quite as fancy as this as they usually kept to their small town of Eldon when they dined out. The exterior boasted a harmonious blend of modern design and a touch of rustic charm, drawing in her attention. Sleek, floor-to-ceiling windows graced the façade and offered a tantalizing glimpse into the vibrant world within. A delightful sidewalk patio extended in front, featuring wrought-iron tables and chairs adorned with plush cushions. Lush greenery, carefully arranged in ornate planters, added a touch of nature to the urban landscape.

Stepping through the opulent doors of Subito was like entering a realm of refined enchantment. The interior design was a symphony of modern elegance and timeless charm, carefully curated to provide an unforgettable dining experience. An impressive chandelier hung from the ceiling, casting a soft and inviting glow over the space, framed art pieces lined the walls, and the atmosphere was an exquisite blend of warmth, sophistication, and conviviality.

The host was the epitome of polished professionalism and genuine warmth. With a poised demeanor and a welcoming smile, he exuded an air of sophistication. A smile greeted them as they wandered closer toward him, and his eyes lit up with enthusiasm as they engaged in friendly conversation.

"Good evening. Would you be the Morris party of two?"

"Yes, we're here for our six o'clock reservation. It's for our fifth wedding anniversary."

Tom was always the first to speak up for the two of them. Catherine didn't mind. After all, it would save her draining her social battery before dinner. Over the last ten years, it had grown hard for her to trust and interact with new people. Despite knowing she only needed to speak with this new man once, it would remain socially taxing for her.

"Ah yes! I recall our conversation, Mr. Morris. If I may suggest, our lamb chops are exquisite this time of year. And I must recommend the calamari as an appetizer. It's the perfect palate cleanser."

"Thank you. We'll take your recommendations into account when we order. Lamb sounds like a lovely meal." Tom's voice exuded confidence.

Again, it did not bother Catherine that he hadn't consulted her on if she wanted the lamb to eat, and she knew he probably wouldn't before he ordered. Tom nearly always ordered for them both, and she had become used to it over the years.

"Perfect! Please, allow me to show you to our private dining area. I'm sure you will love the atmosphere of the oak room."

The host guided them to their table with grace. As they proceeded further into Subito, the main dining area unfolded before them in all its grandeur. The open kitchen allowed guests a captivating view of the culinary magic happening behind the scenes. Stainless steel surfaces gleamed, and state-of-the-art cooking equipment were a testament to the restaurant's commitment to excellence. Catherine watched as skilled chefs orchestrated their craft, creating gastronomic masterpieces with precision and artistry.

Tom extended his arm, guiding Catherine toward a small table in the secluded Oak Room. As they settled into their chairs, a sense of coziness washed over her. The intimate setting encouraged couples to draw closer, and the room's windows framed the outside world as a tranquil scene that provided a serene backdrop to the evening's festivities.

Catherine's fingers brushed against Tom's as they exchanged tender smiles.

"Happy anniversary, my love." His beautiful blue eyes held hers.

Catherine's gaze filled with curiosity as she stared back at him hoping to rekindle her love for him. "Happy anniversary, Tom. I can't believe it's been five years already."

Tom nodded, a small smile playing on his lips. "Time flies, doesn't it? But every moment with you has been a cherished memory, and I can't wait to see what the future holds for us." The timbre of his voice was deep and warm.

An impeccably dressed and dedicated server interrupted their intimate conversation. A warm smile graced his lips. "Good evening, Mr. and Mrs. Morris. All of us here at Subito are glad to have you as guests for such a wonderful celebration of love. My name is Clint, and I will be your server for the evening." With a delicate flourish, he presented the menus, beautifully bound books that promised a symphony of flavors and textures. "This is our menu. It contains well-thought-out lists of all the culinary delights our cooks can create. To begin, please allow me to guide you through our drinks list on the second to last page. Do either of you have anything in mind that you would like to start with?"

"What do you have for wine?" Tom asked.

Catherine looked at him with a frown. He was supposed to be the one driving tonight, and they'd already had some at home prior to coming here. Still, Tom was going to do what Tom wanted and Catherine sighed, knowing full well there was no telling him what he could and could not do. If he wanted to have a glass of wine, he would. She figured it would be absorbed by their meal in any case, so she shouldn't have to worry too much about it. If worse came to worse, she could always drive them home as she wasn't planning to drink.

"Well, our most popular are Riondo, Moët & Chandon Impérial, Mumm Napa, and Meranda-Nixon Catawba Estate. Do any of those pique your interest, Mr. Morris?" the server dutifully replied.

"I'm not too sure. What's the most expensive you carry?" Tom's electric blue eyes perused the menu.

He was clearly unaware of the shocked gaze Catherine was sending his way. Tom had never been a big spender. Quite the opposite, in fact. Catherine's eyes glossed over the menu with intent. She had become immensely interested in the prices, all of which she found to be way out of Tom's normal spending range. Some items didn't even have price tags, which usually meant if you had to ask, you couldn't afford it. What did Tom have up his sleeve? Sure, it was their anniversary, but to spend so much? Something was definitely going on.

"Ah, that would be our Nicolas Feuillatte. It is the best

champagne on our menu. They make it from brut rosé in France. It is a hundred dollars per six ounces. If you are curious about its taste, I've been told by many customers that it reminds them of a tropical vacation, and I'd have to agree. Would you like to try a glass, Mr. Morris?" The server tilted his head.

"No, no."

A wave of relief washed over Catherine.

"I would like a bottle for the table."

Catherine's eyes widened. Had Tom gone mad? This was nothing like the husband she had been married to for five years. Even in the years she'd known him before that, he'd never ordered anything so extravagant.

The server clasped his hands together, a wide smile forming across his pale face. "Of course, Mr. Morris. Is there anything else I can do for you? Appetizers?"

Tom waved the man off. "No. I think we would both like some time to peruse your menu. Thank you for the offer."

The server bowed and took his leave.

Catherine's mind was alive with curiosity. The intimate, luxurious ambiance of the restaurant now seemed suspicious, as if they'd been transported into a world of luxury that Tom surely had not meant them to have. At least, he never had before. What was he up to? A seed of doubt took root, casting a shadow over her mind that should have been filled with nothing but pure joy.

On the other side of the table, Tom had pulled out his phone and was typing away, sending a message to an unknown person, which wasn't unusual. Tom was always conducting some sort of business or answering the questions of various townspeople who phoned him or texted him for advice at all hours.

Catherine's wandering thoughts trapped her gaze on her normally cheap husband. The selection of the venue, the ordering of the expensive champagne, it didn't fit into the life she'd known with him. She couldn't help but feel a nagging sense of unease, and finally, she voiced her concerns.

"Tom." She kept her voice soft but determined. "Can we talk about something?"

Tom looked up from his phone, his dark brow arching slightly as he sensed the seriousness in her tone. "Of course, dear. What's on your mind?"

Catherine took a deep breath, trying to gather her thoughts. "Please don't take this the wrong way. I'm having a wonderful time, and I truly appreciate the effort you've put into making tonight special. But, well, I couldn't help but notice that the cost of that champagne is not what you would normally spend on such luxuries."

Tom's expression shifted from curiosity to understanding. He set his phone on the table and turned to face her fully. "I suppose it is odd for me to order something so above our means normally. Are you worried I can't afford it?"

Catherine nodded; her gaze fixed on the tablecloth. "Yes. I'm also a little worried about you. This isn't your normal behavior." She played with the fabric napkin, folding it between her fingers as she continued to avert her gaze. "I know this is a special occasion, but I wouldn't mind if you wanted to spend less. I mean, the gas price to get here alone must have been crazy. Do we even have the budget for all this?"

She continued to sit, waiting for him to answer, but Tom remained silent. Finally, she turned her head toward him and raised her eyes to find him staring at her with a smile and something unreadable in his eyes. As her gaze met his, his smile widened.

"I appreciate your concern, sweetheart. I should explain. My decision to celebrate here was made with careful consideration, and I've already taken everything into account, so don't worry your pretty little head over it. How about we just enjoy the evening? When the champagne arrives, you will have a glass to celebrate, and I'm sure that will go a long way to helping you enjoy the evening."

Catherine smiled, knowing he wouldn't answer her on the money subject any further. For now, she needed to dissuade her husband's next line of conversation. "I'm sure it would, but you know I can't have alcohol with my medication." Her forehead creased in worry as she bit her lip.

Tom's lips curled into a playful pout. "Ah, yes, your medication. Always impeding life's brief pleasures." He sighed and shook his head as his fingers tapped on the table.

Catherine chuckled. "It's not just about the medication, Tom. You know I'm a lightweight with alcohol, even without the meds."

Tom leaned forward, resting his sharp chin on his fist. "Darling, this isn't just any champagne. It's a celebration in a glass from France. A symphony of bubbles that dance a tropical tune on your tongue and whisk your worries away. You heard Clint, it's like joy in liquid form," he said, apparently trying to entice her into trying it.

Catherine raised an eyebrow; a hint of amusement filled her at his words, and she smiled. "Joy in liquid form, huh? You make it sound like some kind of happiness elixir."

He nodded, a humorous grin tugging at the corners of his lips. "Exactly! An elixir that can transform you from mundane to magical, if only for a moment. You'll have boundless amounts of fun. After all, I know it makes you more fun to be around." He sent a sly wink in her direction.

Her cheeks flamed. It didn't surprise her at all that Tom was probably planning to take advantage of her loopiness later if she were to mix the alcohol with her medication. There were certain things about her husband that she expected. Like his voracious sexual appetite. And not just with her—when she didn't exactly fall in line with his ideas, he went looking elsewhere.

The reminder of his infidelity left a sour note on her tongue. She didn't exactly love Tom anymore, but she was married to him, and she believed in her vows. She wanted to try to make things work, and he'd promised her he would be faithful after the last time. So Catherine gazed at him with a mixture of intrigue and caution. "You certainly have a way with words, Tom. But I shouldn't let your eloquence sway me this time. I already shared a glass of wine with you at home. That is more than I should ever have with this medication."

Tom feigned a dramatic sigh, placing a pale hand over his heart. "Catherine, sweetheart, you make it sound like I'm trying to lead you astray. All I want is for us to enjoy our anniversary to its fullest. Besides, I'm here at your side, what could actually go wrong other than you loosen up a bit? It's our fifth anniversary, darling, let's live a little." He reached for her hand and squeezed her fingers.

Catherine laughed. "You're quite the charmer, Tom. I'll give you that. Alright, I won't deny that this is a once-in-a-lifetime opportunity to taste joy in liquid form."

Leaning back in his chair, Tom regarded her with a victorious expression. As their animated conversation meandered to an end, Tom shifted slightly in his seat and leaned closer to Catherine. "Excuse me, darling, I need to use the men's room." He raised her hand and kissed the back of it before standing.

As Tom walked away, Catherine's gaze fell on his phone. A subtle curiosity tugged at the edges of her mind, the allure of exploring the digital realm of Tom's life becoming increasingly tempting. Who was he talking to all the time? And who was so important that he had to answer them tonight of all nights? Her fingers toyed with the fabric of the tablecloth, her thoughts momentarily divided between the present desire to look away and the potential secrets held within the phone before her.

Her gaze flickered to the phone once more, a surge of temptation flooding her senses. Her heart raced with the exhilaration of the forbidden, and with a mixture of anticipation and guilt, Catherine reached for the phone, her pulse quickening as her fingertips brushed against the smooth surface. As she held the device in her hands, a moment of hesitation washed over her. Did she really want to know who Tom had been texting with? Catherine set the phone back down, her sense of propriety ultimately prevailing over her curiosity.

But just as she was about to release the device, a soft vibration shook it in her fingers—the unmistakable alert of an incoming message. Catherine froze, her heart skipping a beat as her eyes widened in surprise. She focused her gaze on the screen; her internal struggle reignited. The message notification illuminated the screen, casting a soft glow on Catherine's features as she stared at it, torn between curiosity and the guilt that threatened to engulf her.

She glanced toward the bathrooms, then tapped the screen to see who had messaged her husband. Her heart dropped at the name that flashed on the screen for half a second. She regretted looking at it now. She drew her hand back, leaving the phone in its original position.

Tom returned, his smile warm and inviting as he took his seat next to her. "Everything okay, sweetheart?" His voice was laced with concern as he reached for her hand.

Catherine offered him a reassuring smile she didn't really feel at that moment. "Yes, everything's fine." She quickly decided not to let the woman's text ruin her evening with Tom and brightened her smile. "I was just lost in thought for a moment."

Tom nodded, his eyes lingering on her for a beat longer before their conversation resumed its natural flow. The waiter returned a moment later with the champagne, and Tom placed their dinner orders, opting for what the host had suggested when they'd first arrived. For the remainder of the dinner, Tom had put his phone away and focused solely on her, his loving gaze lingering on her throughout the meal. Despite the text message and the way her head swam from the champagne, Catherine felt it had been an amazing meal and one of the best nights she'd had in a long time.

"This has been wonderful, Tom," she murmured as they headed to the car.

Tom squeezed her fingers and tugged her a little, causing her to stumble. "Careful, now, sweetheart, the evening isn't over yet."

THREE

Catherine's consciousness slowly drifted back, like a swimmer rising to the surface of a murky pond. Her head felt heavy, her thoughts muddled, and her body was sore as if every muscle had been stretched to its limit. She groaned softly, her eyes fluttering open as she tried to make sense of her surroundings. A blinding light pierced through her squinted eyelids, and she instinctively raised a hand to shield her vision. The sharp ache that shot through her arm brought a surge of memories crashing in. The screeching tires, the blaring horn, the sickening sensation, and the sound of metal colliding with metal—it was all there, like a nightmare that refused to release its grip.

Catherine's heart raced as panic threatened to overwhelm her. She struggled to sit up, her breath coming in ragged gasps as she attempted to survey her surrounds, but nearly everything seemed fuzzy. The once pristine interior of Tom's car was now a twisted mess of broken glass, crumpled metal, and debris. Smoke wafted in from the cracked windshield, a ghostly haze that made her cough.

"Tom?" she croaked, her voice barely audible. Her gaze darted around, searching for any sign of him. And then she saw a figure outside the car. She thought it might be Tom, but he no longer looked like his elegant self; his torn and stained clothes clung to his body, and sweat and—was that blood?—matted his pitch-black hair as he stood illuminated in the streetlights. One arm cradled the other, which was bleeding, his shirt soaked crimson. She called out for him again.

He returned to the car in a few long strides, his pale fingers gripping her shoulders through the shattered driver's window with a strength that surprised her.

"What—?" Catherine started as she realized she was no longer buckled in.

But before she could finish, Tom pulled her toward the driver's seat. Her head throbbed as if in a vice, and her vision started to blur at the pain. Tom gripped her body, pulling her over further, sending another wave of shock and pain through her that caused her world to go black once again.

Catherine's senses slowly returned to her in fragments, but her consciousness continued to dance on the edge of reality. The world around her was a haze of fuzzy shapes and muffled sounds, like a disjointed dream that refused to coalesce. Her head throbbed with a relentless intensity, each pulse sending a jolt of pain through her body. Images of the accident—the twisted metal and shattered glass—replayed in her mind on an unabating loop, and as she lay on the stretcher, the pain in her body was a constant reminder of her vulnerability. As her vision gradually cleared somewhat, Catherine realized she was no longer in the car, but reclined on a stretcher. A fresh wave of uncertainty washed over her. What on earth had happened?

A uniformed police officer walked up to her, his expression stern and unreadable. A somber-faced paramedic stood quietly by his side. Catherine's heart skipped a beat as she watched them approach, her thoughts racing to make sense of their presence. Tom. Had something happened to Tom? She felt a heavy weight settle in her chest, a knot of anxiety that tightened with each passing moment.

She noticed a pair of handcuffs glinting in the officer's hand. Oh no. Were she and Tom being arrested for the accident? A sense of dread settled over her like a heavy shroud. She wanted to protest, to insist that she had done nothing wrong, but her words caught in her throat. She felt a surge of panic, a visceral fear that threatened to overwhelm her.

The paramedic was gentle as she guided Catherine's wrist to the side of the stretcher. The police officer then stepped forward, speaking words she couldn't understand, his movements deliberate as he placed the handcuffs around her wrist. She felt the cold metal against her skin.

Catherine's world was a fog of disorientation as she focused on the noises of the crowded street. It buzzed with life around her—the blare of a car horn, the chatter of paramedics, the distant hum of footsteps. But despite the cacophony of activity, Catherine felt an overwhelming sense of isolation. She couldn't move or defend herself, and her thoughts were a jumble of fears and doubts. And she still didn't know where Tom was. Was he in handcuffs too?

A sudden sound cut through the noise of the crash—a woman's voice, filled with desperation and anguish, screaming at someone to wake up. Catherine's heart leaped into her throat as she tried to look up. The woman's voice was a piercing cry, a plea that reverberated through the air like a banshee's scream. Catherine felt a surge of empathy for the woman, her heart aching at the rawness of her emotions.

"Wake up! Please, wake up!" shouted the woman desperately.

It was as if the woman's cries were a mirror reflecting the turmoil in Catherine's heart.

The air was thick with tension as the paramedics hoisted

Catherine into the ambulance. As she awaited the ride to the hospital, her mind was a whirlwind of madness. All of a sudden, her heart rate quickened as she picked up a conversation just outside. Tom. She could hear him speaking. He was okay.

"Good evening, sir," a measured voice began. "I'm Detective Sheldon. I want to discuss the events leading up to the crash. I'd like to hear your side of the story."

"Of course." Tom's voice was a mere whisper.

"Can you confirm you were present in the car with a Mrs. Catherine Morris at the time of the crash?"

"Yes, Catherine was with me." Tom's voice was remarkably steady.

"And can you tell me about your interactions with Mrs. Morris before the crash?"

Catherine felt a pang of sympathy for Tom, at what he would have to confess to. This was devastating.

"I tried to tell her to slow down, that I was feeling sick from the champagne we had at dinner. Catherine wasn't even supposed to be drinking. Her medication reacts poorly with it, but I couldn't stop her. She just doesn't listen to me, ever."

Catherine's world seemed to spin. What was he talking about? She recounted the moments leading up to the collision—the stop sign Tom had ignored, the car in the intersection, the screeching tires, the feeling of helplessness as the car careened out of control.

"And what was the nature of your words with Mrs. Morris during this time?" the detective inquired.

Catherine's thoughts swirled as she tried to recall their conversation. She remembered the adrenaline-fueled chaos of the moment. Tom looking over at her, ignoring the road as she'd asked him to reduce his speed. She remembered her voice, her urgency, her attempt to tell Tom to slow down. But the words that had passed between them felt like fragments, disjointed and incomplete.

"We were... we were arguing." Tom's voice was soft. "I remember telling her to slow down, to be more careful."

Catherine wanted to scream at the top of her lungs that he was lying, but the accusation was a shock, a betrayal that cut through her like a knife. She was speechless. She had trusted her husband, had believed that their shared experiences would forge an unbreakable bond. But now Catherine felt a sense of betrayal that left her reeling.

"And can you provide more details about this argument? What were the circumstances that led to it?"

"We were both stressed." Tom's voice tinged with regret. "She ignored my attempt to tell her to pay attention to the road and that there was a stop sign. Then we hit the other car. I think Catherine even tried to drive away from the scene, but I must have blacked out as I'm not sure what happened until you arrived."

"Mr. Morris, are you saying your wife was attempting to flee the scene of the crash?"

Catherine felt the knot in her stomach tighten as the weight of Tom's words settled in.

"Yes, I think so."

Catherine strained to hear her husband.

"She panicked."

"Let's go back to before the accident. Did Mrs. Morris heed your advice to slow down?"

Catherine's mind replayed the memory of Tom's aggression when she'd told him this very thing. She remembered the chaos, the cacophony of fear and adrenaline, the feeling of being trapped in a nightmare.

"She... She didn't listen." Tom's voice sounded strained. "She was drunk and just wanted to get home. I'm sure she didn't realize how fast she was going."

"Thank you for your honesty, sir. We're working to reconstruct the events of tonight, and your account will be an important piece of the puzzle."

Catherine had hoped that Tom sharing his side of the story would bring clarity, a sense of resolution. But now, as she sat in the cold, sterile ambulance, she felt anger, hurt, and confusion. And fear. Would the police believe him over her? She was in handcuffs, they clearly thought she was to blame. In a flash, she remembered Tom pulling her into the driver's seat, remembered the pain his grip produced, despite his bleeding arm. She suddenly realized that he was always going to blame her.

The moving ambulance was a screeching hell, the blaring of the emergency siren and the rhythmic beeping of machines providing a chaotic backdrop to Catherine's thoughts. She lay on the stretcher; her body still weary from the emotional and physical toll of the night. The weight of uncertainty lingered like a heavy cloud, casting a shadow over her consciousness. Catherine's mind was a landscape of conflicting emotions—the accusations, the betrayal, the echoes of Tom's words, which seemed to reverberate through every corner of her thoughts.

She closed her eyes, seeking a moment of reprieve. She had believed her bond with Tom would weather any storm. But now Catherine felt a profound sense of loneliness, a realization that even the strongest connections could fracture in the face of adversity. As the darkness of the night enveloped the area, she felt as though she were adrift in a sea of uncertainty, the waves of doubt and fear threatening to overwhelm her. And amidst the chaos of her thoughts, one question loomed large—how could she reconcile the accusations, the betrayal, with the person she had believed Tom to be?

FOUR

Catherine felt the gentle caress of sunlight filtering through her curtains, casting a warm glow across her room. She stretched languidly, a soft sigh escaping her lips as she relished the comforting hug of her soft bed. Slowly, she let her eyes flutter open, blinking away the remnants of sleep as she took in the familiar surroundings of her cozy sanctuary. As she swung her legs over the edge of the bed, her feet met the plush embrace of a soft rug. A contented smile graced her lips as she reveled in the sensation, a sense of tranquility washing over her.

Her room was a haven of pastel hues, adorned with delicate artwork and mementos that held cherished memories. Tom had ordered the walls to be painted a soothing shade of pale blue, reminiscent of a clear summer sky, and a soft, melodious tune played in the background, enveloping her in a cloak of serenity. With a graceful movement, Catherine rose from the bed, her limbs fluid as she embarked on her morning ritual.

The scent of freshly bloomed flowers filled the air as if nature itself had conspired to greet her awake. They infused the air with a delicate aroma that stirred her senses and seemed to beckon her onward. Making her way to the window, Catherine drew back the curtains, revealing a breathtaking view of a lush, vibrant garden. The dew-kissed petals of roses, daisies, and tulips glistened like precious gems, each bloom a blessing of her choice. Birds chirped merrily, their songs harmonizing with the gentle rustling of leaves in the soft breeze. Catherine's heart swelled with an overwhelming sense of gratitude as if the world had come alive solely to offer her a moment of enchantment.

Catherine headed to her vanity. She stood in front of the mirror, her skincare products laid out before her like an array of fragrant offerings. The morning light streamed through the window, illuminating the bottles and jars that held the promise of a glowing complexion. Annoyance tinged with curiosity danced in her eyes as she anticipated the sensory overload that lay ahead.

She gently splashed her face with cool water, the sensation awakening her senses further. She reached for a cleanser that boasted natural botanical extracts, promising a refreshing and revitalizing experience. After that would be an exfoliant, a toner, serums, and, finally, a moisturizer. The combination was undeniably luxurious, though used together, the different products created a cacophony of aromas that challenged her olfactory senses. Yet, she persisted, knowing that Tom's pleased demeanor would be worth the sensory journey.

He had said it was so she didn't develop any skin issues, but Catherine had concluded that Tom didn't want her to lose her youthful appeal. The thought sickened her—especially as she was only twenty-three—so instead she focused on the task at hand. With the skincare routine complete, Catherine stepped back from the mirror and took a deep breath. She could still detect traces of the various scents swirling around her. They had settled into an unharmonious blend, like the notes of an elementary school symphony that hadn't found their rhythm.

After pampering her skin, Catherine proceeded to her shared bedroom, which held a closet containing a treasure trove of elegant attire. Except that the closet was always locked, Tom picking out her clothing each day and leaving it—and only it—for her to wear. That day he had picked out a skin-tight, long-sleeved black dress. Catherine would have loved the choice for a fancy get-together despite the short skirt length. However, she knew she was to stay within the walls of her home. Tom had decided it was best for her to focus on house chores today. That meant no outside contact with anyone and no daily allowance. Catherine let out a huff of frustration. Still, her fingers danced over the thin fabric, whispering promises of comfort and style. However, as she slipped into the dress, she felt an instant transformation that wasn't welcome, as if the garment itself had the power to squeeze the life out of her.

With her formfitting attire donned, Catherine made her way to the kitchen, the aroma of freshly brewed coffee beckoning her forward. The nightmarish quality of her morning routine continued as she found a folded note atop a prepared mug of Tom's favorite coffee blend, the rich aroma enveloping her in an overpoweringly warm embrace. She discarded the note on the counter for later, not wanting to ruin her appetite for breakfast. The note was a list of his daily commands to complete before he came home, and she wanted nothing to do with the man any time soon.

The first sip of coffee sent a disgusted shiver down her spine, a moral moderation that seemed to melt away any lingering traces of sleepiness. As she focused on not sipping the coffee, Catherine wandered into the dimly lit living room, her heart heavy with a burden that seemed too great to bear. The morning's silence echoed the emptiness she felt inside, a void that had flourished over the years of her marriage to Tom. She gazed at the wedding picture on the mantelpiece, a snapshot frozen in time— a time when hope and love had prevailed over reason and doubt.

As the years had passed, she regretted the decision her father had made for her at the tender age of fourteen. Now, she felt trapped in a marriage she didn't desire, yet unable to escape because she had given up everything to marry the man her father had deemed appropriate for her. She had actually come to love Tom by the time they'd wed, though, at least she'd thought she had.

In the beginning, Catherine and Tom being together had seemed like a fairy tale—a whirlwind romance that everyone in town exclaimed over. Tom was charming, confident, and a successful lawyer—a man her father could be proud to call son.

Catherine hadn't known when she was fourteen that her father had approved of Tom's interest in her. All she'd known at the time was that Tom was a successful lawyer, and he'd taken an interest in her academically. He'd encouraged her to do well in school, and by the time she'd turned sixteen, they'd become good friends. Her father had passed away when she turned eighteen, leaving her alone in the world except for Tom.

They'd gotten engaged within six months of her father's death and married just after she turned eighteen. The early days of their marriage were no less enchanting. They had traveled to New York City for their honeymoon, dined at restaurants, and enjoyed a life of moderate luxury. Tom showered her with gifts and surrounded her with a circle of affluent friends. From the outside, their life together appeared idyllic—a picture-perfect couple basking in their happiness.

As time passed, however, Catherine noticed the cracks beneath the surface of their perfect life. Tom's demanding nature became more pronounced with each passing day. He was a man who had built his success on ambition and relentless pursuit of his goals, but that same drive spilled over into his personal life. He expected nothing less than perfection from Catherine, demanding that she be the ideal housewife—attending to his every need, managing the household flawlessly, and standing by his side at every social event.

Tom's controlling nature extended beyond the domestic realm. He often decided things about Catherine's life without consulting her, asserting his dominance in every way. Catherine felt suffocated, as if she were living in a gilded cage—trapped in a life that glittered on the surface but left her feeling isolated and unfulfilled as the years passed.

Catherine had once been an independent, ambitious girl with dreams and aspirations of becoming a lawyer herself. However, over time, Tom's demands had eroded her sense of self-worth and autonomy. She had given up the idea of a career, believing that supporting Tom's endeavors was her new purpose. Yet, as the years passed, she realized she had sacrificed too much of herself. The more she acquiesced to Tom's demands, the more he seemed to take her compliance for granted. She had become a shadow of the vibrant girl she once was, her dreams buried beneath the weight of her husband's expectations. The confident, self-assured Catherine of her youth had vanished, replaced by a woman who questioned her own worth and capabilities.

In addition to this... The knowledge that leaving Tom was simply not an option exacerbated Catherine's inner turmoil. Since her father's death, she had become financially dependent on him. Tom was the one making an income, leaving Catherine to feel helpless, as though he'd trapped her in an inescapable power dynamic.

She had no income of her own, no career to fall back on, and no support system outside the circle of Tom's acquaintances, except for maybe her friend Donna. The fear of the unknown held her back, as did the fear of becoming homeless. Leaving Tom meant relinquishing the security that he provided. Catherine had become ensnared in a web of dependence and expectations, making the prospect of escape seem like an unattainable dream.

. . .

Catherine slowly opened her eyes. The sterile scent of disinfectants permeated the air, and the soft beeping of machines echoed in the background. The bright lights of the hospital room pierced her wide eyes, causing her to squint as she tried to make sense of her surroundings. Her head felt heavy, and a dull ache throbbed through her body. As the fog of unconsciousness lifted, Catherine's mind pieced together the events leading up to her hospitalization—the blurring roads, the screeching of tires, the missed stop sign, and the crunch of metal.

Panic washed over her as she remembered she had been in a car crash. She could feel her body had been left bruised and battered, her skin a canvas of pain and healing, the worst of it surrounding her shoulders and breasts. As she lay in her hospital bed, she realized the tender spots that dotted her body —the souvenirs of the accident that had shattered her world. Each bruise told a story of impact, of force meeting flesh, and of the fragility of life.

Catherine tried to sit up in the small hospital bed, but her body was still too sore. It throbbed with pain as she waited patiently for one of the staff to notice she was awake. The memory of the accident was a little hazy in places, and she hoped someone could provide her with some clarity. But as the door swung open, her anxiety heightened as she saw the stern expressions on the faces of the two police officers who entered, walking with purpose. They identified themselves as officers Anderson and Rogers. Their uniforms were crisp, and their badges gleamed under the harsh fluorescent tubes. Catherine felt like a deer caught in headlights, unsure of what to expect from their appearance in her room. She clutched her bandaged arm and looked between them.

"Mrs. Morris, we need to ask you some questions about the car accident." Officer Anderson's voice was firm and accusatory.

Catherine's mind raced as she tried to recall the details of the collision, but her memories remained elusive due to the tranquilizers coursing through her veins. She felt disoriented and overwhelmed, the pressure of the situation bearing down on her.

"I... I remember little." Her voice trembled and sounded weak to her ears. "Where is my husband? Is he okay?" Surely Tom could sort this out. He was a lawyer, plus he was friends with the sheriff and his deputies.

Officer Rogers exchanged a glance with his partner, a hint of skepticism in his hazel eyes. "We'll get to that, ma'am. Right now, we need you to tell us what happened before the accident. Did you see anything unusual on the road? Were you under any influence?"

Catherine tried to think back, but the events leading up to the crash were a jumble of disjointed images. She shook her head, frustrated by her inability to provide simple answers. "I don't remember. I was so sick, and then suddenly Tom was speeding..." Her voice trailed off, and she frowned as she recalled hearing her husband say at the scene that he hadn't been the one driving, that he had blamed her for everything. These police officers were under the impression she had been driving the car.

Officer Anderson leaned forward, his expression intense. "Mrs. Morris, we need you to try harder to remember the truth. Don't lie to us, it's not going to go well for you if you do. Your drunken behavior caused a serious collision, and we need to determine what happened because an innocent woman is dead."

Catherine's heart pounded in her chest. The officers' accusatory tones only added to her confusion and distress. "Please, I remember very little of the accident. I wasn't even driving. I'm not allowed to drive on my medication. Tom always drives." She squinted, attempting to escape the absolute need for rest. "Tom... he can tell you." Perhaps last night her husband had panicked in the moment. Surely by now he would have come to his senses.

Officer Rogers let out a sigh, growing annoyed. "We understand you're worried about your husband's well-being, but we need you to cooperate. We found you in the driver's seat last night, so what do you mean you weren't driving? And can you think of anything, anything at all, that might help us understand what happened?"

Catherine's mind searched desperately for any piece of information that could be relevant. She remembered the sound of screeching tires, the sight of the shadowy road through the windshield, and the car in the intersection. But the details were still too fuzzy to form a coherent picture. "I'm trying, but everything is so jumbled in my head." Her voice was tinged with frustration.

As her mind reeled from the emotional turmoil of the police interrogation, a gentle knock on the door interrupted her thoughts. Before she could respond, it opened, and a warm smile greeted her.

"Hello, Mrs. Morris. My name is Margaret, I'll be your nurse. I'm here to check in on you." As the nurse glanced around the room, her chocolate-brown eyes narrowed as they landed on the presence of the two officers, a hint of annoyance on her face as she approached them. Her demeanor was polite but firm as she addressed them. "Excuse me, Officers, but what are you doing in here? You were told the patient needs to focus on her recovery, not deal with stressful interrogations. She's in a vulnerable state and needs time to recover. The questioning can wait until she's in a better condition. She's not going anywhere in her state."

Catherine was immediately put at ease.

Anderson glanced at Rogers before turning back to the nurse. "We understand your concern, Nurse, but we need to gather information while it's still fresh in her mind. The sooner we can solve this case, the better."

Margaret crossed her arms, her stance unwavering. "I know your investigation is important, but Mrs. Morris's health and well-being are my priority. She's just been through a traumatic experience, and your accusations will cloud her anxious and recovering mind in such a way that she will agree to anything. I'm sure you want your investigation to be truthful and not questioned by the medical society, seeing as if you push this right now, I will be more than happy to make sure there is a medical inquiry as well, and I'm sure it will put you both in a bad light."

Officer Rogers stepped forward, trying to defuse the tension. "We don't mean to add to her stress, but we need her cooperation to sort this out. The sooner we can find out what happened, the sooner we can find closure for everyone involved."

Margaret took a deep breath, her brown eyes unwavering. "I hear you, but she's not in a position to provide the information you're looking for right now. We haven't even fully assessed all her injuries. She's disoriented, emotionally overwhelmed, and asking about her husband, who she cannot see at the moment. I think it's best if you come back at a later time when she's more able to cooperate."

"Okay, fine, we'll back off for now. But we'll need to talk to her again once she's in a better state."

Margaret nodded. "Thank you. I'll let you know when Mrs. Morris is ready for further questioning."

As the officers walked away, Margaret returned to Catherine's side with a reassuring smile. The evening sun dipped below the horizon, casting a warm glow over the hospital room. Catherine lay in her bed, her body tender from the car crash. The pain medication and tranquilizers had worn off, leaving her in discomfort. The police interrogation had added to her emotional turmoil.

"Sorry about that, Mrs. Morris." A soothing smile crossed Margaret's face. "You look like you're feeling uneasy. Let's get you some rest and relief from the pain. How about I help you into a more comfortable position?"

Catherine nodded gratefully as the nurse adjusted her pillows and elevated her bed.

She gently placed a hand on Catherine's shoulder, offering a reassuring touch. "Now, you need to rest and allow your body to heal. Sleep will help you feel better and give your body the time it needs to recover."

"I know, but I'm just so anxious. The pain is getting worse, and I can't stop thinking about everything that happened." Catherine's voice was filled with exhaustion and worry.

"It's completely normal to feel this way after such a traumatic event. Your mind and body need time to process everything. Let's see if we can ease your anxiety too. The doctor has ordered some pain relief I can give you via your IV. That's if you would like to try that."

Catherine nodded, agreeing. "I think I'd like that. I can feel the bruises. Is anything broken?"

"You've got a few broken ribs, your arm is sprained, you've dislocated and bruised your shoulder, and you also have some massive bruising across your chest, stomach, and hips."

Catherine frowned. "You told the officers I hadn't been fully assessed, though."

The nurse smiled and nodded. "I did indeed. They don't know otherwise," she murmured, picking up the syringe and sticking it in a vial. She turned back and plunged the needle into a piece of plastic attached to the IV cord leading to Catherine's arm.

Catherine felt a coolness invade her veins.

"Would you like me to turn the lights off?" Margaret asked.

"Yes, please," Catherine replied as she felt the pain starting to dull. Her eyes began to drift shut.

"Rest now, and I'll be back to check on you after a while." Margaret hit the lights, dimming the room so that only the glow of the computer screen illuminated it.

Catherine nodded, but her eyes were already closed as she heard the click of the door.

FIVE

Two days since the anniversary

Catherine woke to find herself surrounded by the sterile white walls of the hospital room. She tried to remember why she was there, but her mind was a blank canvas, painted over with confusion and uncertainty. The throbbing ache in her head intensified as she tried to sit up more, but a sharp pain in her side stopped her. She glanced down to see a bandage wrapped around her chest, and slowly, the memories trickled back. She was in the hospital because of a car accident, wasn't she? However, other details were hazy, like fragments of a broken mirror, reflecting distorted images.

As her senses adjusted to the surrounding reality, she realized she wasn't alone as a nurse passed by her doorway.

Catherine cleared her throat, her voice weak and scratchy. "Excuse me, Nurse. Can you please tell me where I am? And what happened to my husband?"

The nurse, whose name tag read "Emma," turned around with a kind smile. "Oh, you're awake. You're at Ohio Valley Medical Center. I'm sure you're worried about your husband.

You were both in a terrible car accident, but don't worry; you're both safe now."

"He's okay? Oh, thank you so much for telling me." Catherine's brows smoothed as she relaxed into the hospital bed.

"Do you need anything? Are you in pain?" Emma's professional demeanor was softened by a touch of compassion.

"I do hurt, but I think I'm alright for now. Can I see Tom, please?" Catherine's voice filled with longing.

Emma hesitated for a moment, exchanging a brief glance with another nurse who had come into the room. "I'm sorry, but Tom doesn't want to see you right now." Her baby blue eyes filled with sympathy.

Catherine felt as though someone had doused her with icy water. "What do you mean he doesn't want to see me? Is he okay?"

Emma sighed softly. "He's physically fine, but emotionally, it's been tough on him. The accident and the other driver's death were traumatic events, and he needs some space from you and"—she hesitated—"well, what he called 'your behavior.'"

Tears welled up in Catherine's eyes, but she blinked them away, refusing to show weakness. The accident had taken its toll on her memory, leaving gaps and fragments that refused to fit together, but she remembered hearing Tom blaming her for the accident. He obviously hadn't come clean yet.

Her mind became a battleground of swirling thoughts and uncertainties, and a nagging doubt emerged—what if she *was* the one driving? The question gnawed at her conscience, like a persistent itch she couldn't scratch. She tried to push the thought away, dismissing it as a product of her fractured memories. Yet the doubt persisted, growing louder with each passing second.

She grappled with the question, seeking any glimpse of clarity that would dispel her doubts. The two officers who had visited her the last time she was awake had said she was the driver, but she knew that couldn't be true. She never drove. Or very rarely did, at any rate.

Now, sitting alone in her hospital room, she tried to focus on the moments leading up to the accident. Had she been driving? She recalled having the thought earlier in the evening that she might have to if Tom drank too much, but had he? She didn't think so, but what if she was wrong?

Rubbing her temple, she focused on the trip home that night. She could hear herself arguing with Tom, heard their raised voices, but the details of who was behind the wheel remained obscured. She couldn't place either of them in the car.

Frustration and anxiety bubbled within her as she attempted to unravel the tangled web of memories, and as she tried to force herself to remember, other forgotten memories returned like echoes from the past, including unsettling recollections. She couldn't ignore the memories that were coming back to her—moments when Tom had manipulated her perceptions, twisted her reality, and made her doubt her thoughts and feelings. She remembered instances where Tom had invalidated her experiences, undermined her emotions, and made her question her own sanity. She had always tried to please Tom, first as a girl of fourteen who hero-worshiped him, and then later because he was her husband, and because he loved her and looked after her so well. He was older than her and, as he always said, he knew best. The times she disagreed with him, it didn't seem worth raising. Besides, he could have a temper when things didn't go his way. But she had always thought he'd had her best interests at heart.

Lying in her hospital room, she admitted to herself that Tom had frequently manipulated her throughout their nine-year relationship. Who was to say that he wasn't doing this now? That he wasn't attempting to manipulate everyone—and everything—involved in this incident.

The soft hum of the hospital machinery and the occasional

murmur of nurses outside were the only sounds that filled Catherine's room. She had lost herself in thought, reflecting on her experiences and Tom's lies, when the door swung open, revealing a muscular figure in a crisp suit. Catherine's heart skipped a beat as her eyes settled on the man standing in the doorway. It was immediately clear that he was a police officer, despite the fact he was wearing a suit and not a uniform. She vaguely recalled seeing him before, but she wasn't sure where.

"Good afternoon, Mrs. Morris," he began, his tone calm and assertive. "I'm Detective Alan Sheldon. Your nurses say it might be hard for you to talk too much, but that I could ask you some questions if you were feeling up to it. Before I begin, are you feeling well enough to do so?"

Catherine's mind raced, and her heart pounded against her chest. "Of course, Detective."

Detective Sheldon sat down in the chair for guests, his chestnut brown eyes assessing her. He had an aura of experience that seemed to seep from his every pore. Catherine's thoughts flitted back to the accident, her memories still fragmented and tangled.

"Did someone really die in the car crash, Detective?" Catherine's voice was steady despite the anxiety churning within her. She knew she had to share her recollection of the car accident before it was too late, revealing the truth—that Tom had been driving during the collision. She was positive about that now.

Detective Sheldon's voice was calm and reassuring. "Do you think you can handle the answer to the question you're asking, Mrs. Morris? You can ask me anything, as long as you feel you can handle the answer. Your mental state is very important while I'm questioning you. If at any time you feel you need to take a break, never hesitate to tell me."

Catherine gripped the hospital sheets. "I... I need to know if the car crash killed anyone."

There was a brief pause, an uncomfortable silence that stretched on for what felt like an eternity. Finally, the detective spoke, his tone gentle but hesitant.

"Mrs. Morris, I understand your need for answers, and I'll be honest with you. Yes, there was a fatality caused by the accident."

Catherine felt as if the ground had shifted beneath her feet, her breath catching in her throat as she recalled the woman's voice from that night shouting at someone to wake up. The weight of Detective Sheldon's words left her shaken. She hadn't been prepared for the confirmation, and her mind struggled to process it. Her voice trembled as she forced out the next question that had jumped forward in the line of questions she had about that night. "Who... who was it? Who was killed?"

Detective Sheldon seemed to measure his response carefully before speaking. "It was a passenger in the other vehicle, Mrs. Morris. A young woman who was at the wrong place at the wrong time, just like you."

Catherine's heart ached at the thought of a young life cut short. She felt a surge of guilt and sorrow that she couldn't quite put into words. The reality of the consequences of the accident hit her with a force she hadn't expected. "Oh my gosh." Catherine's voice quivered with emotion, tears welling up in her eyes. "I can't believe any of this is happening. Who was she?"

Detective Sheldon's tone remained compassionate. "I understand, Mrs. Morris. Her name was Melissa Legrasse."

Hearing the young woman's name made everything even more tragic. She wished she hadn't asked as she felt tears slip down her cheeks.

"Now, it's important to remember that we're working to uncover the truth behind what happened, Mrs. Morris, but first I need you to tell me what you know. Is there anything you can remember?"

Catherine had been grappling with her doubts, but the

reality of another person's life lost cast a shadow over everything. She wished she could turn back time and undo the events that had led to that fateful collision. "As I told the other officers, I don't remember a whole lot. We'd gone to Cincinnati for dinner. It was our fifth anniversary. Tom insisted on us having champagne. I hadn't wanted any because of my medication, but he persisted, and I gave in. I wasn't feeling well when we got on the interstate, and Tom was going so fast. I... I asked him to slow down." Catherine shook her head, trying to piece it all together. "Everything is jumbled." She raised a hand to her forehead, which was pounding again.

The detective's eyes narrowed, and he frowned at her.

"Detective Sheldon." Catherine was filled with heavy remorse as she thought about the woman whose life was gone. "I'm sorry, but can I talk to Tom? I want to see if we can do something for the young woman's family. Did she have family?"

The detective didn't say anything as he stared at her, a look of speculation on his face which made her uncomfortable. Finally, he spoke, his tone measured.

"I apologize, Mrs. Morris, but you can't speak to your husband. He is the primary accuser in this case. He claims you were the one driving the car and that your actions caused the accident."

Catherine had known that Tom had said she was driving, but to hear that he hadn't corrected himself was a betrayal worse than when she'd realized he'd been unfaithful to her throughout their marriage. She couldn't wrap her head around the fact that he would do this. That he would lay the blame for that young woman's death on her. Tears flowed faster down her cheeks as she met Detective Sheldon's gaze.

"Tom is saying that I was driving? But I wasn't. I don't understand. What am I supposed to do?" The weight of her husband's accusations threatened to suffocate her. She had done nothing wrong, but it felt like someone had pulled the ground out from under her. Catherine wiped at her tears, her emotions raw and exposed. That anniversary dinner was supposed to be a new start for them, but this... "I thought we were on a path toward healing, toward rebuilding our relationship. But now... now it's like everything is unraveling." Another wave of panic swelled within her. Her breathing grew shallow, and she felt as though the walls were closing in, as though she was losing control of her mind.

Catherine's therapist had equipped her with techniques to manage her anxiety when she was first diagnosed with Social Anxiety and Panic Disorder, as well as Major Depressive Disorder (MDD), and as panic tightened its grip, she tried to focus on her breathing. But the panic attack was relentless, its intensity growing with each passing moment. Catherine's breaths came in short, rapid gasps as her panic escalated. The room seemed to spin around her, and she clutched at the edges of her bed, desperate for an anchor to reality.

Tears streamed down her face as she fought to regain control. Everything outside her window seemed distant, and the darkness that had clouded her mind felt all-encompassing. Catherine's thoughts spiraled into an abyss of fear and doubt. She had been through this before—she knew the signs of a panic attack. But this time, the emotions were more intense, the fear more palpable. She needed help, and she needed it fast.

Detective Sheldon looked concerned by her distress and got up and called for a nurse, and soon, a voice from the side of the bed spoke up in a calm and reassuring tone as she held a bottle under her nose that smelled like lavender. "Don't worry, Catherine. We're here for you. Take slow, deep breaths if you can."

But the panic had taken hold. Moments later, the door to her room swung open, and another nurse rushed in. Catherine took in both nurses' appearances. They were both clad in scrubs, their faces portraying concern and professionalism.

"Catherine, let's try the five, four, three, two, one method... Can you name me five objects in the room?" the nurse asked.

Catherine's vision swam. Everything was fuzzy and unfocused. She couldn't make out anything but blobs of things and that sent her heartbeat into overdrive. She began to sweat, and fear threatened to overwhelm her.

"She's not responding. We need to sedate her," a female voice said from her left.

Catherine noticed the blob of a person moving on her right. "Hi there, Catherine. You remember me? It's Emma." Her voice was calm, but Catherine was too deep into the attack to be soothed. "You're having a panic attack."

You think? She wanted to shout, but of course, there was no getting those words out. If there were, she wouldn't be in this position in the first place.

Emma continued. "We're going to give you a tranquilizer so you can calm down, okay?"

Catherine's whole body began to shake with the sweats, she felt a chill come over her and her teeth began to chatter as if she were freezing to death. She thought she nodded, but she wasn't sure if she actually did.

Emma's voice was soothing as she said, "It's okay, Catherine. You're safe here."

She guided Catherine to lie back on the bed, but Catherine fought her, she didn't want to lie down. It felt wrong as her body locked up and became almost rigid.

"I've got you, it's okay. We're going to make this stop." The blob of Emma turned to the other nurse. "Get that sedative in the IV now." The Emma blob stroked Catherine's hair and gently said, "Catherine, I want you to focus on your breathing, and this will all be over in three... two..."

The world faded to black once again.

SIX

Three days since the anniversary

The rain had been falling incessantly for hours, creating a persistent symphony of drops against the windows of the Ohio Valley Medical Center. The sterile white walls seemed to close in on her as Tom stood in the doorway of her hospital room, wearing an expression of distaste.

Catherine lay on her side, her lips pulled into a frown, her chest rising and falling rhythmically as she watched him through her eyelashes. Tom's electric blue eyes, which she'd once thought were so loving but now seemed icy cold, were fixed on her, his gaze unwavering. She knew if he could force her back to full health, he would do it in a heartbeat. She was of no use to him in her current state.

Doctor Matthews, a stern and bespectacled man in his fifties, had been Catherine's attending physician since the accident. She'd found him to be kind and gentle. He stood beside Tom, his light brown eyes wary as he studied her husband. "Mr. Morris." He adjusted his glasses. "I know this is a trying time for you, but your wife is not well. We must consider what's best for Catherine."

Tom's knuckles turned white as he clenched his pale fists. She could tell he was very angry, though his voice came out even and reasonable. "I know what's best for her, Doctor; she's my wife, and we've been dealing with her disorders for years now. She needs to be at home, surrounded by the things she loves. This hospital room is suffocating her."

He sounded so reasonable. As though he actually cared for her. Catherine doubted that was the reason he wanted her home. She didn't know what he was really after, but it wasn't to take care of her or make her life easier.

Doctor Matthews sighed, crossing his arms. "Mr. Morris, I understand your concerns about her mental health, but Catherine's condition is still critical. She's heavily injured and dealing with severe trauma to her chest and abdomen. Moving her could exacerbate her injuries and hinder her chances of recovery."

Tom's expression wavered with a mixture of frustration and desperation that made Catherine's heart rate kick up a little. Why wasn't he listening to the doctor? Why was he trying to move her?

"She wouldn't want to be here, hooked up to machines. She'd want to be in our home, with me, in our bedroom, with her favorite paintings on the wall."

The doctor's gaze softened slightly, and Catherine knew he was going to give in eventually. Tom was going to talk him around. It was what he did, and he was good at it. He had the accolades to prove it.

Still, for now, Doctor Matthews tried valiantly to sway him. "I empathize with your desire to create a comfortable environment for her, but we have the expertise and equipment here to provide the best care possible."

Tom's fists clenched and unclenched, and Catherine

watched his jaw tick. She knew he was angry. He would never back down. "Doctor, I won't just sit here and watch her waste away in this sterile prison-like environment. I'm taking her home." His voice was firm and brooked no argument.

Doctor Matthews shook his head with a sigh, and Catherine knew that was it. He was giving in. Stronger men than he had argued with Tom and lost.

"I strongly advise against that. You will be jeopardizing her chances of recovery; she needs a professional caregiver."

Tom's voice became even firmer as his eyes bore into Catherine. She had a feeling he knew she was awake. "I've decided, Doctor. I'm bringing her home, even if I have to do it against your wishes. I will hire a professional nurse to administer medication and look after the equipment, but I will be bringing my wife home as soon as possible."

Doctor Matthews sighed again. "Fine, Mr. Morris. If you're insistent, we'll make the arrangements and find a qualified nurse for you. However, I must reiterate that this is against medical advice."

Tom nodded, spun on his heel, and left the room without another look at her or the doctor.

Catherine could feel tears building. She didn't want to be moved. Tom had accused her of driving that car, and she didn't want to go with him. But she didn't feel as if she had a choice. After a little while of thinking about it, she decided it would be better to just pretend to be unaware of his manipulations. Maybe before she could be moved, the kind detective would step in and stop him from taking her from the hospital.

Despite her hopes, two days later, a medical team carefully transferred Catherine from the ambulance stretcher to the new hospital bed that Tom had installed in their downstairs guest room. Her body was a patchwork of bruises, her left arm was in a cast, her ribs were wrapped tightly, and her health was being supported by tubes and wires. It hurt to move, and her breathing was shallow due to the pain of the broken ribs.

The EMTs left after ensuring Catherine was stable in her new environment. Tom didn't say a word to her but spoke to the young, pretty nurse who flitted into the room. She fiddled with the IV line, and Catherine felt her eyes droop. She looked at Tom as he stood in the doorway, waiting until the nurse was finished. When she left, he merely flicked off the light to the room and wandered away after her as Catherine drifted back to sleep, the state she most preferred these days.

The midnight moon filtered through the curtains, casting a gentle glow over the room. Catherine stirred in her sleep, the thin veil between dreams and consciousness slowly lifting. As her eyelids fluttered open, the overhead light flicked on, momentarily blinding her.

She blinked, her vision adjusting to the light, and gradually, her surroundings came into focus. She was lying in a comfortable bed; the sheets were crisp and white against her skin. It dawned on her that she was at home, ensconced in the guest room that Tom had prepared for her.

Finally, her eyes latched onto a woman standing tall in the quiet of her room. She didn't know who she was, but the woman's presence exuded a sense of rage and hurt. She displayed the hospital emblem on the left chest pocket of her crisp white doctor's coat. Underneath the coat, she wore a light blue scrub top with a subtle pattern of tiny stethoscopes. The color brought out the arctic hate in her gray-blue eyes and complemented her fair complexion. The top's V-neck design revealed a delicate silver chain with two dog tags, a subtle personal touch. She navigated through the room with agility, wearing fitted but not restrictive light blue scrub pants. On her feet were a pair of white sneakers. The woman had dark, cherry-red hair pulled back into a neat bun, ensuring that her scarred cheek was clear for patient interactions and procedures. A few strands, however, escaped to frame the scar on cheek, softening her appearance, and adding a touch of approachability. A silver stethoscope dangled from her neck.

With each step she took, the woman embodied persistence and power. The guest room seemed to shrink in her presence as she came to stand at the side of Catherine's bed. Her eyes were pools of intensity, the gray-blue color deepening into a stormy cloud shade, her lips drawn into a stern scowl. Catherine felt a shiver run down her spine as the woman's gaze bore into her.

"Good evening, Catherine." Her voice was clipped, devoid of warmth, and sounded harsh to Catherine's ears.

Catherine stared up at the woman. Meanwhile, the woman's gaze was unwavering, holding a depth of emotion Catherine couldn't quite decipher.

She took a step closer to the bed, her voice measured. "It's time you face justice for what you've done. Whether you're prepared doesn't matter to me."

Catherine's heart raced; she could feel panic building in her chest, but she did her best to fight it. "What do you mean? Who are you?"

The woman's lips deepened into a somber scowl. "You make me sick. I'm not surprised you don't even know what you've done. Do you even understand the weight of your actions?"

Catherine tilted her head, her eyes showing her confusion. "What actions are you talking about? I don't understand. Who are you? What is this?"

Her gut was telling her this was not someone Tom had hired. There was no way he would have a doctor here at the house in the middle of the night. Besides, what doctors make house calls these days? The woman had to be an imposter, but why was she here? And how did she even get into the house?

"You need to leave." Catherine's voice was barely a whisper as the panic made her throat tighten.

A heavy silence settled in the room, the air thick with tension. The woman's gaze seemed to pierce through Catherine's defenses, delving into the depths of her soul. When she spoke again, her voice was a mixture of sadness and anger. "I lost my sister in that crash. She was someone I loved deeply. The only family I had left in the world."

Catherine's eyes widened as she processed the words. This was the woman she had heard screaming the night of the accident, who she had heard mourning the dead woman amidst the wreckage, her grief palpable in the air. Catherine's heartbeat picked up speed, and her throat tightened further. Any moment now, she'd descend into another major panic attack.

"You took her from me." The woman seethed with anger, her eyes blazing with hatred as she stared at Catherine. "It should've been you. Your lies and deceit end today. Admit to what you've done."

As Catherine looked into the woman's hate-filled eyes, a chilling realization settled over her like a dark cloud. There was a shift in the woman's demeanor, a subtle change in the air. The woman's gaze had transformed from anger and hate into something colder, something darker. Catherine's instincts screamed at her, warning her of the danger that loomed just beneath the surface.

Catherine spoke quickly, trying to keep her voice as calm as possible before the panic could take hold of her, and she wouldn't be able to speak at all. She kept her eyes warily on the woman's face. "I wasn't driving. It wasn't me."

The woman's lips curved into a chilling smile, her expression a mix of calculation and resolve. "You know, Catherine, sometimes the truth is more than your kind can bear. It's better to get rid of a parasite before it festers and infects an entire community."

Catherine's heart squeezed in her chest, another wave of unease washing over her as she tried to process the woman's words. She had a feeling this woman was going to kill her, but she hoped she could stall her long enough for Tom or the real nurse to come in. "What are you talking about?"

The woman's eyes held a glint of something Catherine couldn't quite define, but made her nervous. "My sister's death was a tragedy, one that was never meant to happen. But I'm going to make things right."

"Make things right how?" Catherine brushed a stray blonde hair from her cheek as she tucked it behind her ear. She was nervous, and her voice was barely a gasp of sound now. She couldn't scream for help if she wanted to, as anxiety filled her.

The woman's gaze bore into Catherine's, her voice a chilling whisper. "By taking your life for you taking my sister's. By ensuring that justice is served."

Another surge of terror overtook Catherine, and the panic made her squeak out, "You can't be serious."

The woman's smile was devoid of warmth, her words laced with an unsettling calmness. "Your survival was a mistake. A mistake I intend to correct."

The pain of Catherine's injuries weighed her body down, and she knew there was no getting out of the bed. She couldn't run. Even though she knew it was impossible, with the panic closing her throat, she attempted to scream. It wouldn't have mattered anyway as the woman clasped a firm hand over her mouth, silencing any sound that Catherine might have managed to make.

She was going to die, and there was nothing she could do about it.

Catherine thrashed against her assailant, hoping that the sound of a struggle would alert the real nurse or Tom, but with it being past midnight, she knew that unlikely. Still, Catherine fought for her life, scratching at the woman's hand with her good one. She tried to hit her with her cast, but the woman dodged the blow. She had total control over Catherine in her injured state. The woman's eyes glinted with a chilling resolve as she grabbed Catherine's right arm, pulling it off her, her actions measured and purposeful.

All of a sudden, her attacker's gaze moved to Catherine's exposed right shoulder, and the woman let go of her mouth and arm. She gasped for air as the woman reached over and shifted Catherine's gown to see her left shoulder.

"It's on the wrong side." The woman sounded astonished.

Catherine continued to try to take deep breaths, her body shaking as she snuck a look at her would-be killer.

The woman's expression was full of shock and disbelief. "I'm sorry, Catherine," she murmured, backing up from the bed, her expression filled with confusion.

The woman stood in the middle of the room for another moment, staring as Catherine tried to find five things—the vase on the dresser, the oil warmer full of lavender oil, the chair in the corner, the IV stand, the door—to calm herself down. Before Catherine could recover, the woman gave her one last glance, then turned, and walked toward the open door. And just as quickly as she had entered, she shut off the light and vanished into the shadows of the hallway.

Catherine laid against her stack of pillows, trying to process the encounter. She continued with her task of finding four things she could physically feel as she thought over what had just happened. One minute she was going to be killed by an intruder, and the next, the intruder was apologizing to her.

She grasped the bedsheet with her hand, her fingers tracing over the cotton. She moved on to the comforter, which was thick and soft. From there she moved her left hand to the side and touched the hard wood of the table and then the cool metal of the lamp as she took several deep breaths.

Catherine didn't bother turning on the lamp. The moon

provided plenty of light now that her eyes had adjusted to the darkness again. She reached up and touched the bruise on her right shoulder, wondering at the woman's words. Although the danger and her panic had vanished, Catherine couldn't shake off the lingering shadows of the confrontation. The encounter with the woman had been haunting, a surreal blend of danger, panic, and uncertainty.

Catherine grappled with a question that gnawed at the edges of her consciousness. Had it all been a nightmare? She replayed the events in her mind, each detail etched vividly. The sinister intentions, the chilling words, the woman's enigmatic smile—they all felt too real to be mere products of her imagination. And yet...

It all feels so unreal. Like a nightmare. But it had to have happened as I am awake. I can't be dreaming. Maybe I want it to be a nightmare. The reality of what happened is too much to bear.

Catherine fixed her gaze on a distant point beyond the window. The moon painted the sky with shades of black and white, similar to the darkness that had engulfed her thoughts. As the night unfolded, she found her eyelids growing heavy, and she drifted off to a much-needed sleep, despite the lingering sense of unease.

SEVEN

One week since the anniversary

Catherine's current bedroom was a haven of serenity, tucked away on the first floor of the house that she shared with Tom. From her bed, she had an unobstructed view of the world beyond her room. The bed sat opposite the large bay window adorned with lavender blackout curtains, which were currently open since she hadn't wanted them closed. The window looked out onto the front lawn and beyond to the busy street. Catherine found she could lose herself in the landscape that stretched out before her. As the first rays of sunlight broke over the horizon making the room lighten more, Catherine stirred beneath her warm cocoon of blankets. She blinked away the remnants of sleep, her eyes immediately drawn to the window like a moth to a flame. The sky was a canvas of soft pastel hues and fluffy white clouds that seemed absurdly bright in the morning sunlight.

The houses that lined the street across the way were of a similar structure to theirs. Across the street was a bus stop bench, which sat just off the sidewalk halfway between two of the houses in her view. She drew her gaze to a figure seated on the bench. An elderly man, his face etched with wrinkles that spoke of a lifetime of experiences. She recognized him as Mr. Harley, her neighbor three doors down. He sat there; his gaze fixed on something further down the road. She wondered about his thoughts, his memories. Did he, too, find solace in staring out at the early morning light? Did he reflect on days gone by, on loved ones lost and dreams unfulfilled?

Probably not, she thought. He was most likely just focused on catching the local bus to the market for his groceries. He lived alone since his wife had passed away. Catherine watched the small white bus arrive, pulling to a stop just in front of him. A moment later he was gone, leaving the street and sidewalk empty once more.

As the day progressed, Catherine's view transformed. The sky shifted from soft pastels to a vibrant blue, the sun now casting its golden glow upon the world. From her vantage point, she watched as cars zipped by with vibrant energy as people headed to work. Eldon wasn't a huge town, and many of the residents worked elsewhere. Some even made the long drive into Cincinnati, choosing to live rural and make the commute.

Several of the neighbors, though, worked in town and would walk to work or to the store instead of driving. She could see Miriam Glenn sauntering down the walkway, her empty shopping bags tucked under her arm as she scanned her phone's screen. Minutes later, Lynn James and her husband Patrick walked hand in hand, oblivious to Catherine's observations. They were probably on their way to work at the bakery they owned about three blocks away.

Throughout the rest of the day, between the nurse visiting with medication, check-ups, and her meals, Catherine used the window like many would a television. She made up stories in her head about her neighbors and where they were going, what they were talking about, and what their plans for their day would be.

As evening draped the small town in twilight hues, Catherine realized she hadn't seen Tom all day. She had grown accustomed to him returning home at five o'clock, which was an hour ago. Somehow, she missed the familiar sound of his footsteps and longed for the days when she thought of his arms as a comforting embrace. It had been a long time since she'd felt that way about him.

Had it only been a week since she'd thought they were going to make a new start on their anniversary? It seemed like a lifetime ago now. So much had occurred since that night out. The crash, Tom trying to gaslight her into thinking she'd been driving, and that intruder trying to kill her. She'd thought about telling Tom or her nurse, Eleanor, about the woman who'd snuck into the house dressed as a doctor, but had decided against it. They probably wouldn't believe her and would say her medication had caused her to hallucinate. It hadn't, but it wasn't worth listening to them try to come up with reasons to dismiss her.

Her thoughts turned back to Tom and where he could be. It was odd that he wasn't home. Tom was nearly always home on time unless he had a dinner or a case he was working on. But if so, she felt sure he would have mentioned it. Had he texted?

With a furrowed brow, Catherine looked toward the nightstand for her phone but then realized she didn't have it. It hadn't been returned to her after the accident. She wondered if it was still in Tom's Camaro, and then where the Camaro actually was. Had Tom gotten the car back? Had he taken it to the body shop for repairs, or did the cops impound it?

She shook her head. That should have been a giveaway right there that she hadn't been driving. The car was Tom's, and she wasn't even on the insurance to be able to drive it. She wasn't even allowed to drive, period. Unless it was an emergency, he would never allow it. Besides, that car was his baby. Anytime she had shopping to do, she had to walk or take the bus like Mr. Harley. It didn't matter that there was another car in the garage, she wasn't allowed behind the wheel.

A pang of unease settled in Catherine's chest. She pushed herself further up in bed, her gaze drifting to the space beside her where a chair sat. It was the one Tom and Eleanor used when they would visit.

Why hasn't he come home? Or is he home and avoiding me? Why would he be avoiding me? she wondered as she adjusted the pillows behind her. *No, he can't be home. I'd have heard him, he's not that quiet.*

Her gaze turned back to the window; it was calm outside, and there was very little movement within her view. Just a gentle breeze that ruffled through the leaves, making the branches of the tree in the yard shudder and wave to her. As the sun started to set, filling the sky with bright oranges and pinks, a sound pierced through the stillness of the evening—the soft purr of an engine.

Catherine's gaze turned toward the edge of the window where she could see a dim set of headlights breaking up the shadows as it moved up the street. The car slowed, and she could see the silhouette of their other car, a black Lexus sedan, pulling into the driveway. Her breath caught in her throat as she heard the car come to a stop. The engine shut off, and she heard a car door open and close. And then, there he was—Tom, walking up the front path from the driveway to the door, his figure illuminated by the soft glow of the sunset.

A mixture of relief and anticipation flooded her senses as she waited for him to come see her. She had unconsciously been counting down to this moment without realizing it, the time when Tom's footsteps would echo through the hallway, a melodic cadence that signaled his presence. In her mind, she could almost hear the rhythmic sound, like a whispered promise of connection amid the quiet world.

The minutes seemed to stretch on, each one an eternity of waiting. And then, finally, she heard it—the soft sound of a door closing, the creak of the front step, and the unmistakable shuffle of shoes against the hardwood floor. She heard the murmur of voices coming from the kitchen, where she imagined he'd stopped to say hello to Eleanor, who was probably cooking her dinner. A moment later, just as she had imagined, Tom's familiar figure stood in the doorway.

"Tom." She smiled. "You're later than normal. Where have you been? How was your day?" Catherine asked.

The final question was one he'd trained her to ask. He always expected her to ask about his day and have dinner on the table for him when he came home. Things were a bit out of sorts, with her in a hospital bed right now.

"Sweetheart, we need to talk. It's important." Tom's voice was steady but tinged with a nervousness that was uncharacteristic of him.

Catherine wondered what he had to say now, but she knew what was expected of her, so she replied, "Of course. Come sit." She gestured toward the chair that had been moved next to the bed.

Tom followed her request, sitting in the cozy chair, leaning back as he looked at her.

Catherine broke the silence. "What did you want to talk about?"

Tom cleared his throat, and he turned his gaze from her. His eyes drifted to a photo of the two of them laughing together at a neighbor's pool party on the bedside table. "Catherine, do you remember the night of the car crash?"

Catherine gulped. She'd been afraid he was going to bring that up and start in with his manipulations now that she was feeling a little better. This was what she'd wanted to avoid by staying in the hospital. Still, she answered him. "Yes, but some is still a blur, to be honest. And I don't remember much about our evening beforehand." The last part was a small white lie. She did remember most of what happened at the restaurant prior to getting back in the car to come home.

Tom's fingers tapped a nervous rhythm against his knee as he steadily avoided her gaze. She'd never seen him like this. He was always confident. "I need to tell you something. Something that you might not want to hear."

She locked her gaze on him. She knew what was coming, what he was about to say. She braced herself for it, knowing that he was about to try to gaslight her. "What is it, honey?" She tried to keep her voice soft and pliant, she didn't want to give herself away and let him know she knew exactly what he was up to. Not yet.

"I was in the passenger seat during the accident," Tom began slowly, his voice quiet but steady. "I woke up shortly after the impact, and... I saw you trying to restart the car to flee."

Catherine turned her gaze back to the window as anger at him filled her. The events of the past week had been tumultuous, full of pain and doubt, but one memory kept resurfacing in her mind—a memory that held the key piece of the puzzle she had been struggling to put together. The recollection that Tom had pulled her into that driver's seat. Added to that was a stranger's comment about the unmistakable bruise on her right shoulder, a bruise that pointed to the truth that Tom had been avoiding and trying to make disappear.

Catherine's fingers brushed against her right shoulder, the touch evoking a vivid remembrance of the night marked in her mind by the terror of high speeds, disorientation, bleeding, and injuries. As the details of that night settled over her, chills covered her body. The events that had followed the accident still weighed heavily on her mind, but there was one crucial fact that stuck out—Tom had been the one to cause that crash. He was the one who was speeding. He was the one who wouldn't slow down. He was the one who ran that stop sign. Not her.

She recalled when she first regained consciousness, and the emergency services weren't there yet, that the damage to the car had been pretty severe. She remembered looking for Tom and seeing him outside the car. Then he'd walked to the driver's side, reached in through the broken glass, gripped her shoulders, and pulled her across to the driver's seat.

Catherine continued to stare out the bay window, her gaze fixed on a group of neighborhood children playing a game of tag in one of the yards across the street. It was twilight out, and with the streetlights on, there was still plenty of light for the kids to play. They'd probably be called in for dinner soon if they hadn't eaten already. She wished she had what they did. The simple enjoyment of playing and hanging out with friends. Instead, she was stuck in this bed, in this house, in this marriage with a man who was domineering and currently determined to get her to take responsibility for something she hadn't done.

With a controlled exhale, she decided she couldn't let this lie fester any longer. She needed answers, clarity, and, above all, honesty. She took a moment to gather her thoughts, her fingers nervously tapping against her casted arm.

"Tom, I've noticed that something's been off with you lately. You've been acting contradictory, avoiding certain topics. I can't shake the feeling that you're hiding something from me." She shifted her gaze from the window to him.

Tom's expression shifted, a flicker of fear crossing his features. "Catherine, I..." he started, but just as she thought maybe he was going to confess, his eyes grew dark, and his lips firmed into a tight line. "I don't know what you're talking about."

Catherine kept her voice steady, her gaze unwavering as she stared at him. "Tom, please don't lie to me." She knew showing her anger would trigger his temper, so she tried to keep it from her voice. "There's a bruise on my right shoulder and across my chest to my left hip that says I was in the passenger seat. The medical staff at the hospital have seen it. You were driving drunk and crashed the car. Why are you lying to me? Why are you trying to convince me and everyone that I was the one driving?"

Tom clenched his fist and then drummed his fingers on the armrest of the chair. He took a deep breath, his gaze steady as he met her eyes. "Lately, you haven't been a proper wife."

A flicker of confusion flashed through Catherine's mind. *Where had that come from, and what did it have to do with him lying to her?* she wondered. She stared at him, confused by his words.

"What do you mean I haven't been a proper wife?"

His jaw twitched, and his gaze was hard as his voice came out in a harsh whisper. "I mean, you're not being the wife I thought you'd be."

She felt a blow to her heart and self-esteem, what was left of it. Catherine had always done everything he'd asked of her. She was exactly how he'd told her to be and had allowed him to control her life—what more did he want? Then it dawned on her. He was trying to distract her from the facts of the accident because she wasn't falling in line with his current manipulation. She was asking questions. Questions he didn't want to answer.

Tom stood up from the chair. He moved over to the dresser and picked up a syringe that had been tucked between the picture frame and the vase of flowers and then turned off the overhead light, leaving the room bathed in only moonlight. The moon had fully risen as they'd spoken, and Catherine could no longer hear the joy and laughter of the children outside playing tag. It was quiet and she was alone with a man she no longer recognized.

Catherine froze, her heart pounding in terror. Fear had claimed her voice as panic filled her. She had spent days physically and mentally fighting to survive her injuries, and now, seeing Tom coming toward her with who-knew-what in that syringe, she knew she could no longer win. He was going to kill her for not going along with his narrative. She wanted to cry out, she wanted to fight him, but there was nothing she could do. He was too strong for her to fight against.

Tom reached out and snagged Catherine's IV line in his hand, pulling the clear wire toward him with determination. He traced his thumb over the line toward the medication port, his gaze fixed on her face, which she was sure was filled with the horror she felt at his actions.

"Catherine." His voice was heavy with the weight of unspoken words as he stared into her eyes. He shook his head. "I just wish you would have accommodated me. I hate having to do this. It could have been so different if you had just cooperated and taken responsibility for the accident. Now I have no choice."

Just as Tom lined up the syringe needle with the medicine port, an unmistakable crash of glass echoed through the room. Catherine cried out, and Tom's arm jolted, causing the syringe to slip from his grasp and bounce against the hardwood floor, almost disappearing beneath the bed. Tom turned around to see what had happened, kicking the syringe fully under the bed in his hurried movement.

Catherine's bedroom lay ensconced in a hushed darkness, the moonlight gently filtering through the now-broken window that drew her gaze. The room exuded an air of quiet terror. Catherine's panicked breathing was the only sound that dared interrupt the silence.

They heard footsteps, and the door to the guest room opened. Eleanor stood there, holding a tray, and her eyes widened as she took in the scene.

Tom spun from the window and stalked past her out of the room, jostling the nurse.

In the distance, a clock struck eight, each strike a lash to Catherine's heart. She'd been mere seconds from death a moment ago; she knew it. But then something or *someone* had intervened and shattered the window, causing a different outcome than what Tom had clearly intended. She had been saved.

Her nervous gaze moved to Eleanor. She could see that the woman was bringing her dinner, but she knew she couldn't eat a thing.

"What happened to the window?" Eleanor's eyes widened as she set the tray down on the dresser and flipped on the overhead light. "Are you all right, Mrs. Morris?" She hurried over to her. "Just breathe, Mrs. Morris. Remember your breathing techniques..."

It was too late; Catherine's mind was spiraling in the aftermath of the fear she was experiencing.

"Mrs. Morris?" Eleanor fussed. "Can you tell me five things you see?" she asked as she moved to the locked box on the bathroom counter of the ensuite bathroom.

Catherine attempted to find something to focus on, but all she could see were black spots in her vision among fuzzy outlines.

"Okay, hang on, you'll feel better in just a second," Eleanor murmured.

A moment later, Catherine felt the cooling sensation of a sedative flowing through her veins, and her world descended into darkness as her heartbeat slowed and the panic left her.

EIGHT

Eleanor had confined Catherine to her hospital bed after the shattered window and panic attack incident. While Catherine had slept, Eleanor and Tom had apparently discussed moving Catherine's bed to another room. Tom had swiftly agreed, according to Eleanor, but it took a couple of days to rearrange the other first-floor guest room and to move her, which frustrated Catherine no end because she couldn't even enjoy looking out the window, which was now boarded up.

When the room was ready, Eleanor took it upon herself to transform it into a haven of comfort. She adorned the walls with Catherine's photographs of her parents and colorful paintings that Catherine had brought from her family home after her dad had passed away and the place had been sold. Eleanor placed a cozy armchair by the window overlooking the serene garden on the side of the house while the bed faced the larger front window, which had a similar view as the other room.

Catherine's mood lifted as she sat in the armchair. Her overall outlook shifted from a state of fear to one of hope, knowing Eleanor was there for her and had said she wanted to make sure she stayed calm and didn't have any more panic attacks. Catherine hoped that would be the case. As long as Tom didn't try to murder her again with whatever was in that syringe. When Eleanor had left her alone last night, after cleaning up the glass from the window, Catherine had gotten out of bed and, despite the pain from her broken ribs, had reached under the bed and grabbed the thing. She'd squirted the clear liquid straight into the toilet and flushed it away, then dropped the syringe in the medical waste box Eleanor used for the syringes of sedatives she administered to Catherine when she had her panic attacks.

An hour later, Catherine moved from the chair and returned to her bed, reclining against the pillows to watch the activity out the front window. As she observed her neighbors go about their day, she saw a beige sedan turn onto her street and slow as it neared the house. It stopped, and after a car driving in the opposite direction passed, she heard it turn into her driveway. This window didn't offer a view of the front walkway, but she heard the doorbell ring a minute or so later and wondered who might have come to visit.

Soon she heard the soft tap of footsteps in the corridor outside her room and looked to the doorway. Detective Sheldon stood there, his chestnut brown eyes meeting hers with a mix of professionalism and warmth. "Good afternoon, Mrs. Morris." His voice sounded reassuring. "I hope I'm not disturbing you."

Catherine managed a smile, her nerves settling slightly. "Not at all, Detective. Please, come in."

As he entered the room, his gaze swept over the sunlit space. Once he was seated across from Catherine, he said, "Mrs. Morris, how did you come to leave the hospital? We were unaware that you were allowed to come home."

Catherine gave him a tight smile. "My husband was rather

insistent with the doctor. You'll find that Tom tends to get his way in most cases."

Detective Sheldon frowned. "I see. Well, would you be able to answer some more questions about the accident?"

"I'm more than willing to answer your questions," she replied. "Although, I will tell you I only remember fragments, Detective."

He leaned forward slightly, a look of empathy on his face. "That's completely understandable, Mrs. Morris. Traumatic events can cloud our memories. I'm here to put together the puzzle, one piece at a time."

Catherine's fingers traced the edge of the blanket draped over her lap. "I want to help, Detective. But I have to be honest —I don't fully understand exactly what happened and in what order."

Nodding, his expression turned thoughtful. "It's okay, Mrs. Morris. Sometimes, even the smallest details can hold significance. If you're comfortable doing so, could you tell me what you do remember about that evening, leading up to and including the accident?"

Catherine closed her eyes briefly and then refocused on the detective. She gave him a slight nod, then began. "I remember leaving the restaurant with Tom. He'd ordered an expensive bottle of champagne at dinner. I had one glass, but my medication doesn't mix well with it, which is probably why some things are still unclear to me. Tom drank the rest of the bottle, not wanting to waste it."

"It was your wedding anniversary, is that correct?"

"Yes, our fifth."

"So, you had some champagne, and then what happened?" he asked patiently.

"After dinner, we headed for the car. Tom had to help me into it; as I said, my head was fuzzy. I remember there was an argument... we argued because everything was moving so fast, and I was getting ill. Tom made the turn toward Eldon and continued to speed—"

"You've said that before, that Tom was driving... but you were found in the driver's seat." He arched a bushy eyebrow at her, his pen poised over his notebook.

"I am aware of that, as nobody can seem to get past that fact, but there is an explanation. Do you want me to continue telling you all I remember, or do you want me to jump ahead to that?"

"Sorry, you were saying Tom continued to speed?"

Catherine nodded. "Yes, the road was only two lanes, and I was frightened because Tom was going as fast as he had been on the interstate. I was asking him to slow down, and we were arguing when he drove through a stop sign, and then..." Catherine's voice wavered as she spoke, the emotions of that moment resurfacing. "All I recall is the sound of metal hitting metal."

Detective Sheldon's gaze remained steady upon her. "I appreciate your willingness to discuss that night. I know this is a tough conversation to have."

Catherine nodded, her fingers curling slightly around the edge of her blanket as she waited for him to go on.

"In my line of work, I've encountered various scenarios involving accidents. Sometimes, factors that might not be immediately apparent can play a role in how events unfold."

Catherine tried to catch up with the implication of his words. "What do you mean, Detective?"

"Mrs. Morris, are you sure you only had one glass of champagne prior to the accident?"

Catherine's breath caught in her throat. He didn't believe her. He still thought she was driving. Not only that, he thought she'd been drinking and driving! She blinked, her mind struggling to process the gravity of the situation. "As I said, Detective... I... I did have one glass of champagne," she stammered, feeling a mixture of surprise and defensiveness. "And I'll admit to having a small glass of wine before we even went to dinner earlier that evening, but that was all I had."

Detective Sheldon's expression remained neutral; his focus unwavering. "Mrs. Morris, please know that I'm not making any assumptions. It's my responsibility to find out exactly what happened that night."

Catherine's fingers loosened around the blanket. "I appreciate that, Detective."

"When you answered my first question," Detective Sheldon continued, "you said something that intrigued me. You said you were in an argument with Tom, while he was driving, before the accident."

She wondered where he was going with this, if the detective was trying to gaslight her into thinking it was still her fault because of the argument. She wouldn't put it past Tom to try something like that, but she'd hoped this detective would be unbiased and at least listen to her.

Hesitantly, she said, "Yes. We had an argument." Catherine winced as she shifted positions.

The detective looked at her with concern. "If you're still comfortable, Mrs. Morris, could you restate what that argument was about?"

Catherine took a deep breath and nodded. "As I said before, it was about Tom speeding." She felt a tinge of vulnerability and knew it had come out in her voice. "I was feeling sick and was nearly passing out from the mixture of alcohol and my medication. Tom had said he would get us home quickly. I recall he said something about not having any antacids in the car. He was already speeding at that point, and I didn't want him to go any faster, so I kept telling him to slow down. After he made that turn off the interstate, I started feeling sicker. He wouldn't listen and told me to... to shut up. Then I pointed out the stop sign he was in the process of running through, but it was too late, and he crashed into that other car."

Detective Sheldon nodded; his pen scratching notes on his
paper. "Thank you for sharing that, Mrs. Morris. Arguments
can amplify stress and emotions, which can affect our focus and
reactions." He raised his eyes from the paper to look at her.

Catherine's gaze met his. "Are you suggesting that the argument might have contributed to the accident?" She started
feeling sick at the idea that he might be about to charge her for
being the underlying cause of the accident because she'd argued
with Tom.

"It's my duty to explore all the possibilities, Mrs. Morris.
Emotions can influence our actions in unforeseen ways. By
understanding the context of the argument, we might uncover a
potential link to the accident."

Catherine tamped down the fear she felt, taking a few calm-
ing, deep breaths. "I hadn't thought about it that way, Detective.
In the heat of the moment, my focus was solely on getting Tom
to slow down. I never imagined doing so could have played a
role in the accident."

Detective Sheldon's demeanor was respectful. "Thank you
for your honesty, Mrs. Morris. I understand these conversations
can be difficult, especially when the implications are sensitive.
The circumstances of accidents are often complex, and it's
important to address all potential factors." He leaned back in his
chair, his pen poised above his notebook. "It's clear to me that
the accident had a profound impact on you, both physically and
emotionally. Was there anything else you recall about that
night?"

Catherine contemplated his question. "There is something
else I remember—a moment after the accident that has been
haunting me."

"Please, Mrs. Morris, share whatever you remember. Every
detail, no matter how small, can hold significance."

"I remember waking up right after the crash," Catherine
began. "Tom wasn't in the car, and the driver's seat was empty.

My hearing wasn't great, so everything was muffled, and my vision was hazy. I remember seeing him outside of the car. He reached in through the driver's side window, which was broken. I think he unbuckled me; I know I didn't do it myself. He told me he was going to pull me out of the car through the window."

Detective Sheldon nodded patiently.

"So then," Catherine continued, her words gaining momentum, "Tom gripped my shoulders and pulled me into the driver's seat over the parking brake. I remember because it hurt worse than anything I'd ever experienced." Catherine could hear the shakiness in her voice as she recalled the overwhelming stab of pain when her broken forearm hit that parking brake, the memory resurfacing in vivid detail. "I passed out from the pain after that."

"You believe he put you in the driver's seat to avoid taking responsibility for the accident himself?"

Catherine nodded, her throat tightening with the weight of the memory. "Yes, Detective. I was disoriented, and everything happened so fast, but I do remember that."

Detective Sheldon's pen paused in midair, the significance of Catherine's words sinking in. "Tom physically put you in the driver's seat just after the accident." He said it as though he was trying to make sure he clearly understood the implication of her words.

Catherine's gaze dropped to her hands, her fingers gripping the blanket. "Yes, Detective. It's that memory I've been grappling with. I don't understand why he would do that. Tom has always been a very responsible man, so this doesn't make sense to me." Of course, ever since that night, Tom has been behaving in more and more bizarre ways. He'd tried to murder her the other night with that syringe!

"Mrs. Morris, this adds a layer of complexity to the events."

"Detective, I can prove what I'm saying—I've got evidence that proves I wasn't in the driver's seat during the accident."

Detective Sheldon's eyebrows lifted slightly; his curiosity piqued. "Please, Mrs. Morris, share whatever you have."

Catherine took a deep breath and leaned forward, steadying herself as she pushed down the right shoulder of her gown, then gently lifted the bottom of the fabric to reveal the faint but distinct bruising on her midsection and left hip where the buckle had left a square bruise from the impact. "Look, Detective." Her voice was tinged with urgency. "These bruises, they're from the seat belt. They prove I was in the passenger seat during the crash and not driving. If I had been, they'd be on the other side, wouldn't they?"

Detective Sheldon's eyes widened as he took in the evidence before him. "Mrs. Morris," he began, his voice measured, "this evidence is significant. It does contradict our initial assumption and the version of the story your husband told, which was that you were driving the car and caused the accident. I should have followed up your injuries with the hospital. I'm sorry I didn't." He shook his head, his teeth clenched.

Catherine felt a wave of relief that finally someone believed her.

Detective Sheldon's expression held a blend of empathy and responsibility. "Mrs. Morris, I think there is something you should be aware of, in light of this evidence."

"What is it?"

"I mentioned that your husband told a completely different story. What I haven't said was that he's had a number of your neighbors come forward to give testimony about that night as well."

Catherine frowned. Why would her neighbors be giving testimony? The accident took place almost an hour from Eldon. They were nowhere nearby when it occurred, but then, if Tom told them to, they probably would do whatever he asked.

Still, she asked, "What do you mean, Detective? What have they said?"

His gaze remained steady. "Your neighbors, Mr. Lewis, and his wife; your husband's law firm partners, Mr. Durbin and his wife; as well as Mr. Banks and his wife; and your husband have all claimed that you have a serious alcohol problem. They all claim that prior to your evening out, you drank an entire bottle of wine during a small cocktail party here at your house. Your husband also claimed that you were the one who drank the entire bottle of champagne while he only had a seltzer water. They were all adamant that you get belligerent when you drink and that you won't listen to reason. Your husband said you demanded that you drive home because he was too slow and you were feeling—" his cheeks turned pink, "er... frisky?"

The implications of what Detective Sheldon was saying were staggering. She had been betrayed, not only by her husband but also by the people she'd thought were her friends, people she had shared her life with.

Catherine's voice was barely above a whisper as she processed the information. "An alcohol problem? That's... that's not true, Detective. I've always been sure to drink responsibly, especially because of the effects of my medication. I hate the way it makes me feel, and the only drinks I had were at Tom's insistence because he said it was a celebration."

"I am coming to believe your version of the events of that night, given the evidence of those bruises. It did seem odd to me that your husband would drag those people into Cincinnati to give testimony about something they weren't around to witness; however, I had to make a record of what they said because, at the time, we believed that version of events." He shook his head. "The question I now have is why he would do something like that."

Catherine wondered the same thing, but she didn't have an answer. She merely hoped that this nightmare of events would finally be over after this. She felt immense gratitude that he believed her. Suddenly, she gasped, her eyes widening.

"What is it, Mrs. Morris?"

"Detective," she said, "I've just remembered something." She gave a half laugh. Could it really be so easy to clear her name once and for all?

"Please, Mrs. Morris, share whatever information you have. Every detail is crucial in our pursuit of the truth."

Catherine took a deep breath and nodded. "Tom installed a dashcam in the Camaro a few months ago. Did you find it?"

His eyes widened. "The wreckage of your car was impounded as evidence. We're waiting for Forensics to examine it, but the team has been behind due to staff shortages. I've been told your husband has been trying to gain access to it and that he has been persistent in his efforts to retrieve personal items from the car, even though it is considered a piece of evidence in an ongoing investigation." Detective Sheldon stood. "Mrs. Morris, I hope you'll excuse me... as long as you feel safe here. It's essential I get to the impound lot right away. I think your husband is trying to frame you."

NINE

Catherine sat by the window, her gaze fixed on the soft hues of the setting sun as it filled the sky with shades of pink and orange. Eleanor bustled around the room, tidying up. She was a constant and comforting presence. Catherine relied on Eleanor not just for her medical expertise but also for her companionship and the brief moments of laughter they shared amidst the pain and struggle.

"Everything seems in order for the evening, Catherine." Eleanor glanced at the checklist on her clipboard. "Your pain medication is right here for when you need it."

Catherine nodded, not knowing how to tell the sweet woman about Tom's evil ways. She kept her eyes fixed on the horizon. "Thank you, Eleanor. You've been so kind to me."

"It's all part of the job. But I've enjoyed our time together too. You're a strong woman, and you're making remarkable progress. I couldn't be happier with how far you've come in such a short amount of time."

Catherine's lips curved into a faint smile. "I couldn't have done it without you."

As the sun dipped below the horizon, casting the room into

a soft twilight, Eleanor pulled up a chair beside Catherine. "I wanted to let you know that I'll be leaving for the evening. Tom said he can handle the night shift, as he'd like you to join him for dinner. He also asked that I remove the IV for the evening."

Catherine felt a pang of fear at the thought of Eleanor leaving her in the house with her abusive husband. But all she said was, "I'll miss you, Eleanor."

Eleanor placed a hand on Catherine's shoulder, her touch gentle and reassuring as she set about removing the IV. "I'm just a call away if you need anything. And I'll be back first thing in the morning to check on you." Eleanor's voice was soft as she retook her seat. "You know, sometimes we meet people at certain times in our lives, and they leave a lasting impact. You've left an impact on me, Catherine. Your strength, your determination—it's been inspiring to witness."

Catherine felt a lump in her throat, making it difficult to speak. "You've been my rock, Eleanor. You've made this journey so much more bearable."

Eleanor's smile held a hint of sentimentality. "Life is full of chapters. Some are brief, like this one, while others stretch on for longer. But each chapter adds to the story of who we are."

Catherine nodded, her eyes glistening with unshed tears. The room seemed to hold a sacred silence, a space where words weren't necessary to convey the depth of their feelings. And with that, Eleanor left.

Soon, the sound of footsteps approached her room, the door creaked open, and in walked Tom, the man she was coming to despise. He wore a crisp suit that stressed his broad frame, and his bright and determined eyes were shining with something Catherine couldn't quite decipher. He had always been an egotistical man; a quality Catherine had grown to find exasperating.

"Good evening, dear."

Catherine sighed and drew her body in once more, a faint

frown gracing her features. "Evening. What's got you all dressed up?"

Tom crossed the room and sat on the edge of the bed. "Well, I have planned a dinner tonight with my colleagues and some friends from the neighborhood."

"Okay. So why are you in my room?"

Tom's smile grew wider. "You're going to be the hostess for the evening. You know, greet the guests, make sure everything runs smoothly. It's just that you have that special touch everyone loves."

Catherine's eyes widened, a mixture of surprise and uncertainty flickering within them. "Me? Hostess? Tom, I'm not exactly in the best shape right now."

Tom gently took her hand in his, his eyes softening. "Catherine, you've been thinking of no one but yourself since the accident. I think you are selfishly holding your recovery back. This could be a great opportunity for you to interact with others, to heal yourself, and come to understand the truth."

Catherine held in the groan she wanted to let out. The idea of being a gracious hostess was intimidating, but the prospect that one of the guests might believe her side of things was appealing. Tom's words had her worried he was going to continue to push the narrative that she had been drinking and driving and had been the one to cause the accident. But she used to be social and outgoing when they'd first married, so maybe she had a friend amongst these guests.

"I don't know, Tom," she hedged. "What if I can't handle it? What if I fumble for something or get tired? I don't want to embarrass myself."

Tom squeezed her small hand with his large one, making her feel fragile. "Catherine, there you go, thinking all about yourself again. You've faced challenges head-on before, and you've always come out stronger. Besides, I'll be right there with

you, and I know my friends and colleagues will be understanding."

Catherine could see his unwavering annoyance reflected in
his eyes. She knew there was no getting out of this. He was
going to get his way. Even if he had to force her from this room
in her nightgown. It would be easier to just go along, and at least
if she did, he'd let her go get dressed instead of continuing to
lecture her. "Okay, I'll be your hostess. But you have to promise
to help me get ready and be my backup if things get too overwhelming."

Tom grinned; excitement filled his eyes. "Deal! It's going to
be a wonderful evening. Just you wait and see, sweetheart." He
strode out of the room and returned quickly, holding a dress on
a hanger.

Catherine's gaze fixed upon the gaudy dress that hung from
Tom's finger. It was a calamity of navy blue silk, adorned with
massive jewels that traced dizzying patterns along the bodice.
She knew her husband had carefully chosen it as he did everything she wore. The question she had was why he'd chosen
something so tacky. He usually had impeccable taste, so she
could only assume he'd done this on purpose to cause her
embarrassment. She met his gaze and knew he was waiting for
her to argue with him over it, but she wasn't going to give him
the satisfaction. She'd wear the damn dress.

Catherine stood and moved to the bathroom where he had
put her makeup and beauty regime. She began getting ready
nervously. She knew Tom had ulterior plans for this dinner, but
she hoped it would also be a chance to spread her authentic
version of events from beyond the confines of her hospital bed.

After doing her hair and makeup, she needed a rest, so she
sat at the edge of the bed, taking deep breaths.

Tom's face was a mix of eagerness and determination as he
sat waiting for her. "Ready to get dressed yet?" His voice was
laced with annoyance.

Catherine nodded, her frown growing wider as he held the dress up in her face.

Tom's hands were rough as he helped Catherine slip into the dress, and she loathed the reassurance of his touch. The silk felt cool against her skin, and she took a deep breath, abhorring the moment. Tom worked to fasten the intricate buttons along the back, cinching in the waist against her bruised midsection, causing her a lot of discomfort. His touch was rushed and impatient, and she flinched as he jerked on the dress. The buttons seemed to resist his manipulations, and Catherine winced when his fingernails scratched against her skin.

"Tom, be careful."

Tom's movements faltered for barely a moment. "Sorry." He didn't sound sorry though. "We need to get this done quickly. I don't want to leave the caterers unsupervised, and you've taken too long. You need to get in there."

"I don't want to be injured further," she gritted out. "Can you take your time? My ribs are still healing; you need to be careful."

Tom sighed; his frustration clear. "There you go again. We're going to be late for everyone's arrival because of you."

"Tom, I'm willing to do this so long as it doesn't injure me further. I know you want tonight to go well, but I need you to remember that sometimes other people's needs matter more than any event."

Tom huffed. "Shut up, Catherine. I swear if you keep making things about you, I'll shut you up for good."

Catherine held herself rigid at his words. Her heart stilled for a moment and then began to beat irrationally in her chest. *Did he mean that? Is he still planning to kill me? If he is, why make me do this? What is the point*, she wondered. She pressed her lips together firmly and let him finish without her saying another word, even though it hurt.

Once Tom finished fastening the dress, Catherine stood

before the mirror, feeling gauche and insecure. The jewels cascaded down her figure, making her look like some floozy. She turned, loathing the way the fabric pulled with each movement. She felt ugly, a sensation that went beyond the external appearance and resonated deep within her.

Tom stared at her reflection, a satisfied smile on his lips. "You look stunning, Catherine. I'm glad you finally dropped your selfish desires to make this moment special."

The knock, louder this time, echoing through the house. Catherine stumbled to the front entrance, her high-heeled footsteps echoing on the wooden surface. With a sigh, Catherine turned the knob and opened the door, fully prepared to politely greet whatever guest might wait on the other side.

Standing on the doorstep were four well-dressed individuals, all exuding an air of professionalism that was hard to miss. Richard Banks, one of Tom's senior partners at Durbin, Banks & Morris, stood there holding a leather briefcase in one hand and extending the other in a friendly greeting. He was tall and impeccably groomed with salt and pepper hair.

"Catherine, so glad to see you again," he said with a warm smile. "I'm sure you remember my wife, Rachel."

Catherine showed composure and offered a polite smile despite knowing all four of the people on her front step had told the police she had a drinking problem. She shook Richard's hand and then Rachel's. "Yes, of course. It's a pleasure to see you both." Her smile was a practiced fake. "Come in." Catherine stepped aside, allowing the Banks and then the Durbins, Carl and Linda, to enter. She closed the door behind them and gestured toward the living room, where there was plenty of seating for everyone. "Please, have a seat. Can I offer you anything to drink?"

"Red wine would be great," Rachel said with a pleasant

smile as she and the other three settled into the plush white chairs and matching sofas.

Catherine nodded and headed toward the kitchen. Her arm still in a cast, she returned moments later carefully balancing a tray with four glasses of red wine and a platter of appetizers put together by the caterers. Setting the tray on the coffee table, she was about to take a seat when a sudden knocking reverberated through the hall to the living room.

As she approached the front of the house, the sound persisted, more insistent now. She pulled the door open, revealing two familiar faces—a man and a woman, both around her age and exuding an air of casual confidence. The man, Stewart, had sandy blonde hair and a friendly smile, while the woman, Kelly, had honey-blonde hair and a dull glint in her steel-blue eyes.

Stewart extended a hand. "Hi there, Catherine. Great of you to invite us to dinner. Where is the old bugger? I have some catching up to do."

Catherine returned the handshake, giving them a smile that didn't reach her eyes. "Good evening, Stewart, Kelly. Tom should be in the living room by now. Come on in."

Kelly sighed; her eyes were filled with boredom. "You're serving drinks, aren't you? I would kill for a glass of wine."

Catherine nodded, allowing them to enter. "Of course, I've just poured some red for everyone. I'd be happy to get you a glass." She closed the door behind them and gestured toward the dining room. "Please, make yourselves comfortable."

As they settled into the open seats in the living room and began chatting amongst themselves, Catherine couldn't help but feel a bit frustrated. She knew none of the guests so far would take her side against Tom; even Kelly's dig about serving drinks made Catherine think she was only there to antagonize her. Tom had surrounded her with his faithful friends and colleagues, and she wondered why he had even bothered to have her there. After all, the caterers were working in the kitchen and the dining room and would be maintaining the guests' needs aside from the drinks she was expected to provide, which Tom could have easily handled.

The aroma of dinner wafted through the air, mingling with the soft strains of classical music playing from speakers in the corner of the living room. She could hear the catering staff moving about the dining room with a sense of purpose. As Catherine sat in an open seat, there was another sudden knock on the front door.

She stood up carefully once more and walked from the living room to the entrance, her footsteps soft. Taking as deep of a breath as she could in the formfitting dress, she opened the door to reveal two faces she recognized—their next-door neighbors, Mark and Shannon Kellogg. Mark, a tall man with graying hair and a friendly smile, stood on the doorstep while Shannon offered a wave from behind him.

Catherine's lips curved into a polite smile as she greeted them. "Hello, Mark, Shannon."

Mark's smile widened, and he extended a hand in greeting. "Hi, Catherine. Thank you so much for inviting us for dinner."

Catherine shook his hand. "Of course, come on in."

Mark and Shannon entered with a sense of familiarity, their presence bringing an air of neighborly warmth into her home. She closed the door behind them and followed them into the living room where Tom had finally taken up residence and was playing the gracious host. The tinkling of glasses and soft laughter filled the atmosphere as guests mingled in the small group.

Kelly, who was about three years older than Catherine, sat beside Tom on the sofa, her vibrant red dress catching the light and making her appear as if she was the embodiment of a summer sunset. Although her smile was sloppy, her laughter was like musical notes that danced through the air. She was the life of the party, drawing the attention of everyone around her, including Tom, who seemed captivated by her presence. Catherine knew he had known her for years, and while their friendship had always been strong, there was something different about their behavior tonight. Her playful glances, the way she brushed a strand of hair behind her ear while she laughed—it all seemed to suggest she was flirting with him. As the evening progressed, Tom gravitated toward Kelly. She engaged him in flirtatious banter, their conversation flowing effortlessly while few people even noticed or spoke to Catherine. That suited Catherine fine as she observed their guests.

Every now and then, she noticed a spark of something ignite between her husband and the honeyed blonde woman. Catherine felt a tight knot of unease form in her chest. She and Tom had been married for five years, and she knew he'd been unfaithful, though he'd never acted so disrespectfully to her in public. However, tonight was different. The way Kelly looked at Tom, the way she touched his arm when she laughed—it was all too intimate, too familiar, and too public.

Catherine clenched her hands around her glass of water, her knuckles turning white. Kelly's laughter rang out once again, and Tom's head turned in her direction as if drawn by an invisible force. Catherine's grip on her glass tightened further, the fragile object feeling as if it might shatter in her hand. She had always been a composed woman, but the doubts that were now clouding her mind were making her question everything.

"They'd do just about anything for you, Tom." Kelly laughed as she turned to her husband. "He's related to most of the town, you know."

"Is he?" Stewart replied, looking curious.

Catherine frowned. "What are you talking about?" she asked, her voice barely a whisper that no one answered.

"Tom's family founded Eldon. Nearly half of the town is related to him." Kelly's admiring gaze was back on Tom.

Catherine felt like she was choking on air. "No," she whispered, trying to remember everything she knew about Tom, everything that he'd told her over the years, "he said he was an only child and had no living relatives."

"I do have an older brother who lives up in Cleveland, and four older sisters here in town," Tom acknowledged as he raised his glass of wine to his lips. "I'm the youngest by about ten years."

"You've got more cousins, aunts, and uncles than I can even keep track of," Kelly teased Tom, running her hand over his arm possessively before looking at Stewart. "Even Sheriff Mason is like his second cousin on his mom's side, Stewart," Kelly added.

"Really, I would think that would help in a situation like yours," Stewart said, his gaze flicking toward Catherine.

Tom chuckled. "Indeed."

Catherine was drowning. That was the only thing she could feel at that moment. She was floored that the man she'd married had somehow blinded her to the truth of his life. And she couldn't understand why. Why would he lie to her about his family connections? Why had he focused on her when she was so young? Why did he marry her? None of it made sense to her.

"How is that possible? You told me you were an only child like me," Catherine said, making her voice louder.

Tom arched a brow and looked at her as though she were the crazy one. "Don't be ridiculous, sweetheart. I never said that. You've met my sisters and my cousins. You went to school with a couple of my nieces and nephews, you know that." He sighed and shook his head, before sharing a look with Kelly. "You see what I'm dealing with? She never remembers things I tell her. She lives in her own selfish little world."

Catherine silently gasped in shock. He was lying to them, to her. He'd never introduced her to his sisters. He'd never mentioned nieces and nephews who'd gone to school with her. She hadn't known anyone who said they were related to him.

She looked around the room in horror, knowing these friends of his were judging her. She felt so alone in the room. Nobody cared that her whole view of her life had just been shattered. And for what? Why would he do that to her? Lie to her? Had he wanted her that isolated? For what reason?

She pressed her fingers to her temples, trying to recall every conversation, every interaction with people in town and in school. Could she somehow have forgotten? Could the accident have messed with her long-term memory? She didn't think so, but then, what else could explain all this? Unless Tom was gaslighting her again.

The conversation went on around her, and as the night wore on, they adjourned to the dining room, and the wine continued to flow freely, not that Catherine had any. The conversations grew livelier around her, while their guests all continued to ignore her. Catherine felt like an outsider looking in. She watched as Tom became engaged in a spirited discussion about traveling with his friends, his enthusiasm clear in the way he leaned forward and gesticulated. Occasionally, someone in the group's attention would stray surreptitiously toward Catherine as though they finally remembered she was there, and then they'd quickly look away. She wondered if they were afraid to acknowledge her or if they were doing it on purpose to make her feel small.

Catherine noticed that Tom's gaze lingered everywhere except on her until the table decided they needed more wine. Then, he actively sought her out instead of one of the catering staff.

"Catherine, get us another bottle of wine, would you?"

Catherine's stomach soured. They'd been through six bottles of wine already, and the more they drank, the louder they got, and her ears were starting to hurt as much as her heart did. However, by the look on Tom's face, she knew she couldn't say a word about it. Giving him a tight smile, she nodded and carefully rose from the table without a word.

As she walked toward the kitchen, Catherine's attention was caught by the group's hushed conversation again once she was through the doorway, out of sight. Her instincts told her that their discussion was about her. She discreetly adjusted her position, just on the other side of the door, while straining to catch the pieces of conversation that drifted her way.

"I'm sure you've all heard about the accident," a voice, barely more than a whisper, carried through the cracked door. "She killed that woman with her recklessness."

Another voice chimed in, and she recognized it as Kelly's. "It's a shame, really. I don't know how you can put up with living with such a monster, Tom."

Catherine's heart skipped a beat, her palms growing clammy. She strained to listen further.

The first voice continued, and she realized it was Rachel speaking, the words like a dagger to Catherine's heart. "Well, there's no doubt she's been arrogant lately. I mean, look at the way she's dressed, and not following doctor's orders to stay in bed. You must be so unhappy with her, Tom."

Her actions? Tom wasn't happy? She had hoped that someone would have some sympathy for her plight, but, of course, they all believed Tom's version of events. Her mind raced, piecing together memories and moments, wondering if any of these people had ever been her friend.

Another voice—Shannon's—joined the conversation, her tone dripping with condescension. "Honestly, I never thought you two were a good match. Mother and Aunt Isabelle never thought so, either. Catherine was so young when you married, and as we all know, she's always been a bit too... egocentric... and full of herself. Take tonight, for example, saying she never knew we were family. What rubbish. I will never understand what you saw in her, nor why you allowed her to keep us from the wedding in the first place. Mother was quite hurt you didn't allow her to see her favorite nephew get married."

"I know, but Catherine was insistent on not having any family there since hers were all deceased. I should have demanded, but I was trying to be accommodating. You know I was distraught not having any of you around on such an important day."

"Aunt Isabelle and Mother should have stepped in," Shannon said, sounding annoyed. "Catherine never even went to college; she just expected you to take care of her. I've always found her to be very selfish and manipulative. You could do so much better, Tom."

"There are days when I wish they had stepped in," Tom said, sounding regretful.

Catherine's hands clenched at her sides, her nails digging into her palms as she struggled to contain the surge of hurt and anger. The words stung, each syllable like a venomous dart. And to hear herself dismissed as *selfish* when she had done everything that he had ever asked of her. She hadn't gone to school because he hadn't wanted her to. And he had asked her to marry him, and she'd thought she was in love. She had been a kid when she'd met him, and he'd wooed her, manipulated her more like, and with her father's permission. She was what he'd made her to be.

A third voice—Richard's this time—added its perspective, the words like salt rubbed into a fresh wound. "Well, it's clear she's not as caring as some of the other women here tonight. Kelly, it was so sweet of you to think about our needs, hiring Subito's Catering Service for Tom's dinner party. Now you are someone who knows how to make an impression."

Kelly's name, amid the discussion, and the fact that she had chosen Subito's Catering intensified the turmoil with Catherine. Once upon a time, Catherine had considered Kelly a close friend, or as close a friend as Tom would allow her to have. But after tonight, well, Catherine could see that had never been the case. And Shannon? His cousin? He'd never said. Never once had he mentioned that Shannon Kellogg and her mother, Amanda Westerly, were relatives. And Isabelle Porter was his aunt as well? She'd been Catherine's eighth-grade teacher; never once had she been told that Tom was her nephew. He had certainly never called her Aunt Isabelle. She was almost positive that he had been gaslighting her about his family now. There was no way she would have blocked knowing about his family. She had clear memories of him telling her she was an orphan, just like he was, when her dad died and that they should stick together.

The conversation continued, the voices weaving a tapestry of doubt and insecurity around Catherine. The happy sounds of the party seemed to blur into the background as she grappled with the harsh judgments being cast upon her. She knew she had to return before Tom came looking for her, and there would be hell to pay, so she hurried deeper into the kitchen to the wine cabinet and pulled out another bottle before pasting a smile on her lips and returning to the dining room.

The dinner party had been a success, according to Tom, as he declared it a culmination of the elegance and opulence that was expected of him. Of course, he, too, gave credit to Kelly for it and her securing Subito's to cater. As the last guest departed, a sense of exhaustion settled over Catherine. The horrid evening of having to play hostess to this group of hateful people had taken its toll on her. She yearned for nothing more than the embrace of her bed, a mantle of comfort and solace in the midst of the bustling house. She needed to get away from Tom and all of his lies.

Catherine returned to her room, dying to get out of the dreadful dress. She didn't bother to ask Tom for help, even though she probably needed it. It took her longer than she would have liked to get out of the garment, and it hurt trying to contort herself to reach all the buttons, but eventually, she stepped out of it and got it on a hanger.

She glanced at herself in the full-length mirror, the reflection revealing a woman who had battled and survived, her long blonde hair cascading in gentle waves down her back. Beneath the exterior of pain was a woman longing for quietude. With a graceful movement, she pulled the drapes on both windows shut, plunging the room into a swathe of darkness before the flick of a switch illuminated a single lamp on the bedside table, casting a warm and gentle light. She finished undressing, removing her bra, pulling on her light blue silk nightgown and went to the bathroom to remove her makeup and brush her teeth.

A moment later, she sat at the edge of the bed; the events of the evening played in her mind like scenes from a vivid dream. The laughter, the conversations, the clinking of glasses—all held a certain dark magic, a tapestry woven from the threads of disconnection and alienation. Slipping beneath the covers, Catherine felt the embrace of the sheets against her skin, a sensation akin to being wrapped in a cloud. She closed her eyes, the fatigue of the day and all the things she'd learned during the dinner finally caught up with her. In the gentle liminal space between wakefulness and slumber, her thoughts danced on the edge of her consciousness.

The night was restless, and a persistent unease, the tendrils of a nightmare creeping into the depths of her subconscious, plagued Catherine's sleep. Her room transformed into a realm of shadows and whispers. As the moonlight filtered through the curtains, a faint glow settled upon Catherine's form, her body tangled in the sheets as if caught in a web of turmoil. Her breath came in shallow gasps, her brow glistening with a sheen of sweat. The room felt oppressive to her as she lay in the still-

ness as if the air itself was charged with an otherworldly
tension.

As the sun began its ascent, a soft whimper escaped her lips,
a haunting melody of distress that pierced the silence. In the
realm of nightmares, Catherine found herself once again
standing on the precipice of a memory, a landscape marred by
shadows of the past. Her eyes fluttered open; her breath ragged
as the tendrils of the dream dissipated. She was back in her
room, the soft light of dawn casting gentle patterns upon the
walls, which was odd because she clearly recalled drawing her
curtains closed before getting into bed.

The remnants of the nightmare clung to her, a vise-like grip
on her heart that refused to let go as she tried to understand
what was going on. With a trembling hand, Catherine reached
for the tissue box on the bedside table, her fingers fumbling as
she pulled out a tissue to wipe away the tears that had filled her
eyes and spilled down her cheeks. The dampness on her face
was a bitter reminder of the emotions that had stirred within
her, a visceral echo of the dreams that had taken hold of her
mind. Drawing in a shuddering breath, Catherine sat up, the
sheet and blankets pooling around her waist.

The events of the past weeks had once again begun to
unravel the fabric of her life, revealing the deepening darkness
that continued to lay hidden beneath the surface. The memories were a mosaic of suspicion, doubt, and fear, each piece
forming a puzzle she was reluctant to solve. Her husband, Tom,
had been the captor of her heart. The emotions she had once
held for him—love, trust, companionship—were completely
entangled in a web of deceit.

A montage of memories played in her mind. Their friendship when she was a girl, their courtship, the vows they had
exchanged, the dreams they had shared—they all seemed
distant now, like a faded photograph of a time that no longer
existed. A life that no longer existed. He had already broken her

heart with his infidelities, but now—well. Now he was attempting to frame her for actions she hadn't committed. Hell, he'd even tried to kill her for not complying with his lies.

She knew she only had one option left. For her own safety, she had to get away from this house. She had to get away from Tom, and these people, and this town, and clear her name.

But she had no idea how she would achieve it.

TEN

Catherine sat closer to the window, her fingers tracing the edge of the blanket that covered her lap as she gazed out at the garden in the side yard. The sun was just starting to rise, casting a warm, golden glow over the town. But her mind was far from the picturesque scene outside; something tangled her in a web of doubt and uncertainty.

Tom's behavior had been gnawing at her, gnawing at the very foundation of their relationship. When she first met Tom all those years ago, he had been nothing but charming and outgoing. His amiable smile and friendly nature had drawn her to him, and she had hero-worshiped him.

He had encouraged her in those early years to do well in school, to engage in conversations with him about all sorts of things, but mostly about law, which was his favorite topic. She'd felt so grown up and mature to have a friend like him when she was just a girl. She remembered her friend Laura thinking it was weird that she was friends with someone fifteen years older than her, but she hadn't. Tom had said she was mature for her age, and she'd believed him.

Of course, she never told anyone they were dating when she was sixteen, though her father knew. He and Tom had agreed that once she completed school, she and Tom could be married. Things hadn't worked out exactly like that since her dad died just two days after she turned eighteen. Instead, Tom had helped her pay for her dad's funeral and sell the house, but there was nothing left after that. Her dad had taken a second mortgage out on the house, and it took everything to pay off all his debts, at least that was what Tom had told her.

During that time, she had trusted him to know what was best, to take care of everything for her, and why shouldn't she have? He was older and wiser than she was. And when he'd said there was really no money for her to go to school, she'd believed him. He'd said that she could take out loans if she really wanted to attend, but there was really no point in doing so when they were getting married and she was going to be a stay-at-home wife. She'd, of course, agreed.

So, instead of attending college, they'd gone to the courthouse and gotten married. Catherine recalled how happy she'd been to be his wife in those early days. Tom had taken her to New York for their honeymoon and bought her a nice wardrobe suitable for the wife of a prominent lawyer. He'd just made partner at his law firm at the time, and he had wanted her to impress the other partners and their wives.

He wasn't so controlling in the beginning; that happened over time. By the end of their first year of marriage he'd put a lock on the closet door and decided that he would be the one to choose what she wore each day because she couldn't be trusted to look her best on her own. He had her on a diet to keep her from getting fat—his words, and bought her a treadmill that he expected her to use for an hour every day.

Little by little, he took over her life. Telling her what to wear, what to eat, how to live, what she could do each day. Every aspect of her life was controlled. Even her therapist had been chosen by him because he'd said she needed one when she started having anxiety and panic attacks about a year into their marriage, which led to the diagnosis of MDD.

Things had gotten worse over the past year, though. Something had changed, and she wasn't sure why when she was doing everything that he asked of her. It had started innocently enough, at a casual dinner party at Mark and Shannon's house. The atmosphere was relaxed, laughter filling the air as the group shared stories and jokes. Catherine had watched as Tom engaged with everyone, his laughter mingling with those of the other guests. But it was the way he interacted with the female guests that caught her attention.

Catherine's heart skipped a beat as she recalled Tom's playful banter with the women. It had been the first time she had noticed how he behaved toward them. He had exchanged knowing glances and shared inside jokes. She recalled thinking his rapport was just a little too comfortable for her liking. She had felt a twinge of unease that she hadn't experienced before. It had been the first major crack in the rose-colored glasses she'd worn when she looked at her husband.

The memories of the times Tom had treated her poorly resurfaced like ghosts from the past that refused to be forgotten. The tears in their relationship had started to show, and one incident in particular still left a bitter taste in her mouth. They were at a restaurant, to cheer her up after the psychiatrist had diagnosed her with MDD, anxiety, and panic disorders. The dim lighting and soft music created an intimate ambiance, but as the evening wore on, the conversation took a sharp turn.

"*You know, Catherine.*" His gaze had been steady on something out the window. "*Sometimes I wonder if we're really meant to be together. You're always so anxious, so caught up in minor details. Can't you just let loose for once? You're just so annoying."*

Catherine's heart had dropped, and her smile had faltered as the weight of his words had settled in her chest. She hadn't been able to control her emotions, she had a mental illness. Tom's words had felt like a betrayal. He had claimed to love her, but his words had made it clear he didn't.

The memories of Tom's hurtful remarks accumulated like stones in a wall, each one building onto the last until it became a formidable barrier between them. There was the time he had forgotten her birthday—a day she had been eagerly expecting, hoping for a surprise that never came. She had smiled through the disappointment, masking her hurt, but deep down, she had wondered if she was truly as important to him as he claimed.

Then there was the argument they had when discussing their future, and she had mentioned wanting to have a child when Tom's dismissive words had cut like a knife.

"You're so fucking focused on having a kid when you should be focused on me and helping me build my career and the firm. Not everything is about you. You should be concentrating on us and how you can be a better wife to me."

Catherine had felt her heart shatter in that moment, the realization that Tom doubted her commitment to their relationship, leaving a scar that hadn't fully healed. She had fought back tears as his words had hung in the air like a cloud of doubt over her heart.

As the memories continued to flood back into her mind, she realized that they were part of a pattern, a pattern of disregard and disrespect that had eroded her self-esteem. It wasn't just the words that had wounded her; it was the way Tom had made her doubt herself, question her worth. She had lost sight of her value, her needs—if she'd ever really known them—in her desperate attempt to please him throughout the years.

Catherine couldn't help but wonder how she had let herself

endure such moments of hurt for so long. She had justified
Tom's behavior, convincing herself that it was just a rough
patch, that they could work through it. She'd been stupid, she
thought, looking back at the past nine years of her life with him.

As she sat there, a newfound clarity emerged. Catherine
suddenly realized she deserved better than a relationship that
chipped away at her self-esteem, which left her feeling insignifi-
cant. She deserved better than a husband who tried to frame
her. Better than a husband who had tried to kill her. Possibly.
She wasn't sure what was in that syringe. She supposed it could
have been something non-lethal, but she doubted it from the
way he'd been acting.

Now that she was looking back at her life and how things
had played out, she recognized the many unhealthy demands
Tom had placed on her. The first was when he had asked her to
give up her weekly café meetups with her friends when she'd
been fifteen. Tom had insisted her dedication to her friends was
a sign that she wasn't fully committed to her studies, which now
she realized he'd used as a way to manipulate her into spending
more time with him. Back then, she had questioned her priori-
ties, deciding she was being selfish for seeking out company
from people her own age.

Eventually, Catherine had distanced herself from nearly all
her friends because Tom had insisted that they were dragging
her down, holding her back, making passes at him. Now, the loss
of those friendships was a constant reminder of the lengths she
had gone to in order to appease Tom.

The only friend who had remained steadfast was Donna,
and Catherine had assumed it was because Donna was shy and
reserved and didn't push for Catherine to spend time with her
daily. Donna had gotten married last year and worked in Tom's
law firm as a paralegal. Seeing it now, Catherine figured the real
reason Donna was allowed to be her friend was because she was
smart and could talk to Tom about law. He saw her as his friend

who also spent time with Catherine, not the other way around. Of course, he always made sure they didn't spend too much time together.

Catherine realized she had no idea what her life would have looked like if she had been allowed to develop on her own. She suddenly wondered why her father had allowed Tom into her life. If he were alive, she'd have demanded answers, but it was a useless line of questions now. He wasn't here to answer them.

Her mind turned to the car crash, and a chilling idea had taken root—the possibility that Tom had planned to kill her that night. It wasn't a thought she entertained lightly, but she remembered how odd Tom had been acting that day. First, he'd put together that cocktail party before they'd gone out, insisting that she have a drink with him and "their" friends in celebration. Then, he had taken her to one of the most expensive restaurants in Cincinnati. He had ordered the most expensive champagne and food on the menu, which was completely out of character. On top of that, his demeanor had been more giving, and his words had even had a sexual undertone, which he'd not used on her in more than a year. She recalled sensing an underlying tension in him, a darkness lurking beneath the surface that she couldn't quite put her finger on that evening.

As Catherine played back the events of that night, a sinking feeling settled in her gut. She could see it all now. Tom's tone of voice as he'd spoken to her, his aggression on the road. How he'd looked at her, his gaze full of what she now recognized was apathy. She remembered he had sped up suddenly, his grip on the steering wheel tightening as she'd yelled at him about the stop sign.

Catherine's memory of the impact was hazy, a blur of chaos and pain. But she remembered the airbag hadn't gone off. Why not? She didn't have the answer to that. The other thing that stood out was the image of Tom's face as he'd gripped her and pulled on her so that she would be found behind the wheel. The anger and determination that was there.

Catherine's mind swirled with thoughts and emotions. She knew without a doubt that Tom wanted her to take the fall for the car crash—to be rid of her. The thought had lodged itself like a thorn in her consciousness. She couldn't escape the chilling notion that the person she had trusted most was capable of such deception. A shiver went down her spine.

She needed to get out of this house.

But how?

The weight of her thoughts hung heavy in the air, a reminder of the journey she had embarked upon. The IV pole stood like a sentinel beside her, a constant reminder of her limitations. Eleanor had returned earlier, before sun up, and reattached it to make it easy to administer her sedatives when Catherine became overwhelmed. She'd hoped to keep it off, but Eleanor had said it would make things simpler, so Catherine had complied.

Through the window, she could see slivers of the outside world—a tantalizing glimpse of life beyond the confines of her room. Her gaze lingered on that window, yearning for a more unobstructed view, a connection to the world she felt so removed from. She longed for a closer view of the sun painting the sky with its golden hues, the dance of leaves in the breeze, and the ebb and flow of life happening just beyond her reach. The urge to experience a more complete view of the world outside was too strong to ignore any longer. Yet, her body protested with every movement.

She'd done too much the night before. She should never have been out of bed and hosting that dinner party. She'd overdone it, and now she was paying for it.

The pain was a reminder of the car crash, but the need to see beyond the window was stronger than the discomfort. Catherine's gaze fell on the IV stand. It was both a lifeline and a hindrance—tethering her to her room since the accident, except for her excursion last night into the hell that Tom had put her through for dinner.

She took a moment to steady herself, her breath coming in shallow gasps as her muscles protested any movement. Last night had seriously taken its toll on her body. Summoning her inner strength, Catherine reached out for the IV stand, her fingers curling around the cold metal. She could feel the thin tube leading to her IV site, a lifeline that she was temporarily commandeering. Gritting her teeth against the newest aches and pains, Catherine stood and maneuvered the IV stand, inch by inch, closer to the front window. Each movement was a battle, a testament to her determination. She felt as if last night had set her recovery back by weeks. After what felt like an eternity, Catherine positioned the IV stand near the front window. She stood there, her body trembling, a mixture of pain and triumph coursing through her veins.

She could feel the warmth of the sun's rays against her skin, a sensation that was both invigorating and soothing. She watched as the leaves danced in the gentle breeze as people passed by on the sidewalk, their faces illuminated by the sunlight. A flicker of movement caught her attention. Her brow furrowed in curiosity as she focused on a van parked on the street in front of the Browns' old house, which stood empty. The white exterior of the van glinted in the sunlight, but that wasn't what drew her eye. Beside the van, something seemed out of place—a lone lawn chair, positioned on the curb as if waiting for someone to claim it. Intrigued, Catherine leaned forward slightly, her eyes narrowing as she wondered who had put it there. The van seemed unremarkable, a vehicle like any other. But the lawn chair piqued her curiosity. Had it been there long? Probably not, the neighbors would complain if they thought some transient had taken up residence on the street. Could one of the neighbors have bought the van? Might it be one of the teenagers? She snickered. They wouldn't like that either.

Catherine's gaze remained fixed on the van and the lawn chair as she spun different scenarios for who it belonged to. As she stood there, Eleanor came in.

"Catherine, what are you doing up?" she fussed. "Let me at least pull the chair over here if you want to change your view." She shook her head and hurried to move the armchair.

Catherine sat down and smiled at her. "Thanks, Eleanor. I just wanted to see something different."

Eleanor patted her shoulder. "I'll be back in a bit with your lunch." She checked the IV and then left the room again.

Catherine turned her gaze back to the van and the lawn chair, a new movement catching her attention, causing her heart to skip a beat. A redheaded woman emerged from the van; her hair vibrant like a freshly grown cherry dancing in the sunlight. Catherine's eyes widened in surprise and apprehension as she watched the familiar woman step onto the pavement, her movements confident and purposeful. She wore a casual yet practical outfit—a fitted white tank top, a pair of camouflage cargo pants, and a pair of dark boots. She held her hand up to her forehead like a visor as she stared at Catherine's house, scanning it from one side to the other.

As if sensing Catherine's presence, the woman's gaze fixated on the guest room window, her eyes locking onto Catherine. A wide, noticeable smile curved her lips, and she raised her hand in a friendly wave.

Catherine stared at her, her anxiety rising at the unexpected interaction. She could hardly believe that the woman who had planned to kill her was now looking right at her as if she were happy to see her. Catherine let her gaze drift from the woman to the lawn chair, trying to make sense of what was going on. Was this woman who had once seemed so determined to kill her now watching over her? How did that make sense?

Catherine recalled the night Tom had been messing with her IV and the mysterious rock crashing through the window that stopped him, and she began to wonder if that really was the case. Her heart raced as she considered the possibility. Could she have somehow sensed or seen the danger and intervened to protect Catherine from Tom? The idea was unsettling and strangely comforting. Returning the woman's wave, Catherine felt a surge of gratitude. The exchange felt like a bridge between their worlds, a moment of shared understanding.

As the redheaded woman approached the lawn chair, she picked it up with practiced ease, her movements confident and deliberate. She positioned the chair so it was facing Catherine's window, and then, with a last glance in Catherine's direction, she settled into the seat, her posture relaxed as she leaned back. It was as if she was intentionally sharing this moment with Catherine, inviting her to be a part of her world, if only from a distance.

Catherine's heart swelled with a mixture of wonder and gratitude. The woman's presence was a reminder that even in her current circumstances, she could still find unexpected moments of connection and joy.

As Catherine continued to watch, the woman reached into a bag beside the lawn chair and pulled out a book, her focus turning to the pages before her. The sight brought a smile to Catherine's lips—she no longer felt so alone.

ELEVEN

The sun hung low on the horizon later that afternoon, casting a warm golden hue over the tranquil suburban neighborhood. From her bed, where she'd returned after eating lunch, Catherine heard a car pull up to the house. A few minutes later, she heard the rap of knuckles against the front door, the sound resonating through the entryway. After a moment, there was the sound of the door swinging open, and heavy footsteps reached her ears.

"Good afternoon, Mrs. Morris," Detective Sheldon greeted with a polite nod.

She regarded the policeman standing in her bedroom door-way. "Detective Sheldon, what brings you here?"

He offered a small smile as he held up a sealed gray evidence bag. "I'm here to return this."

Catherine's eyes widened in surprise as she accepted the bag, her fingers tracing over the plastic. She opened it and looked inside, where she found her clutch and her phone. "My things. Where did you find them?"

His expression was serious as he drew the chair over to her bedside and sat down. "We found your phone under the passenger seat along with your purse when we inspected your husband's impounded car. I thought you might want them back."

Catherine gave him a smile. "Of course. Thank you for returning them. Did you find the dashcam?"

"We've located the dashcam, and we've analyzed the footage it captured on the day of the crash."

Catherine's fingers stilled as she processed the significance of the news. "What did the footage show?"

Detective Sheldon leaned forward. "The footage caught the crash, and we saw how the other car was struck and pushed, spinning it away from your car. It also revealed that shortly after the crash, Tom moved from the driver's side over to the passenger side, then he walked back again to the driver's side, and returned once more to the passenger side and didn't move until our officers arrived."

Catherine frowned.

"I know it's a bit late for this, but I've brought a female officer to photograph your bruises. Well, what bruises you still have, seeing as it's been nearly two weeks. If you will agree to that, that is. It'll be better for evidence, but with the current developments—the video evidence, I mean, you don't have to."

Catherine nodded, determined. "I want to help in any way I can, Detective. And you can still see the bruising, it went pretty deep. They're kind of a yellowish-brown color now."

He nodded appreciatively. "Thank you, Mrs. Morris." He motioned for the woman standing in the hallway to join them. "Mrs. Morris, this is Officer Reynolds," Detective Sheldon introduced.

Catherine offered a small smile. "Nice to meet you, Officer Reynolds."

She returned the smile. "Likewise, Mrs. Morris. If you're comfortable, we'll proceed with photographing the injuries."

Catherine took a deep breath, her fingers twisting together slightly. "Yes, I'm ready."

The detective stepped out of the room, and Officer Reynolds prepared her camera, adjusting the settings before approaching Catherine with the utmost care.

"May I?" Her voice was gentle.

Catherine nodded, her posture tense as she braced herself for the discomfort of the process.

Officer Reynolds ensured an accurate capture of each angle and detail of Catherine's bruises. After taking the photographs, she stepped back and offered a reassuring smile. "Thank you for your cooperation, Mrs. Morris. These will be valuable for the investigation."

Catherine let out a heavy breath, her shoulders relaxing slightly. "You're welcome. I just want to do whatever I can to help."

Detective Sheldon rejoined them. He spoke up, his tone appreciative. "Your willingness to cooperate and provide evidence is crucial, Mrs. Morris. We're dedicated to uncovering the truth, and your help brings us one step closer. I was also wondering if I could ask you a few questions about your husband."

"Of course, Detective. Ask away."

Sheldon nodded; his pen poised over a notepad. "Have you noticed any changes in his behavior lately?"

Catherine sighed softly and winced. "Tom has always dedicated himself to his work and his friends. He's a confident and generous person, often spending long hours at the office to ensure we have everything we need to live a comfortable life. He's always been a private individual, never telling me about his day or about things he says will hurt me to know. But over the past year, Tom has changed. He had an affair a few months ago, which I found out about and confronted him over. He swore he'd ended it;

however, he spends more time with female guests at our home and often flirts with them. He receives calls and messages that he is reluctant to discuss. He keeps things from me all the time."

Sheldon jotted down notes as Catherine continued.

"Any time I ask him about one of the calls, he brushes it off, saying it is a big legal case, but these past few months his demeanor has been different."

"Has Tom ever mentioned any personal or financial troubles?"

Catherine thought about it for a moment before answering honestly. "No, but Tom refuses to discuss financial things with me. Our life seems stable, and as far as I'm aware, we've never had problems in that area, but then I don't have access to our finances, so I wouldn't really know. As for personal troubles, all I can say is he's been growing distant from me, and it's been going on for a long time now. Long before he had the affair I know about."

Sheldon asked, "Can you tell me how you and Tom met? How did your relationship begin?"

Catherine's voice softened, and her cheeks heated. "I grew up in this town, and he had his eye on me once I turned fourteen. Tom is older than me by fifteen years."

He raised his eyebrows at that. "That's a big age difference. And wait, you said you met at *fourteen*?" He looked appalled and horrified.

Catherine wished he'd been around when her father had introduced her to Tom. Maybe things would have been different if another adult had realized what was going on. "Yes, my father introduced me to him when I was fourteen. I should explain." Catherine paused. "My mother died when I was twelve. My dad was a bailiff at the courthouse. He met Tom at work and invited him to have dinner with us. I had always been interested in Dad's stories about court proceedings and had thought I wanted to be a lawyer. When I met Tom, it was a bit like meeting a hero, you know?"

"Okay?"

"So, Tom was really kind to me back then, he encouraged me to do well and study hard. We became friends of a sort in those early years. He took an interest in me and encouraged me to go into law. He asked me out on a date about three months before my seventeenth birthday, with my dad's permission. After that, we started seeing each other romantically. I was planning to go to college, and he continued to encourage me to pursue law school, but then, a couple of days after my eighteenth birthday, my dad died. There was no money to go to school, and the house had to be sold to pay off his debts. Tom asked me to marry him, so I did." She shrugged.

Detective Sheldon let out a stunned breath. "Okay. Um... can you tell me what the early years of your marriage were like? Did you notice any significant changes in Tom's behavior during that time?"

"The first year was great, at least I thought so. Tom focused on his career, and I supported him. He'd made partner by the time we married, and he was going after bigger cases, drawing attention from Cincinnati. I hadn't noticed anything different, hadn't really put anything together until this past year."

"I see. Have you ever suspected that Tom might be involved in something secretive or illegal?"

Catherine was a bit surprised by that question. Did he suspect that Tom had been trying to kill her? Or was he talking about something else? "I don't know. I had never thought so. But..." Catherine pressed her lips together firmly, considering her next words. "Do you think my husband... Do you think Tom was trying to kill me with the car crash?"

The question hung heavy in the air, the weight of its implications palpable. Detective Sheldon's gaze never wavered as he studied her. "Mrs. Morris, it's my duty to consider every possibility in this investigation," he began carefully. "I want to assure you we are working diligently to gather all the evidence and information before making any conclusions. At the moment, I cannot say what Tom's motives were at the time of the accident, but I have to agree that it does look as though he's been trying to frame you for it, and that makes me very suspicious."

Catherine's eyes welled up with tears, her voice choked with emotion. "I can't believe I even asked that question, Detective. It's just that things haven't been right for a long time, and with my medication anxiety and panic attacks, well... sometimes I don't always know what's real and what isn't. Things have been off since that night. Since before that night, actually, but worse since then."

Sheldon's tone was compassionate as he replied, "I understand that this is an incredibly difficult time for you, especially given your mental health issues, Mrs. Morris. I'm going to end my questions for the evening and let you rest, but I want to assure you that I will find out the truth. I will figure out what happened that night and if what you suspect is the truth, I'll protect you as best I can."

Catherine wiped away a tear and nodded. "Thank you, Detective. I need to know if it's even a possibility that those were his intentions that night. Thank you for caring enough to find out the truth and for letting me go through this at a pace I can handle."

TWELVE

Two weeks since the anniversary

Catherine sat on her bed, absorbed in her phone screen, her fingers dancing across the keyboard. The rhythmic clatter of keys was her sole companion, the only sound that reached her ears. Until a hesitant knock echoed through the room, pulling her attention away from her phone.

"Come in," Catherine called out, her brows knitting together in confusion.

The door creaked open, revealing Tom standing in the doorway with a solemn expression and a small group of their neighbors. He cleared his throat. "Hey, Catherine." His voice was laced with unease. "Mind if we have a word with you?"

This was curious and disturbing. Catherine gave him a nod after a brief hesitation. "Of course. What's on your mind?"

Tom and the group of five took a step into the room. He glanced around, his hands fidgeting at his sides for a moment, before finally meeting Catherine's gaze. "It's about the accident." His voice was soft but firm, as though he wanted to appear gentle in front of the people he called friends.

The memory of the screeching tires and the sickening crunch of metal resurfaced, sending a shiver down Catherine's spine. She had been trying to avoid thinking about it, wanting to be in her best health when Detective Sheldon came back.

"What about it?" Catherine began to feel nervous as she looked at the faces of those Tom had surrounded himself with. Her gaze moved from Shannon and Mark to Donna, who was looking anywhere but at her, to another set of neighbors, Jim and Barbara Miller. There were more people in the hall, but she couldn't see who they were.

Tom narrowed his eyes, his gaze roaming over her face. "I think it's time for you to take responsibility for the crash, Catherine. You can't keep avoiding it."

Her mind raced with a flurry of negative thoughts. She had been wrestling with the decision of whether to continue her relationship with Tom, replaying his actions repeatedly, searching for a way to absolve him.

"I don't know what you're talking about." As her panic and fear rose, her throat began to close, causing her voice to come out just above a squeak. "I wasn't driving... I know I wasn't driving."

Jim stepped closer; his gaze unwavering. He was a large man, built like a linebacker, and was very intimidating. His voice was gruff and harsh as he said, "None of us believe that. You can't change what happened. You were found in the driver's seat."

She shook her head, her eyes moistening as she blinked back tears. "You're wrong," she whispered. "You don't have the facts right."

Just as the weight of the conversation grew, his wife Barbara narrowed her eyes. She settled on the edge of the hospital bed, her expression thoughtful. "He's right. You can't keep ignoring what happened. It's affecting all of us. Our community is being subjected to the scrutiny of the city police, and you know how we like our privacy, dear. It's not right that you continue to fight against taking responsibility."

Barbara's words intensified Catherine's anger. Barbara had always been kind to Catherine in the past, but now Catherine knew that had all been for show. She shook her head, her eyes landing on the round figure of her best friend, Donna, who was awkwardly quiet as she tugged on a strand of her brown hair. The others around Tom begged Catherine to accept the consequences of her actions. Her world was in disarray. The weight of her husband's lies bore down on her shoulders, and anger gnawed at her heart. She felt numb, unable to fully process what was happening. Catherine stared blankly at her best friend, lost in a sea of thoughts. Her throat felt dry and tight. Her heart pounded at the betrayal of everyone closest to her. How could Donna side with them? She had to know that what Tom was saying was a lie.

The memories of the accident, the weight of Tom's responsibility and cunning, the rage from her neighbors' judgment—they all churned within her. She pressed her hand against her mouth, attempting to stifle the turmoil that was building within her. And then, as if a dam had been breached, Catherine's emotions spilled over, the floodgates of her despair opening wide.

She gasped for air, her breaths coming in ragged sobs as tears streamed down her cheeks. Her body convulsed with each cry, her chest heaving as if trying to expel the overwhelming weight that had taken residence within her. "I... I can't do this." Catherine choked out between sobs, her voice cracking with a raw vulnerability. "I can't handle it anymore."

The words were like drops in an ocean of anguish, swallowed up by Catherine's overwhelming distress. The room seemed to spin around her, the walls closing in. She felt a searing pressure building in her chest, threatening to engulf her completely as fear and panic took over.

And then, with a sudden lurch, Catherine's body betrayed her, and she clung to the bed as her stomach revolted. The contents of her stomach spilled forth, a physical manifestation of the turmoil that had taken root within her. She retched and heaved, her body trembling with each convulsion, the taste of bitterness lingering in her mouth as they all jumped backward, gasping in disgust.

Catherine's sobs mingled with the sound of her retching, a symphony of despair that echoed through the room. Her body felt weak and drained, her emotions and physical sensations intertwining in a maelstrom of agony.

She heard Donna call, "Eleanor!"

The sound of approaching footsteps echoed in the hallway. Eleanor entered the room. "That's it, visiting hours are over, everyone out!" she demanded.

The neighbors exchanged quick glances, a subtle unease passing between them.

"We just wanted to help Catherine understand the reality of the situation," said Tom earnestly.

"I appreciate your concern, but Catherine needs her rest. It's important for her recovery," Eleanor said firmly.

Catherine's gaze shifted between her neighbors and the nurse, her heart silently thanking Eleanor for her support and understanding. The neighbors tried to fight back, saying Catherine needed to admit the truth and face justice for her actions. Without a change in her demeanor, Eleanor forced them out of the room.

"I'm sorry, but that includes you, Mr. Morris. After this, I am probably going to have to administer a sedative anyway, so there is no point in you being here."

Tom's brow furrowed; his gaze locked on Eleanor. "But I'm her husband. I need to be here with her."

"Of course, I understand you want to be here, but she needs peace and quiet, and she can't have that with all of you here.

You can say your goodbyes, but then I'll need to ask you to leave so she can recover, and I can clean up the sickness."

Tom, disregarding Eleanor's words, settled in the chair, avoiding the mess of vomit on the floor, his eyes never leaving Catherine's. "Sweetheart, I know you've been struggling with everything that's happened. But I want to remind you of something important. Doing the right thing is never easy, but it's essential."

"What do you mean?" Catherine gazed at him with confusion.

Tom's gaze remained steady and demanding. "I mean that sometimes, the choices we make can define who we are. It's easy to get caught up in fear or guilt, but what truly matters is how we respond." He leaned forward slightly, his narrow eyes staring at Catherine with intensity. "Making things right starts with facing the truth, no matter how difficult it may be. It's about taking responsibility for our actions and seeking a way to make amends."

Catherine's gaze dropped to her hands, her fingers twisting nervously in the sheets. She knew his words weren't for her but for those in the hallway listening. Tom's words were forcing her to confront the choices he had made and the path she needed to take.

As Tom rose from the chair, his presence seemed to fill the room, a reminder of the opposition that surrounded her. He placed a hand on her shoulder, his fingers tightening into the healing bruise as his voice filled with fake sincerity. "Remember, Catherine, there's a way to heal and make things right. It might not be easy, but it's worth it." With that, he turned to leave, his steps carrying him toward the door.

Catherine warily watched him go. The accident had shattered more than just glass and metal; it had forced her to confront the disturbing truth of her relationship with Tom, revealing cracks that had been overlooked for far too long.

Catherine tried to gather the courage she needed to accept the desire to defy her husband. A surge of determination welled up within her. She was seeing things differently these days. She had realized that she had allowed herself to be influenced by his external pressure, by his opinions, without questioning them since she'd first met him.

Catherine searched for something—perhaps a glimpse of the truth that lay hidden beneath the surface. *What if what's best for me isn't what Tom thinks it is? I've been sacrificing my desires and opinions to conform to his expectations since we met.* The words that she had tried hard to suppress finally found their way to the surface. *Love should come with respect for my autonomy, for my feelings and opinions.* Her heart refused to agree with his unwavering lies.

THIRTEEN

The panic attack had taken its toll, leaving her drained and exhausted, though Eleanor decided against sedating her, thankfully. The smell of cleaning fluid lingered in the air. As she gingerly pushed herself into a sitting position, her head spinning in protest, Catherine's gaze fell upon the nightstand. A cup of steaming ginger tea sat upon it. A thoughtful gesture from Eleanor, no doubt.

As she reached for the cup, her cell phone vibrated next to it. Catherine glanced at the screen, noting the unfamiliar number. A twinge of curiosity mingled with a hint of apprehension as she swiped to answer the call that she would normally ignore, but given the fact that it could be Detective Sheldon, she decided to answer it.

"Hello?"

"Catherine? Is that you?" a somewhat familiar female voice came over the line, tinged with concern.

Catherine strained to place the voice. "Yes, this is Catherine."

"Listen, the reason I'm calling is that I saw what happened

in your room. It took me a bit to get a hold of your number. I'm very concerned about you. Are you alright?"

Catherine hesitated for a moment, unsure how to proceed. Who could this be that had seen what happened? Was it one of the neighbors who'd been in the hall? "I'm sorry if this seems odd, but... who is this? You sound familiar, but I can't for the life of me figure out who you are."

The woman's voice held a hint of nervousness as she replied, "Um, well, we have met, yes."

That told Catherine nothing except that maybe this wasn't one of her neighbors. "Who exactly are you?"

"I'm Jessica." The woman's voice was steady but laden with emotion. "Look, I know this is weird, but our lives have been intertwined in a way that I never could have imagined nor wanted."

Catherine's head was still fuzzy from her earlier panic attack, and she was having trouble deciphering what this woman was getting at.

Jessica's voice quivered with a mix of sorrow and determination. "My sister... my sister was the woman killed in the car accident your husband caused."

Catherine's eyes widened. "You were there, too, weren't you?" she said.

"Yes, I was driving when your husband careened his car into the passenger side of mine. Melissa was full of life, dreams, and aspirations. That fateful night, all that was taken away from her, from me."

Catherine's heart ached, the weight of the tragedy hanging between them. She struggled to find the right words to convey the empathy and sorrow that welled within her. "I'm so sorry, Jessica." Her voice was tinged with genuine compassion despite her uneasiness.

"Thank you. My sister's death was a profound loss for me." Jessica's voice grew pained.

Catherine's heart sank as she listened to Jessica's words. The injustice of the death weighed heavily on her, a stark reminder of the vulnerabilities of life. The words hung in the air like a thunderclap, shattering the stillness of the day. "I... I don't know what to say," Catherine stammered, her mind reeling as she wondered why this woman was calling her.

Jessica's voice was intense, a mixture of grief and determination. "I've been doing some digging into your life. I'm sorry if that upsets you, but I needed to know who you are. What kind of person you are. What kind of person your husband is." Jessica's voice sounded a little shaky at first but grew firmer and more determined as she spoke.

The idea that this woman had been looking into her life confused Catherine. "Why?"

"It doesn't matter. What does matter is that I know what's happened to you. I know what kind of life you've been living. And I know you aren't fully aware of what your husband has done. You aren't fully aware of what kind of asshole your husband is because of what's been done to you."

Catherine couldn't believe it. The woman who had tried to kill her a short while ago believed her. Knew what Tom had done to her. She wasn't the only one who saw the truth behind her husband's actions. She wanted to trust Jessica, but she was still scared. "No, I don't have a full idea. However," Catherine finally said, her voice strained, "I'm coming to realize some of what has been happening, and I now see that I know very little about who he really is."

"That is good to hear. I didn't want to have to be the one to drag you into full awareness, but I was prepared to if I had to."

Her words made Catherine smile. "I appreciate that. I also wanted to say thanks."

"Thanks? For what?"

Catherine took a deep breath, her fingers nervously twisting a loose thread in her shirt. "For what you did the other day. For throwing the rock through the window."

"You... You figured out that was me?"

"Yes, once I saw you sitting outside your van across the street. You saved me from Tom that night. I'm not sure exactly what he was going to do, but I know it wasn't good."

"I had to do something. It didn't look right, the way he was messing with your IV like that. And the look on his face. I was concerned. When I saw what was happening, I couldn't just stand by and watch."

Catherine's heart swelled with gratitude. The woman talking to her had been a stranger, a nameless voice on the phone, and now, she was a fearsome symbol of protection. "I really can't express how thankful I am," Catherine said, feeling emotional. "If it weren't for you, I honestly don't know what would have happened."

"I did what anyone would have done in that situation. I've seen things that most civilians couldn't dream of other people doing to one another. Your husband... he's not a good man, Catherine, and I'm not just saying that because he was driving the car that killed my sister. That's part of it, but he's worse than you can imagine."

The weight of Jessica's words settled over Catherine, a profound reminder of the interconnectedness of their lives.

"There's something else I need to discuss with you," Jessica said. "It's the other reason I wanted to reach out, not just to make sure you were okay after that neighborly assault on your peace." Jessica sighed. "You are alright, aren't you?"

"Yes. Tired and a bit weak, but overall, I'm okay. What is it you wanted to discuss with me?" Catherine asked.

Jessica paused. "You've been working with that detective, answering his questions and getting him to understand what really happened, right?"

Catherine frowned. "Yes, of course. Detective Sheldon has promised to find out the truth."

"He is dedicated, compassionate, but... I need you to understand that there are limits to what the police can do."

"What do you mean?"

"The law, as I'm sure you know, is a complex web that can sometimes limit the pursuit of justice. Even with a good detective, there are constraints that can make it difficult to achieve the outcomes we are hoping for."

Catherine's heart sank as she considered the magnitude of what Jessica was saying. The realization that pursuing justice might be hindered by legal intricacies left her feeling helpless. "But Detective Sheldon... he seems so dedicated."

Jessica's voice was somber. "Yes, he is. And I believe he genuinely wants to help. But the system can sometimes work against us. The evidence required, the burden of proof—it's not always as straightforward as it should be, especially in Eldon where there is a distinct lack of trustworthiness."

"What do you mean?"

She paused again. "What I'm saying is that there is a great deal of corruption in Eldon. I just want you to be aware of it and what impact it might have on this case."

Catherine considered the implications of Jessica's words. "But shouldn't there be a way to ensure that the courts hold my husband accountable for his actions?"

"I wish it were that simple, Catherine. We can't control how the legal system functions in certain places. Detective Sheldon is from Cincinnati, and I'm sure he's going to do his best to get justice for us, but considering your husband's standing in this town and how deep the corruption here goes, well... we'll see. We need to continue to seek the truth and to make our voices heard so that this Detective Sheldon doesn't give up or isn't told by his superiors to do so."

Catherine's gaze dropped to her hands. She'd had no idea

that Eldon was so corrupt or that somehow Tom might manage to escape justice.

"It's not just Eldon, Catherine," Jessica continued, her voice gentle but firm. "Not everyone within the legal system can be trusted, even in Cincinnati. The detective you're working with may be sincere, but that doesn't mean we can place blind trust in everyone involved in the case."

"Who else do you mean?"

"I've come to realize that there may be individuals within law enforcement who prioritize other interests over pursuing justice. Corruption, bribery, biases—it's a reality we can't ignore."

Catherine's gaze remained fixed on a distant point, her mind grappling with the truths Jessica had confronted her with. *Tom... he's well-connected within the community. He's known by many of the local sheriff deputies and the sheriff himself. He's involved in community organizations, events, and charities. They have always seen him as an upstanding citizen, someone who contributes positively to the community.*

Catherine's eyes welled with unshed tears. *His connections and influence might sway the course of the investigation or protect him from facing the consequences of his actions.*

She realized now that the path ahead was uncertain, fraught with challenges and doubts.

FOURTEEN

Eighteen days since the anniversary

The past few days had been a blur of pain, discomfort, and the relentless march of time. But now, as Catherine lay in her bed, she felt a glimmer of hope, a tiny spark of strength that seemed to have returned to her weary body. The car accident had left her broken and battered, confined to this room for what felt like an eternity. Through it all, Catherine had fought with everything she had against Tom's constant gaslighting, determined to regain her independence.

Eleanor entered the room, her presence a familiar comfort. She had been by Catherine's side from the beginning, guiding her through the toughest moments of her recovery. With a kind smile, she greeted Catherine and began her routine check-up. "How are you feeling today, Catherine?"

Catherine took a deep breath, her chest feeling less constricted than it had in a while. "Better, I think. Sore, but... better. I think my ribs are finally regaining their strength."

Eleanor nodded approvingly. "That's good to hear. Your progress has been impressive. Your body has shown remarkable resilience, and your determination has undoubtedly played a significant role in your recovery."

Catherine gave her a grateful smile. She couldn't wait to regain her independence and return to a better life than she knew. "I'm glad you think so."

Eleanor continued her examination. "You've done well without the IV for the last few days. Have you felt as though you needed any of the meds?"

Catherine shook her head. "No, I've felt fine."

"That's good to hear. I've been reviewing your recent test results, and you've made tremendous strides. Your rib fractures are healing well, and your range of motion has improved significantly. And from what your therapist has said, I think you're mentally on the mend as well."

Could it be that the moment she had been hoping for was finally here? "Does that mean," Catherine started, "I might be ready to leave this room behind soon?"

Eleanor set aside her clipboard and met Catherine's gaze with a compassionate smile. "You've come a long way since the day of the crash. Your determination and hard work have paid off, and I believe you've recovered enough to no longer require my help."

The clock on the wall ticked away the minutes as Catherine considered what this revelation meant. She should have been thrilled that she had become well enough not to need a nurse, but the prospect of Eleanor no longer being around filled her with dread. If she left, that meant—

Tom.

The name whispered through Catherine's thoughts like a haunting refrain. The weight of her fear over what he might do threatened to consume her.

"Eleanor." Catherine broke the silence that had settled over the room.

Eleanor again looked up from her paperwork, her expression kind and attentive. "Yes? Is there something else on your mind?"

Catherine hesitated. She'd rehearsed the words in her mind a hundred times, but now the moment had arrived, she felt her resolve waver. "I... I've been thinking about Tom." Her voice was barely above a whisper. "I can't shake the feeling that... that I shouldn't be alone with him."

Eleanor's brows furrowed in concern, her eyes studying Catherine's face. "Catherine, it's natural to feel conflicted about my leaving you. But remember, you're on your journey of recovery right now. You need someone to care for you still, and that's your husband. I'm sure you understand my expertise is needed for other people. You'll be more than fine in his capable hands."

Catherine's heart ached at Eleanor's words. She knew the nurse was wrong—she needed to get away from Tom before he killed her. But the understanding that she couldn't survive on her own at the moment gnawed at her conscience. "Eleanor, I can't help but think that maybe I shouldn't be here in this house." Catherine's voice trembled as she tried to make her desperation clear. "I need to talk to someone about Tom, someone who understands what he has done. Do you think you could... call Detective Sheldon for me?"

Eleanor's expression softened, and she sighed gently. "Catherine, I understand that you're feeling conflicted about everything, but speaking to law enforcement about your health-care might not be the best course of action."

Tears welled up in Catherine's eyes as she felt a sense of desperation. She had to do something, anything, to ease the weight of these feelings, to calm her fear and her longing to find the truth. She needed to make Eleanor understand that she truly feared for her life if she was left alone with Tom. "Eleanor, please." Catherine's voice quivered as she spoke, her emotions spilling over as her panic rose. "I'm not asking to talk to him because of my health. I just need someone to talk to, someone who might get me out of here. Out of this hou—"

A knock at the door interrupted their conversation.

Eleanor turned toward the door, her smile widening. "Tom," Eleanor greeted him with a nod. "I haven't seen you in a while. How are you?"

There he was, the person who had destroyed her dreams, her heart, and her life. He looked different—energetic, a touch younger—but the essence of who he was remained unchanged. Tom's eyes met Catherine's, and she felt a rush of fear flood over her. The memories of their recent times together, the pain he had inflicted on her, surged to the forefront of her mind. She had thought about him often, wondering what he was doing, what he was planning, and whether he had found another way to kill her.

"I'm doing well, Eleanor." Tom's voice was wry as he smiled at Eleanor. "However, I'm afraid you must have caught Catherine in a bad mental state. I can take care of her from here if you would like to go home early. I'm sure you've got other patients who need you much more than Catherine does. She'll be fine."

Eleanor smiled. "I know she will." She patted Catherine on the arm and said, "You take care now, Catherine. It has been a treat working here." She turned back to Tom and added, "Call me if she has a relapse. I'll be happy to stop by." With a wave, she was out of the door and down the hall.

Unluckily for Catherine, a new challenge emerged—a challenge that tested the boundaries of her newfound strength. Tom's presence had become more intense, and she feared for her life. However, her body was still too achy and fatigued for her to run. There was no way out. Not yet.

"Tom, just leave me alone." Catherine's voice was tinged with uncertainty. "I don't want you around me. I need some space, so go."

As Tom turned to leave the room, a lack of emotions played across his face. He looked back at Catherine, his blue eyes holding voids of emptiness that struck a dagger at Catherine's heart. Her throat tightened as she watched her husband standing in the doorframe, his figure framed by the light of the day. It was a terrifying moment, a moment that held the weight of their shared history and the realization that their paths were diverging permanently. Tom walked out of the room without a word, his footsteps fading into the distance. Catherine's heart eased as she watched him go.

FIFTEEN

Nineteen days since the anniversary

Catherine fidgeted in her bed, unprepared to face the new day. She reached for her phone on the nightstand to check the time, but it wasn't there. Confused, she scanned the room. A soft knock on her door interrupted her thoughts, and before she could respond, the door creaked open.

Tom stood there, grinning as he held up her phone. "Better not be looking for this. You're not allowed to talk to anyone on your phone today." He stepped into the room.

"No, Tom." Her voice was devoid of emotion. "I wasn't looking for it." She played his puppet in order to save her life for the time being.

Tom slipped the phone into his left back pocket before crossing his arms and leaning against the doorway. "Good. Now, we're going out. Get dressed. I've set your clothes on the chair. If you're not ready in twenty minutes, you better pray to God."

As Catherine swung her legs out of bed, Tom's gaze lingered. Catherine felt disgusted by his perusing gaze. She knew that Tom's intentions weren't pure, but she had no means to stop him. She glanced at the chair and noticed a pair of capri pants and a pink blouse, along with fresh undergarments. Without another look at him, she moved toward the bathroom.

The early morning air was crisp, promising a day of adventure to any normal couple, but Catherine feared what lay in store for her. He held the passenger door of the Lexus open for her, and she got in, her gaze straying to Jessica's white van parked down the street.

Catherine glanced at the passing scenery. The rolling hills, dotted with wildflowers, brought back memories of her child-hood. She recalled visiting these hills with her mother for picnics. Beside her, Tom hummed along to the radio, his fingers tapping rhythmically on the steering wheel.

"So, where are we going?" Catherine asked, breaking the uncomfortable silence that had settled between them.

Tom kept his eyes on the road as he ignored her question. "You need to talk about what happened and admit what you did."

Catherine turned to him; her expression guarded. "I know you were driving the car, Tom. I'm not taking the blame for what you did."

Tom shook his head, his false concern clear. "It really wasn't me driving, and this isn't just about the car crash, Catherine. It's about everything that led up to that night."

"What are you talking about?"

Tom's gaze remained fixed on the road. "I've been watching you struggle with alcohol for years now. It's affecting our life, our relationship, and it's putting your well-being at risk."

Catherine's eyes widened in surprise. Tom wasn't just denying his involvement in the car crash. He was now trying to say she had a drinking problem. The man had to be delusional if he thought he'd be able to convince her that she drank too much. She barely ever had alcohol.

"You know I don't drink, because of my medication."

He reached out, his hand finding hers in her lap, and squeezed it hard. "Sweetheart, I'm not saying this to make you feel guilty. You just don't remember things after drinking so much. I care about you, and I want to help you through this. I don't want to see you hurt yourself or anyone else ever again."

Catherine pulled her hand from his. "No, I *don't* drink."

You're just trying to use me as a crutch to escape your fate.

Tom pulled up to a stop sign and turned to look at her, his expression full of fake concern. "I understand life hasn't been easy for you, sweetheart. Losing your parents so young has really messed with your mental well-being. But facing your struggles head-on is the only way to move forward."

Catherine's resolve strengthened. How dare he bring up her parents' deaths. "Stop it, Tom. You know you're lying."

You need to take responsibility for your actions and seek help.

Tom attempted to give her a compassionate look, but she could see through him now. She knew he was full of baloney and only looking out for himself. She just didn't know what he was planning, and that worried her.

"You don't have to do it alone," Tom continued. "Our friends and neighbors care about you, too, and want to support you through this. We've talked, and we've decided we're going to act as your support group before you go to jail for what you've done."

The sense of unease that had been simmering beneath the surface of this car ride grew stronger. She knew Tom was about to put her through another ordeal with his friends' help, but she needed more time to figure out how to get away from the house.

As Tom drove, Catherine felt tears pushing at her eyelids as she thought back over everything. She really wanted answers, so despite her concerns, she decided to question him.

"Tom?"

Tom turned to her, his expression open and attentive. "What is it, sweetheart?"

Catherine took a deep breath, gathering her nerve. "Why have you done all this? The gatherings, the lies... Why are you doing this to me?"

The weight of unspoken words hung in the space between them as if the car itself were holding on to the truth that threatened to shatter the quiet of the ride. Catherine, sensing the shift in the atmosphere, grew increasingly anxious. Her instincts were telling her that Tom was about to lie to her again, and whatever he was about to say would undoubtedly push them farther apart.

Tom inhaled, his gaze on the road unwavering. "Catherine," his voice was steady but tinged with regret, "the car crash... it *was* you who caused it. I'm sorry, but I'm not the only one telling you this. It's important you know the truth. You were driving under the influence when the accident happened." Tom's voice was gentle, as though he actually believed what he was saying. "I know this is difficult to hear, but it's time to confront the truth. The accident happened because you were driving while intoxicated."

Catherine decided to reveal exactly how she knew he was lying. Maybe that was what he needed to stop living in denial. To stop continuing down this path of blaming her for his actions.

"Tom."

He finally looked up from the road, concern flickering in his electric blue eyes. "What is it, sweetheart? Have you realized I'm right? Are you ready to accept the consequences of your actions?"

Catherine met his eyes. "Detective Sheldon informed me

they have the dashcam recording from the crash. They are launching an investigation into you."

Tom clenched the steering wheel. The tension in the air was intense, thick like the storm clouds that were gathering on the horizon. His knuckles turned white as his grip tightened, his jaw set in a hard line.

Catherine glanced nervously at his clenched fists, her heart racing. Maybe she should have waited until they had gotten to their destination before sharing that bit of information with him. She regretted saying anything.

As the car sped down the winding road, Tom's breathing grew heavy and labored. His fingers tapped a new erratic rhythm against the steering wheel, a manifestation of the turmoil obviously swirling within him.

Catherine stole another glance at him, her concern deepening as she watched his eyes flicker with a mixture of anger and desperation. "Tom, please," she mumbled, her voice wavering slightly. "Please, just calm down."

"Calm down?" Tom's voice was laced with bitter sarcasm. "You think I can just calm down after what you've done?" His anger escalated with each word he uttered.

Catherine felt a lump rise in her throat. The car sped up, and Tom's knuckles turned even whiter on the wheel. His hate-filled eyes darted between the road and Catherine, his frustration mounting with each passing moment.

"I can't believe you, Catherine." His voice dripped with venom. "You're always lying, always trying to make me doubt myself. You took vows when you married me. You aren't supposed to lie to me. You are supposed to honor me. To obey me. But you can't even do that anymore."

Catherine's heart sank. She had never intended for things to get so bad, to stoke the flames of his anger. But the words were lost in the whirlwind of emotions that had engulfed them both. "Tom, I swear I'm not lying. The detective watched the video.

He said they were going to investigate you." Her voice cracked as she spoke.

As the car sped down the road, the anger in Tom's eyes was wild, his focus split between the road and the storm brewing inside him.

"Tom, please, you're scaring me." Catherine's voice was barely audible over the sound of the wind whipping over the car.

"Scaring you?" Tom's laughter was bitter and cutting. "Maybe you should be scared. Maybe you should finally understand the pain you've put me through."

Catherine's eyes filled with tears, her fingers clutching the edge of her seat. She had never seen this side of Tom before—a side that was so consumed by rage that it seemed to obliterate any rational thought. She'd seen him angry, of course, but nothing like this.

The car swerved slightly.

"Tom, please." Catherine's voice trembled.

Tom laughed once more. "Please? You think begging is going to fix this? Begging won't change the fact that you've destroyed my life."

The car veered dangerously close to the edge of the road, the tires grazing the gravel. Catherine's heart lurched as her fingers dug into the seat. "Tom, please." Her voice was stronger this time. "I don't want us to die."

Tom's grip on the steering wheel finally relaxed, though it was clear his anger still simmered beneath the surface. He glanced at her, his eyes softening slightly, but the tension in his shoulders remained. "You think it's that easy, Catherine? You think being scared can just fix everything? Maybe you're right. Maybe I'm overreacting, but you've betrayed me."

Catherine reached out tentatively, placing a hand on his arm. "I'm not betraying you, Tom. I am only telling you the truth. I'm sure you never meant for any of this to happen." She wasn't sure about that last part, but she was willing to say it if it got him to slow down.

Tom's jaw tightened. The storm clouds had grown darker, mirroring the turmoil in his eyes. He let out a heavy sigh, his shoulders sagging with a weariness that seemed to seep from his bones.

Catherine sent up a small prayer that he would be reasonable.

"I don't know, Catherine." His voice was quieter, more contemplative. "I don't know if I can fix this now, but I know one thing—I'll be damned if I spend a day in jail because of you."

SIXTEEN

The car hurtled over the obsidian abyss of one of the backroads in Eldon. Beside Catherine, Tom drove with a manic determination. She desperately wanted out of this car. They were going way too fast for the roads they were on.

"Tom, please!" Her words, edged with a sharp fear, were carried away by the wind that rushed through the open windows. "Slow down! You're going to get us killed!"

Tom didn't respond to her pleas, the car's velocity increasing with each passing moment. The scenery outside the windows was a blur, fleeting images that merged into an indistinct, dangerous whirlwind. The car's speed was beyond reckless. It was as if Tom had surrendered himself to some unholy force, an entity that pushed him to the limits of control.

Catherine was trapped. Her life held precariously in the balance between Tom's determination and the unforgiving road that stretched before them.

"Tom, listen to me!" Catherine's throat was raw from her continuous screaming. Tears streamed down her face, mingling with the wind that whipped through the car. "This isn't you! You need to stop!"

His knuckles were turning a purplish color against the whiteness of his fingers. "Catherine." His voice was laced with an intensity that matched the speed of the car. "There's no turning back now. We're in this together, and there's only one way out."

A gut-wrenching realization settled in. She had known Tom for years, had thought she loved him once, but right now, she barely recognized him. The desperation, the reckless determination—it was as if he was a stranger, a mere shell of the man she thought she knew.

"Tom, please." Her voice wavered. "I'll do anything—just slow down."

Tom's lips curled into a bitter smile, a smile that held a hint of madness. "Anything? Then promise me. Promise me you'll take the fall for this. For us. Promise me you'll bear the burden of my actions."

Catherine looked at him in disbelief. "What? No, Tom, I can't—"

"You can." Tom's voice was firm. "You will. Because if you don't, we're both dead. Do you understand? I will kill us both right now."

The blinding headlights of oncoming traffic danced in the windshield as Tom sped around a slower vehicle. A cacophony of honking horns and screeching tires surrounded them, a symphony of chaos that mirrored the turmoil within Catherine's heart.

"Tom!" Panic surged through her veins, constricting her lungs. "You can't keep driving like this!"

But Tom seemed deaf to her pleas, his eyes set on an invisible destination. He swerved around another car with a ferocity that defied reason. The screeching of tires and blaring of horns seemed distant as if the world itself had distorted into a surreal nightmare.

"Promise, Catherine!" Tom's voice was a guttural growl,

each word dripping with desperation. "Promise me now, or we're both goners!"

The car surged forward, racing closer to the bumper of a sedan in front of them. Catherine's breath caught in her throat. She had never seen him like this, a man possessed by his desperation, willing to gamble with their lives to secure a promise she refused to make.

"Tom, please!" Catherine shouted shrilly, terrified. "You're going to get us killed! Stop this madness!"

Tom's response was a jarring swerve into the opposite lane, narrowly avoiding a collision with the sedan that was now a few car lengths behind them. The blaring of horns intensified; the chorus of anger from other drivers a testament to the mayhem he was causing. Catherine's fingers dug into her armrest, her nails biting into the fabric as her heart zoomed like a runaway train.

"Promise!" Tom's voice was a relentless demand, a refrain that echoed through the car like a haunting melody. He didn't seem to care about the danger he was putting them in, his focus singularly fixed on the pledge he sought from Catherine.

Her tears mingled with the sweat that clung to her skin. She had loved Tom once, and a part of her wanted to give in to his demands just to end the madness, but another part—the part that held on to her dignity and self-respect—clung fiercely to her principles.

"Tom, I can't," Catherine choked out, her voice raw with emotion. "I can't promise something like that. I won't."

Tom's lips curled into a bitter snarl. He abruptly swerved into the other lane and back again, cutting off a pickup and narrowly missing the front bumper of a semi-truck that thundered toward them. The truck's blaring horn reverberated through the car.

The world around Catherine spun in a chaotic blur. She couldn't fathom what had possessed Tom to push them to the brink like this, to jeopardize their lives for a promise that should never be extracted under such duress.

"Promise, Catherine!" Tom's voice was hoarse, the edges of his desperation fraying. His entire body was a portrait of turmoil. "Promise, or I'll make sure we crash!"

Catherine's eyes widened, her heart stopping for a moment at the threat that hung in the air. She stared at Tom, her mind a whirlwind of fear, anger, and confusion. The car hurtled forward, the lines of the road twisting into an indecipherable mess. She couldn't believe she hadn't descended into a full-blown panic attack by now. That would have been just one more horrible thing added to this situation. In fact, something close to calm filled her as she said, "No, Tom." Her voice held a desperate plea, laced with a heartbreaking mix of vulnerability and strength. "I won't be forced into this."

The car inched closer to the back of the semi-truck. "Promise, Catherine!" Tom's voice rose to a fevered pitch, a tormented shout.

The outskirts of Eldon's town proper stretched before them, an expanse of road that seemed to go on forever. Tom's grip was unyielding, his eyes maniacal.

As the car hurtled forward, the wind howling through the open windows, something emerged from the shadows of the trees on the side of the two-lane road. It was Jessica's white van materializing like a specter through a portal. Tom seemed to seethe with rage upon seeing the van closing in on them, his foot moving toward the brake pedal. But it was too late. With a gut-wrenching screech of tires and a metallic crunch, the van swerved, wedging Tom's car against the metal barrier on the right side of the road.

Catherine's body jolted forward, the impact sending shockwaves of pain through her muscles. The airbags deployed with a thunderous whoosh, enveloping her in a cloud of white, and then she passed out.

SEVENTEEN

Catherine's consciousness was a haze, a fog of disorientation and pain that seemed to envelop her entire being. Slowly, the fog lifted, replaced by a throbbing ache that emanated from various parts of her body. She blinked against the harsh light filtering through her closed eyelids, her senses gradually returning to her. As they did, she had a chilling realization—she was trapped. Panic surged within her chest, adrenaline coursing through her veins as she struggled to move. Her breaths came in ragged gasps. She needed to get out of the wreckage, and it had to be through the back passenger door because Tom was blocking the driver's side, and her door was blocked by the barrier.

The flashing lights of emergency vehicles appeared in the distance. Her body ached with each movement, a symphony of pain that seemed to intensify with every breath, reminding her of the previous accident. Despite her injuries, Catherine's determination burned brightly, driving her to get out even when every movement felt like a monumental effort.

She braced herself against the seat for support as she unclicked her seat belt. As she shoved at the airbag, her head stopped spinning, and she set her sights on the back door once again. She felt both hope and trepidation—she needed to get out of the car, to escape into the outside world. It was a daunting task, but it was her only chance to get out of Tom's grasp and find help.

Gritting her teeth, Catherine forced herself to move, her arms trembling beneath her weight as she twisted in her seat. She made a tentative move toward the back, then another, her progress slow and deliberate as she maneuvered her body into the small area between the two front seats. Each move sent jolts of pain radiating through her body, and the distance to the door seemed to stretch endlessly before her, but she pressed on, refusing to give in. With sheer determination, Catherine continued her agonizing journey, her breathing labored, her vision focused solely on the goal ahead. Finally, after what felt like an eternity, she reached the back door. Her fingers grazed the handle, and she tugged at it, her heart sinking when it refused to open. Something must be jamming it. She tried again, putting more force into her effort, but the door remained resolutely shut. Panic bubbled up within her as she realized she was trapped once again. She cast a desperate glance around her, her eyes searching for Jessica or someone who could help her.

Just then, Tom chuckled, his expression victorious. His hand was on the child-lock button. Catherine gave up.

Rain had started to fall and was casting a somber pall over the scene of the accident, the flashing lights of emergency vehicles reflecting off the wet pavement like fractured beams of color. Their car and Jessica's van stood as silent witnesses to the collision that had altered the course of their lives once again. Jessica's windshield was so fractured it resembled a spider's web. Their car's front end was mangled and broken, steam rising from the crumpled hood like a wounded beast's final breath. Shattered glass sparkled like diamonds on the wet road, a stark reminder of the impact's force. Amidst the activity, the wail of sirens grew louder, the sound cutting through the afternoon's stillness. As the red and blue lights of police vehicles pierced the dismal day, the air buzzed with an added tension.

As the brown and tan vehicles came to a stop, the officers emerged, clad in their brown and tan uniforms. Catherine watched one of the deputies approach Jessica from the back window, where she could see and hear them just beyond the door she couldn't get out of.

"Good evening, ma'am. I'm Deputy Williams from Eldon Sheriff's Department. I'll be overseeing the investigation here. Are you okay?"

Jessica stared at him silently.

"Ma'am, I would appreciate your cooperation in this investigation." His tone was professional. "Could you walk me through what happened leading up to the collision?"

"Well, I was driving down this road," Jessica began, gesturing toward it, "And out of nowhere, I saw this car speeding toward me." I'm not sure what was going on, Deputy, but the car continued speeding up, going much faster than the posted speed limit. The driver swerved past a bunch of other vehicles and nearly hit several others in the oncoming lane."

"Are you saying that this driver of the other car, one of Eldon's most prominent attorneys, Tom Morris, was driving recklessly?"

Jessica nodded. "Yes, I am. He was endangering himself and others on the road. I couldn't say if he was doing it on purpose though. Maybe there was a problem with the car. I knew I needed to help stop it before he managed to ram the semi that was ahead of him."

Catherine could tell Jessica was spinning a tale. She was making it sound as if the car was at fault, not Tom, and that was a bit worrisome. But then she remembered what Jessica had said about corruption in Eldon. Maybe that was why she was lying. It wasn't as if Tom would contradict her and make himself look bad. There were plenty of other witnesses to what he'd done pulled up along the side of the road.

"Ma'am, I appreciate your cooperation. However, the heavy rain and challenging road conditions must have been significant factors in what was going on with Mr. Morris's vehicle. Given the circumstances and the challenges posed by the weather, I'll just issue you a warning in this case. I want to stress the importance of driving cautiously during adverse conditions. Also, please be attentive to your surroundings."

Jessica stared at him, and Catherine could see the look of disbelief on her face.

"As part of our procedure, we'll be asking you to leave the scene now." Deputy Williams stared at her, clearly asking her to defy him so he could arrest her. "The investigation will be wrapping up shortly, and we need to clear the area for the safety of all involved."

"I would be happy to, Deputy; however, as you can plainly see, my van is out of commission. How am I supposed to leave? And you haven't even checked on the passenger of Mr. Morris's car. Is she alright?" Jessica pointed to Catherine.

Williams shook his head, his expression stoic. "Someone will see to her momentarily. She seems fine where she is for the moment. As to your van, it will be seen to. We need to ensure that we clear the area for safety reasons, so please gather your belongings and make your way off the scene. Deputy Martin will escort you home." He waved over the other sheriff's deputy.

Jessica looked at Catherine and mouthed, "You okay?"

Catherine shrugged and gave her an uncomfortable look but didn't say anything. Not with Tom sitting less than a foot away. She watched Deputy Martin join Jessica, escort her to her van for a moment, and then away from the scene.

A few seconds later, Deputy Williams approached the driver's window. "Tom, what happened here?" he asked.

"Hey, Williams. Something... Something serious."

The deputy wore a concerned expression. "I'm listening. Tell me everything you know."

Tom's eyes met hers in the rearview mirror. "It's about Catherine..."

Deputy Williams leaned forward; his gaze fixed on Tom's face. "Go on."

"I was driving us to our friends' house on the outskirts of town. You know the Kleins?" Tom's voice was shaky, but Catherine knew he was doing it for effect.

"Yes, of course, I know the Kleins. Good people."

"We were arguing about her drinking problem, like we always do, and the issue about her going to jail, but then things got out of control." Tom went on to recount false events about the crash, claiming the rain-slicked roads, the dim glow of the dashboard lights, and the tension that had escalated between him and Catherine had caused him to be slightly distracted. He described her irritation turning to rage. "And then... she grabbed the wheel." Tom's voice wavered. "I thought she was joking at first, but then I realized she wasn't. She was trying to steer us into oncoming traffic."

Deputy Williams' expression went from concern to disbelief. "Tom, are you telling me that Catherine was trying to... kill both of you?"

Tom nodded. "I can't believe it myself, but that's what happened. She was so scared of going to jail, of facing the consequences of all the dumb stuff she's done. She thought it was better to die than to be caught."

The deputy leaned back. "Tom, this is a very serious allegation," he said finally. "You're telling me that Catherine deliberately tried to kill both of you because she was afraid of the consequences from the other crash?"

Tom nodded. "I know it's hard to believe. I never thought she'd do something like this, but I saw it with my own eyes."

Catherine couldn't believe what she was hearing. She

reached a hand through the space between the door and Tom's seat, hitting the child lock button, and then quickly opened the back door. She pushed herself out. "I can't keep living in fear. I've made my decision. I can't let him define me anymore," she muttered. She smiled sadly, her eyes locking with the deputy's. "I need you to take me into custody." Her posture was tense but resolute. "You've clearly got a case against me, so what's stopping you?"

Catherine had expected to be taken into custody at some point, but tonight, she mostly wanted to be away from Tom. She waited patiently next to one of the sheriff's cars as the two deputies conferred and spoke to Tom and the truck driver again. She couldn't be sure, but she thought she saw Tom pull out his wallet, and fear spiked in her stomach. She wasn't sure what was happening, but she knew it wouldn't be good.

Deputy Williams spoke quietly into the radio, Velcroed on his shoulder, then came toward her. "Mrs. Morris, I've been informed that we won't be taking you into custody."

Catherine's eyes widened; her voice tinged with disbelief. "What? Why not?"

The deputy sighed; his gaze sympathetic. "There's been a change in the situation. We've reviewed the evidence and taken your husband's statement into consideration. While what you did was certainly dangerous and unacceptable, your husband wasn't harmed, and after speaking to him again, he's said he's not pressing charges."

Catherine was speechless.

"We would like to ensure your safety, so after the paramedics check you both over, we'll escort you home and have a wrecker come for your car."

"Thank you," Tom said as he joined her next to the sheriff's car, which was brown and tan and matched the deputy's uniform. "We appreciate your help, Deputy."

EIGHTEEN

Catherine stumbled back into her guest room, her legs trembling under the weight of her fatigue. The drive with Tom had been a torturous journey, and she was in a world of throbbing pain. She became acutely aware of every ache, every soreness that permeated her body. The simple act of shifting on the bed sent waves of discomfort rippling through her as if her body was a canvas painted with bruises and agony. She winced as she attempted to lie down. Her muscles protested the movement as if someone had stretched them to their limits and beyond.

The events of the car ride came back to her in fragments, like pieces of a shattered mirror. The cloudy sky, the relentless speed, and the way the seat belt had become a cruel instrument of torture, slamming into her bruised body with every turn. It was as if the very thing designed to keep her safe became a source of additional agony.

Catherine gingerly touched her chest, tracing the new path of the seat belt's impact. The skin was tender to the touch, a mosaic of pain painted in various shades of red and purple on top of the previous bruises. She blinked, holding back tears as frustration mingled with the pain. She had pleaded with the deputies to take her into custody. She recalled the weight of their scrutiny, their eyes searching hers for any signs of deception. Their disbelief had been a painful echo of the doubt she had been facing since the accident. She had always trusted law enforcement officials to be impartial, to protect and serve. Jessica had warned her, but she hadn't exactly believed that they were corrupt. For some bizarre reason, she'd thought they would help her, that she could trust them.

But now, that trust was shattered, and she felt like an alien in a world that continuously turned against her. Her frustration boiled over into anger. She had begged them to save her, seeking validation for the pain she had endured. But all she was met with were walls of skepticism and indifference from both the deputies and the paramedics who'd looked over her injuries. It was as if her words were brushed aside, lost in a system that seemed more interested in passing judgment than seeking the truth.

She could no longer keep the tears at bay. They fell, unobstructed, down her cheeks.

The door creaked open, and Tom entered her room. His face held a mixture of disdain and determination. His gaze pierced hers, demanding attention. "Hey." His voice was an annoyed sneer against her ears. "I've changed the plans a bit."

Catherine held his gaze as she waited for him to continue. She knew he wasn't here for anything good.

"I've reached out to our friends and neighbors," he said firmly. "I explained what happened, how you tried to kill us, and how bad your illness has gotten."

Catherine's irritation swelled at his words. "Excuse me?"

Tom nodded, the look in his eyes almost gleeful. "And you know what? They've all agreed to come here. They want to help."

Catherine closed her eyes for a moment, Tom's words enveloping her in a blanket of terror. It was as if Tom's darkness controlled her life, as though she were a puppet on strings that he could make dance to whatever tune he wanted. She knew whatever happened next would be torture.

"You don't have to say anything. When this is done, you'll appreciate what we're doing for you," Tom assured her. "They're just as outraged as I am over your inability to control yourself, and they want you to stop harming yourself like this. They're organizing your first therapy session as we speak," Tom continued, his eyes lighting up with a spark of joyful determination. "We just want to help you recover from your alcoholism."

To think that people could be so easily swayed by his lies was a horror Catherine had never imagined. The pain and frustration of the accident seemed to multiply with the overwhelming sense of terror she felt.

"You're not alone in this, Catherine. We'll face this together, as a community. Now please stay in your room while we prepare." Tom smiled smugly as he walked out of the room.

Despair threatened to take over all Catherine's emotions. She shifted slightly on the bed, wincing as soreness reminded her of the trials she had faced during the last several hours. Her body was on the mend, but her mind was close to its breaking point. She sighed, trying to gather the strength to face whatever Tom had in store for her.

The door to her room creaked open, and Catherine turned her head to see Donna entering with a tray in her hands. Her best friend's warm smile was a balm against the ache within, and Catherine managed a weak smile in return.

"Hey," Donna greeted softly, her voice carrying a sense of worry.

"Hey," Catherine replied in a mere whisper.

Donna placed the tray on the nightstand and sat on the edge of the bed, her hazel eyes wide with concern as she looked at Catherine. "I brought you some tea."

Catherine's heart swelled with gratitude for the simple

gesture. The pain in her body had left her parched, and the idea of a restorative cup of tea sounded wonderful. "Thank you."

Donna handed her the teacup, her fingers gentle as they brushed against Catherine's. "I talked to Tom."

Catherine's brow furrowed in irritation. "About what?"

"I convinced him to let me come keep you calm and help you before the others arrive," Donna replied, her hazel eyes sparkling with determination.

Catherine's heart skipped a beat as she processed Donna's words. Knowing her best friend had advocated for her, that she had persuaded Tom to allow her to take care of her, was a testament to the strength of their bond. "You're going to help me?" Catherine's voice held a mixture of surprise and gratitude.

Donna nodded, a warm smile gracing her lips. "I know you need some time to rest and heal, Cath, and I want to help."

Catherine looked at Donna, her heart brimming with emotion. "Thank you. You do not know how much this means to me." Maybe now she'd be able to get away from Tom.

Donna reached out and placed a hand on Catherine's arm, her touch gentle and reassuring. "Friends take care of each other, and I'm really worried about you." Donna sank down into the chair next to the bed. "Can we talk?"

Catherine's heart quickened at the request, and she wondered what Donna might want to discuss. She nodded, a mixture of curiosity and apprehension swirling within her. "Of course."

Donna's expression softened; her hazel eyes empathetic. "Look, I know something's been going on with you. You've been in these two accidents within a few weeks of each other and... well, with what Tom's been saying... I just don't know what to believe. I can't imagine you ever doing what he's accused you of."

Catherine's breath caught in her throat. Donna seemed to be asking for the truth, actually wanting to hear and listen to

Catherine's side of things. That went a long way to filling the void of loneliness she'd felt for the last few weeks. She glanced at the door and then back to Donna. "Let me start with that first accident," she said.

Donna looked concerned. "Okay. What happened?"

Catherine's fingers clenched the blanket tightly, her throat feeling dry as she continued. "Tom was driving that night, not me. He was speeding. I tried to tell him I felt sick, and I begged him to slow down, but he wouldn't listen."

"You're saying that... the car crash was Tom's fault? He hit that woman's car, not you?" Donna's brow furrowed as she tried to understand.

Catherine nodded. She kept her voice soft so it wouldn't carry down the hall. "Yes. I had blacked out during the crash, and when I woke, Tom was out of the car. He noticed waking, reached through the window, and pulled me into the driver's seat. He told me he was trying to get me out. I passed out again from the pain, and when I woke up again, I was on a stretcher, and I heard Tom tell the cops I was driving. I wasn't, Donna, I swear I wasn't. You know I don't drive, because of my medicine."

"I know you don't normally, and that car was Tom's pride and joy, so I couldn't imagine him letting you drive it," Donna whispered back. "Do the cops know you weren't driving?"

Catherine nodded. "Yes, I have proof, which they've seen, and I can show you."

Donna's hazel eyes searched Catherine's face. "Proof? Here?"

Catherine unbuttoned her blouse and opened it so Donna could see her shoulders. "You can see the older bruises beneath these new ones. I was in the passenger seat; you can tell from the way the seat belt bruised me."

Donna reached out her hand and drew in a sharp breath. "You were in the passenger seat. There's no way you could have been driving." She shook her head. "But Tom said you'd been drinking and just didn't remember."

Catherine pursed her lips and nodded. "Yes, I know. I did have a small glass of champagne, and it messed with my medication, which was why I felt sick. You know I would never have gotten behind the wheel. And you know I hardly ever drink."

"Yeah, that was what wasn't making sense to me. He's been so insistent though... Cath, he's got everyone believing him. They're all out there... I don't know how to stop what they're planning."

Catherine met Donna's worried gaze with her own. "I know how insistent he's been. That's how the second accident happened."

"What do you mean? Did you grab the wheel like he said?"

Catherine shook her head. "No, of course not. Tom was threatening me. Demanding that I go along with his version of the first accident, or he was going to kill us. I was refusing. Another motorist intervened and stopped our car before he could go through with it. From what she told Deputy Williams, she thought our car was out of control or something."

"That's not what Tom is saying."

"I know. He told Deputy Williams I grabbed the wheel and threatened to kill us both because I didn't want to take responsibility for the other accident." Catherine clenched her fists in frustration. "What am I going to do?" She glanced toward the doorway again. "What are they planning, Donna?"

Donna shook her head. "I think it's some sort of aversion therapy. You know how some of the men in this town are old school when it comes to correcting people?"

Catherine's eyes widened, and she gasped. "They're going to beat me," she whispered.

Donna shrank in her chair as she gave Catherine a slight nod. "I heard Richard say something about *spare the rod, spoil the child...* I know you're not a child, but... I got the distinct impression that was what they were planning."

"I have to get out of here," Catherine murmured.

"There's no way we'll be able to get out of the house before they catch us," Donna whispered.

Catherine knew she was right. But there had to be something they could do. It was then she realized she had an ally or two outside of the house. But she probably couldn't reach Jessica quickly and, besides, her van was who-knew-where, so she probably couldn't help. The other ally was Detective Sheldon, but Catherine had no way to get a hold of him either.

"Donna, can you do me a favor?"

"Always. You know I will help you in whatever way I can. What do you need? Have you thought of something?"

Catherine nodded. "Tom took my phone, or I'd call him myself."

"Who?" Donna asked in confusion.

"Detective Sheldon. Can you call him? He's the detective in Cincinnati who has been investigating that first crash. He knows Tom has been trying to frame me."

"I can try. But what can he do?"

"I'm hoping he can help me if he knows what's going on here. I want him to take me into custody or witness protection, something, anything, so I'm safe from Tom and his 'therapy' sessions."

Donna slowly nodded. "I'll need his number, but are you sure about this? What if he arrests you? What if he disregards the evidence and charges you instead of Tom?"

"I know it's a risk, Donna, but I need to get out of this house. It's too dangerous for me to be left alone with Tom. I think he'll do anything to cover this up. He's already tried to drug me and then threatened to kill me if I didn't agree to do what he asked. I don't think I'll survive his next attempt if I make it through what he's planning out there." She nodded toward the doorway.

Donna stared at her with shock. "Wait, when did he try to drug you?"

"A few weeks ago. He had a syringe of something he was going to push into my IV, but something busted the window and distracted him."

"I wondered about that boarded-up window. Something broke your window right at the moment he was going to drug you? That's weird, right?"

Catherine nodded. "Yes, well, I think someone saw what he was doing and threw a large rock at the window to get him to leave me alone," Catherine shared, keeping Jessica's name out of it. For some reason, she wasn't ready to talk about her.

"Wow. I wonder who." Donna paused, thinking about it. "Maybe it was Mr. Harley? I mean, he's always out walking, but he does tend to keep to himself."

"Maybe. I'm just grateful to whoever it was."

Donna reached for Catherine's hand and squeezed her fingers. "Me too. Okay, so what's this detective's number? How do I reach him?" she asked.

Catherine grappled with her next decision. She only had one card with the detective's number, and it felt wrong giving it up, but she didn't have a pen and paper to copy the number down. She grabbed the card from the nightstand table drawer and pressed it into Donna's hand. "I know this is a big ask, considering Tom's your boss, and you're risking a lot going against him."

Donna's expression softened, her hazel eyes reflecting compassion and support. "Cath, you're my best friend. I'll get a hold of this detective, I promise."

NINETEEN

Twenty-four days since the anniversary

Catherine's muscles screamed in protest with each movement she made. The last few days had been a relentless onslaught, a barrage of beatings that had left her battered and bruised. She had endured more than she ever thought she could.

The dim room felt colder than usual as a group of Tom's friends stood in a circle around the chair that she was seated in. She'd passed out again, and someone had shaken her until she'd woken up. She stared at the stern faces of the men in her room: Tom's two partners, Carl Durbin and Richard Banks, Mark from next door, Jim Miller and his brothers, Greg and Dan. They were all hovering over her, telling her she needed to accept responsibility for her actions as they took turns smacking her around.

Each painful encounter with these men was etched vividly in her mind. She'd prayed for Detective Sheldon to show up, but he never did. Surely Donna had gotten a hold of him by now.

At the beginning of these "therapy" sessions, these men had

lectured her, telling her she needed to take responsibility for her actions and admit to her alcohol abuse. Catherine had argued back and got slapped, which over the past few days had evolved into full-blown beatings that left her blacking out. She had screamed for help, begged them to stop, pleaded with anyone and anything to make the beatings stop, but now she was resigned to them. She could barely see through the black eyes they'd given her, and still they didn't stop.

These men weren't men. They were thugs brought in to murder her so that Tom could get away with what he'd done. She didn't know why they continued to hurt her. She could barely hold her head up, could barely see them through the slits she now had for eyes. She knew she had to smell like the bottom of a dumpster because they hadn't let her bathe, they barely allowed her to use the bathroom, not that she needed to often as they had hardly given her any food or water.

The thugs were relentless and constantly told her she caused the crash with every hit. They demanded that she stop trying to destroy Tom's reputation as he was a fine, upstanding man, a community leader who could do no wrong. She refused to comply. At this point, she hoped for death with each blow. She almost couldn't feel them anymore. Almost.

There was another heavy slap to her cheek.

"Wake up!" a voice demanded.

Catherine squinted at Richard through her bruised and swollen eyes. "Leave me alone," she murmured, but she didn't know if her voice was audible. Her muscles protested as she verged on fainting, but her body refused to give up her life. And despite everything, she didn't really want to die. She wanted to be away from here. Away from them. Away from Tom.

The problem was that Catherine was on the verge of her breaking point. Maybe this would all go away if she just complied and pretended to be guilty. If she just told them what they wanted to hear. She debated with herself, sometimes trying to make the words come out of her mouth, but something held them back each time.

Suddenly, the sound of shattering glass reverberated through the air, and Catherine's head reeled toward the hall. The men, who had been engrossed in covering every inch of Catherine's body in bruises, spun at the sudden commotion coming from the room beyond her doorway.

"What the hell was that?" one of them boomed.

Catherine's body slipped from the hard wooden chair to the floor of its own accord as another crash sounded, and smoke poured through the house. The men fled the room, slamming the door behind them, leaving her behind.

TWENTY

Smoke billowed in from under the door, its acrid scent assaulting her senses. The realization hit her like a freight train —the house was on fire.

A previously untapped source of survival instincts kicked in out of nowhere. Ignoring the protests of her battered body, and with a strength she hadn't known she'd had, Catherine pushed herself to her feet and lunged forward, her muscles screaming in protest as she stumbled toward the door. With her heart pounding in her chest, her breath coming in gasps, she reached for the handle and pulled it open. Beyond her room was a chaotic scene. The living room was engulfed in flames, the fire dancing hungrily across the furniture, carpet, and things Tom had collected, turning horrid memories into charred ruins. The crackling of the inferno mingled with the wailing of sirens in the distance, a haunting symphony of destruction.

The heat was unbearable, sweat mingling with the grime on her skin as she placed a hand on the hallway wall to keep herself standing. She fought to keep her focus, even though she could barely see, her mind a whirlwind of panic and determination. Her lungs begged for fresh air, but the noxious fumes left her gasping and wheezing. Catherine's senses were assaulted by the sound of more shattering glass. She turned her gaze to the source, her heart sinking as she realized that several bottles with flaming rags lay strewn across the floor. The fires they had ignited were spreading rapidly, threatening to engulf the entire room.

Tom stood at the center of it all, his voice strained and urgent, pleading with his friends and neighbors to remain calm. The flickering fire cast eerie shadows on the faces around him, and Catherine realized that it wasn't only the men who had been here. Their wives had been, too, and that just about broke her. How had they stayed quiet as she begged for help? How had they stood by and allowed their husbands to beat her half to death?

"We can't let panic drive us to make hasty decisions," Tom shouted. "We need to stay together and put out the fire."

But his words seemed to dissipate in the smoke-filled air.

"This is ridiculous, Tom, you can't expect us to stay here, you need to let us out!" one of the men replied. Catherine didn't bother to figure out who.

The house was filled with a suffocating blend of fear and uncertainty that seemed to cling to every surface, along with the smoke. Tom's gaze locked on Catherine, who stood in the hallway, desperate to get out.

"Tom! You have to stop this. They're going to kill her, and you're going to get everyone else killed if you don't unlock the door!" Donna pleaded, drawing Catherine's attention.

"Shut up!" Tom stared daggers at Donna. "You shouldn't even be here! You started this fire, didn't you? Admit it!"

"Are you kidding me? I was in here arguing with you when that bottle was thrown through the window!" Donna argued back. "Let Catherine go, Tom. Let us all go!"

Tom's jaw clenched as he faced Donna. "Catherine is staying here." Tom's voice was tinged with frustration, his gaze flickering to Catherine briefly before returning to Donna. "She caused this. She knows what's happening out there."

"How could she cause this, Tom?" Donna demanded, her hands on her hips. "Your buddies all had her surrounded and were beating the crap out of her. Look at her! Look at what they've done to her. She doesn't even know what day it is! She couldn't know what was happening!"

Catherine coughed as the smoke grew thicker. She needed to get out. She couldn't believe these people were all just standing around waiting for Tom to tell them it was okay to leave. It was bizarre that no one would go against him and just leave instead of arguing with him, trying to get him to do what was right.

"Donna, I know you care about Catherine. We all do. But she put us in danger here. We can't just save her and hope the police do their best."

Donna's voice rose as she took another step toward Tom. "Tom, you're going to damn us all if you keep this up!"

Catherine's heart raced as the weight of the situation settled upon her. She had never asked to be a part of this, to be dragged into a world of danger and uncertainty. Her eyes darted between Tom and Donna. She desperately needed to get out of there. While they were distracted by each other, she started hobbling toward the front door.

Just as she did, a familiar figure entered the fray, busting into the room through the front door, which now hung from its hinges. Donna's husband, James, ran in, heading straight for his wife, his normally calm demeanor replaced by a mixture of concern and determination. "Donna, we don't have time for you to stand here arguing with Tom about Catherine, we need to go. This place is going up in flames."

Donna's gaze shifted to James; her eyes still defiant. "Jamie darling, you don't understand. We can't sacrifice Catherine's life just because Tom doesn't want to admit what really happened."

James gripped her arm and started pulling her across the room. "I don't care about anyone but you right now, Donna. You're my wife, and I want you safe. Catherine's going to have to fend for herself for now."

Donna's frustration escalated, her voice rising as James lifted her off her feet. "Tom, please. Don't do this. Don't keep her trapped in here. Let her go!" she called as James carried her out of the house.

Tom's gaze moved to Catherine, a conflicted expression on his face as she stood frozen in the hallway. Panic gripped her as the fire, fueled by an inferno of chaos and destruction, spread through the corridors of the house. She felt rooted to the ground as the wall of flames inched closer. Fear clutched at her chest, making it hard to breathe. She watched Tom's friends and neighbors flee after James and Donna, but still Catherine stood locked in place. She wanted to move, to escape the impending danger, but her body seemed paralyzed. Just as Tom rushed toward the front door to follow his minions, his arm outstretched as if to keep the fire at bay, a figure emerged from the haze of smoke engulfing the front door.

The person was clad in military gear, a gas mask obscuring their face, and they moved with a calculated urgency. Without a word, they lunged at Tom, striking him with a swift punch that left him crumpled on the floor. Catherine's heart raced as she watched the scene unfold, her mind struggling to comprehend the sight.

The figure then turned toward her, their gloved hand reaching out. In a split second, they had crossed the distance between them, toned arms encircling Catherine's waist. The world spun as Catherine was lifted off her feet and put in a fireman's hold. She clung to consciousness, her senses swimming as she was carried, the figure's grip unyielding, away from the encroaching flames.

TWENTY-ONE

Catherine's heart raced as she watched the house burn from her upside-down position. There were few flames visible now they were outside, and the smoke billowing from the broken windows had an eerie quality, more like a thick fog than the raging fire she had expected. She could barely see through her swollen eyes, but she tried to discern any movement within the smoke. She felt an odd sense of hope when she thought of Tom lying unconscious in the house. Would he escape the encroaching threat?

Her mind raced through scenarios, and a growing feeling of desperation gnawed at her. She was terrified that she was in the middle of a nightmare, and none of this was real. But the scent of burnt wood and something acrid hanging in the air as the person carrying her hurried across the street was too real a smell for this to be a dream.

Catherine soon saw she'd been carried to a beat-up, familiar van parked at the curb. Its paint was chipped, and the front was sporting a massive dent in the fender. There also a large crack in the windshield. Catherine relaxed as she realized it was Jessica who had rescued her.

Moments later, Jessica flung open the back of the van and set Catherine down on the floor. As she hopped into the back next to her, Catherine felt a sense of hesitation once again. Trust was a fragile thing, and Jessica's erratic behavior in the past had left her guarded. But curiosity mingled with her wariness, and she cautiously accepted the safety of the van. With a deep breath, she pushed herself up into a sitting position. Jessica pulled the door closed, sealing them within the cozy confines of the van.

"Are you hurt?" Jessica's voice was softer now, concern clear in her pale blue eyes as they met Catherine's. Then she snorted and said, "Of course you are, just look at you. What I mean is, did the smoke mess with you? Can you breathe okay? Do I need to take you to the hospital?"

Catherine hadn't forgotten about the beatings or the aches and pains she felt. However, she focused on taking a few breaths, not deep ones, since her previously broken ribs seemed to be fractured once more. "I can breathe okay. And I don't want to go to the hospital. They'll just call Tom," she whispered.

Jessica nodded, her expression gentle. "Right. Well, let me look at you." She pulled over a green bag and started digging in it. "I was an army medic, so I have some skill dealing with injuries." She shook her head as she began cleaning some of the cuts on Catherine's face with antiseptic. "Your eyes are probably going to be black for a while, but we can get the swelling down. Here."

Catherine took the ice pack Jessica offered her.

"Hold it here." She adjusted Catherine's hold on the pack. "I'm going to undo your blouse and take a look at your ribs."

Unfastening the buttons, Jessica inspected her, gently pushing on the ribs that Catherine knew had to be discolored. The contact was tender, and Catherine sucked in a breath at her touch. Jessica's fingers were careful as they checked for any signs of heavier injury.

After a moment, Jessica's touch withdrew. "I'm going to wrap these, but I don't think they're actually broken like they were in the accident, maybe cracked a little, but not as bad as before."

"How do you know they were broken in the accident?"

Jessica shrugged. "I looked at your chart while you were in the hospital." She rummaged in the bag, and a moment later, Catherine felt her arms move behind her, and then something wrapped around her middle a few times. "There, that should do it."

Catherine exhaled, feeling herself relaxing a little, knowing she was safe. "Thank you."

There was a pause, and then Jessica whispered, "You don't have to thank me. This is what I do. I help those who can't help themselves. I help people like you."

The words may have been whispered, but their impact was profound. Catherine's heart skipped a beat. She had taken a leap of faith in trusting Jessica, and she didn't regret it.

"Hold your hand out," Jessica said a moment later.

Catherine did so and felt two pills drop into her hand. "What's this?"

"For the pain. You're not allergic to anything, are you?"

"No."

"Good." Jessica pressed a small bottle of water into her hand. "Take those."

Catherine put the pills in her mouth and swallowed them down with the water. "Thank you."

Jessica chuckled as she helped Catherine maneuver from the back of the van into the front passenger seat while holding the ice pack to her eyes. Then Jessica took her place behind the wheel. There was an urgency in her movements, a determination radiating from her. Catherine heard Jessica start the engine, the gentle rumble of the van a reassuring sound.

The van started to move and then came to an abrupt stop.

"What's going on?" Catherine was filled with fear and confusion as she lifted the ice pack to stare through her half-open eyes out the front window. The men who had beaten her and their wives were coming straight toward them.

Jessica's grip on the steering wheel tightened, her jaw clenched as she focused on the scene unfolding before them. The crowd of Tom's friends seemed to have grown larger, their faces twisted with anger and hostility. Catherine's breath caught in her throat. They were shouting, waving their arms, and throwing various things at the van. The van's windows were partially rolled down, allowing the sounds of angry shouts, and pounding fists to pierce the air.

"Lock the doors and put on your seat belt." Jessica's voice was firm, a command that spurred Catherine into action as she did the same.

Catherine's fingers fumbled with the lock, and she clicked the seat belt into place. She darted a look at Jessica, her voice shaking. "What's happening? What are we going to do?"

Jessica's expression was grim, her pale blue eyes fixed on the road as she navigated through the chaos. "They must have seen me rescuing you and bringing you to the van. They're trying to stop us."

"I don't understand how Tom got them to do all this," Catherine said, shaking her head. "People don't just do this, do they? I mean... they don't, right?" Catherine's mind spun. People she had once considered friends and neighbors were now an angry, violent mob. Pillars of her reality were crumbling, replaced by a harsh truth that left her feeling vulnerable and betrayed.

"No, normal people don't, but then this isn't a normal town, from what I've discovered. These people... you don't know them, you never did." Jessica shook her head as she stared at them through the windshield.

The van jolted as something hard struck its side, the impact sending shockwaves through Catherine. She shrank back, realizing the extent of the danger they were in. Everything and everyone outside had turned hostile, the very streets she had walked countless times now a battleground. Jessica threw the van into reverse, spun the tires as she turned the steering wheel, and pressed on the gas. As the van sped away from the crowd, the angry shouts and jeers slowly faded into the distance.

There was a crisp autumn breeze as Jessica drove away from Catherine's quaint town of Eldon. The air was tinged with the scent of fallen leaves and the promise of change. Catherine's thoughts were jumbled as they left the small town behind. Ever since the car crash and subsequent death of Jessica's sister, Melissa, Catherine felt as though she had walked through hell and back.

"I'm sorry it took so long for me to intervene. When I realized what was going on, it took me a day to get things prepped for me to rescue you."

Catherine lifted the ice pack and said, "It's fine, really. I'm grateful you came to get me at all."

Jessica's gaze was soft as she glanced over at her. "Catherine, you can trust me." She looked back at the road. "Can you tell me what happened? How did it get to this point?"

Catherine felt a wave of sadness and guilt. "None of this should have happened. It was Tom's stupid mistake, and now I'm caught in something I can't escape."

Jessica pushed on the brake, slowing the van as she placed a reassuring hand on Catherine's knee. "We'll figure this out together. But you need to trust me. Let me help you."

Catherine's shoulders sagged with relief. It would be so nice to be able to share this burden. Jessica seemed strong enough to deal with everything that had happened, and Catherine wished she was more like her. "Okay." Her lips quirked up in a half smile. "Thank you."

"You're welcome." Jessica turned back to the road and pressed the gas again, pushing the van toward Cincinnati. "You can do this, you know. You're stronger than you think."

Catherine nodded, grateful, but also uncertain. "My body is definitely stronger than I could have ever thought it was. Like the Bionic Woman without the bionics."

Jessica snickered. "Look at you making jokes. But seriously, you are. Stronger women than you would have broken by now. Given in and just taken the rap for the bastard."

"I couldn't do that," Catherine whispered, putting the ice pack back over her eyes.

"I know."

"What did you mean that I didn't know those people?" Catherine asked. She'd been wondering about Jessica's comment since she'd made it forty minutes earlier.

Jessica sighed. "Things in Eldon have been hidden from you. Hidden from a lot of people, it seems. I found out through unconventional means, and it would never stand up in court... but Tom... well, he's got dirt on half the people in town, and that's given him a lot of power over them."

Catherine dropped the ice pack and stared at Jessica. "You mean he's been blackmailing them?"

Jessica shrugged. "In a way, yeah."

It took Catherine a few minutes to process this. "So, what's your plan?"

Jessica glanced at her and then back to the road. "Well, for now, I think it's best that you stay far away from Eldon. So, I'm taking us to Cincinnati."

Catherine's brows furrowed. "I figured that, but why? What's there?"

Jessica's lips curved into a smile. "A place to stay. More answers. And possibly a way to unravel this mess. Trust me, Catherine."

Catherine hesitated for a moment before nodding slowly. "I do trust you. I have pretty much since you threw that rock through the window."

Jessica sounded relieved as she said, "Good."

As they neared the city, Jessica suggested Catherine call Detective Sheldon.

Catherine's brow furrowed. "Why do you want me to call him?"

"Right now, he is better equipped to help you than I am. You need protection, and I can't do that and do what I need to do to get the justice we're after. Just tell him what you know, but don't mention me," Jessica replied, her voice serious.

Catherine tilted her head, her fingers tapping nervously on her thigh. "Why shouldn't I mention you? Are you going to be doing something illegal?"

Jessica leaned forward in her seat. "It's better you don't know what I'm doing." She smiled. "It's best if my involvement remains confidential for now."

Catherine's brow furrowed. "Okay, but I don't have my phone. Tom took it, and I never got it back."

Jessica swore. "Then we'll have to get you a phone." She pulled off the interstate at the next exit and found a shopping complex. "Stay in the van, I'll be right back."

Twenty minutes later, Jessica returned and handed Catherine a bag. Inside was an iPhone, all set up and ready for use.

"Thanks, Jessica. The only problem is I don't know the detective's number," she said softly.

"Already figured as much. It's in the contacts." Jessica nodded toward the phone.

Catherine pulled up the contact list and saw three numbers. One was listed as "Bestie," which she recognized as Donna's. She looked over at Jessica with surprise. "You added Donna's number?"

"She is your best friend, right? Figured you might be able to use her to find out what's going on in town if we need to know."

The next number she didn't recognize, and it only said, "medic," but after a moment, Catherine realized it was Jessica's number. The third number was listed simply as Sheldon.

Taking a deep breath, she pressed the button to call Detective Sheldon. Her heart raced with a mix of anxiety and determination as the phone rang, each tone echoing in the van. Finally, a voice answered on the other end, firm but receptive.

"Detective Sheldon speaking."

"Hello, Detective. It's Catherine Morris." Her voice was steady despite the nervous flutter in her stomach.

"Catherine, I'm glad you called." Detective Sheldon's voice conveyed genuine concern. "I received a voicemail that you might be in danger, but it was vague and cut off before they actually said what was going on. I tried your phone, but I couldn't get a hold of you, and when I called your husband, he said you'd had a panic attack and were sedated. Are you well?"

Catherine sighed. Of course, things hadn't worked out as she'd hoped when she'd asked Donna to call him. "Yes, I'm okay now. He was lying because I didn't have a panic attack, and I wasn't sedated."

"I'm glad to hear that, where are you?"

"I got a ride from a friend after escaping Tom and... and some of the people in my town. It's a long story and I should probably tell it in person, Detective."

"In person? Are you in Cincinnati? Do you need me to come to you?"

"My friend has brought me to Cincinnati, so I can come to you. I have some information that might help with your investigation of the accident and of Tom too." She exhaled an exhausted breath as she felt her shoulders relax a little. "A lot of things have happened over the past week."

"I see. Can you give me an idea of what?"

"Detective, I believe Tom is trying to kill me."

TWENTY-TWO

Jessica pulled the van to a stop a few blocks away from the police station and pulled out her phone, texting on it for a moment before she put it away. Raindrops pelted against the windshield, and the rhythmic tap-tap of the rain created a soothing counterpoint to the tension inside her head. Catherine wondered why they were stopped there.

Jessica looked over at Catherine. "Okay, the station isn't far from here. Remember what I told you. Don't mention me to the police. They can't know I'm involved or that I'm investigating Tom."

Catherine nodded, though she was worried. "I understand. But... what about you? What are you going to be doing?"

Jessica's lips curved into a wistful smile. "Don't worry about me. I'll be fine. You just focus on taking care of yourself and healing these injuries, okay?"

"Okay."

As Catherine started to get out of the van, Jessica snagged her blouse.

"Wait." She handed over a wad of cash.

Catherine's fingers brushed over the crisp paper. Her gaze

flickered to the money, then back to Jessica's face. "What's this for?"

"You didn't think I was going to make you walk to the station, did you?" She shook her head and smiled. "The money is for the taxi I've ordered for you," Jessica replied, her voice gentle yet firm. "Just make sure you're safe, okay?"

Catherine swallowed the lump in her throat, her wide eyes stinging with unshed tears. "Thanks, Jessica. I don't know what I would have done if you hadn't shown up."

"Go on, your ride will be here any minute, and I need to go before they show up. If you need anything, call me. Don't hesitate. I promise I'll answer."

Catherine gripped the offered hand like a lifeline. Her thoughts raced, but words eluded her.

"Promise me you'll be careful. And remember, don't fully trust anyone from the police, no matter how friendly they seem."

"I promise." Catherine was overwhelmed with emotion as she said goodbye, and it dawned on her that she had been without her anxiety meds for days now, and even through everything that had been going on, she'd not descended into a panic attack. It was an odd feeling, especially as her life had been so chaotic and bizarre over the last month and a half.

"You okay?" Jessica asked, hesitantly.

Catherine glanced up at her and smiled. "Yeah. I'll see you."

With a reassuring smile from Jessica, Catherine opened the van door and stepped out into the rain-soaked night. A moment later, Jessica waved and pulled away. Catherine took a moment to test her lungs. She was breathing easier now the pain medicine had taken effect.

A car pulled up and stopped next to her. The window rolled down, and a woman looked out. "You called for a taxi?"

Catherine nodded and asked her to drive her to the police station.

"Sure thing, honey, get in." The driver looked at her in the rearview mirror. "I hope you're going to report whoever did that to your face."

"Yes, I am," Catherine said simply, not going into any detail. She pressed her fingers to her temples, attempting to ease the tension that had settled there.

"Here we are, honey. You go tell them who beat the crap out of you, and I hope they throw the book at them."

Catherine thanked the driver and paid her before climbing out. She stood outside the imposing façade of the police station, her heart pounding in her chest. She was worried that if she went in, she would be the one arrested, but she knew it was an irrational fear. She took several deep breaths and calmed herself before going inside. The air in the building was heavy with the scent of polished wood and a feeling of tension, a palpable reminder of the type of place it was.

As she approached the front desk, the receptionist glanced up, her expression one of practiced indifference. "May I help you?"

Catherine's voice wavered slightly as she replied, "I'm here to speak to Detective Sheldon."

The receptionist regarded her with a mixture of concern and surprise. "Are you filing charges against someone for that?" She gestured toward Catherine's face.

"No, I... not exactly." Catherine's nerves caused her to fumble over her words. "I spoke to Detective Sheldon earlier on the phone. He told me to come here. I'm Catherine Morris."

The receptionist frowned but nodded. "Okay, I'll see if he's available. Why don't you take a seat over there." She directed Catherine to a waiting area.

Catherine nodded and found a spot in the corner, her gaze wandering over the other occupants. They all seemed engrossed in their own concerns, enveloped in the processes of the station. The minutes ticked by, each one stretching into an eternity as her anxiety intensified.

Finally, Detective Sheldon approached her. "Catherine?"

She stood; her nervousness evident as she fidgeted. "Yes. Hello, Detective."

Detective Sheldon looked at her with shock. "What happened?"

Blinking back tears from her eyes, which were less swollen now, she gave him a watery smile. "Part of the long story I mentioned."

"Are you okay?"

Catherine shrugged. "As okay as I can be, I guess."

"Why don't you come on back," Detective Sheldon instructed, leading her down a corridor that seemed to stretch into infinity.

He led her past a room full of desks, their occupants engaged in various tasks. Each step felt as though she was walking deeper into the lion's den. She hoped she wasn't misplacing her trust in this man.

They entered a small room with a table and chairs. The walls were all solid, except for one that had a large window looking out into the corridor. As she took a seat, her hands trembling ever so slightly, she wondered if this was an interrogation room. Detective Sheldon sat across from her, his gaze probing.

"Before you begin, I want to make you aware that Tom called the station here, saying you escaped his custody. I didn't quite understand why you were in his custody, seeing as he's your husband, but he didn't clarify. He also said you set fire to his house and fled. He claims there were witnesses who saw you leave the scene."

Catherine had been backed into a corner, a pawn in a game she hadn't chosen to play. She turned to Detective Sheldon, her voice quivering. "That's not true. He's lying. I didn't start that fire."

Detective Sheldon's expression was thoughtful. "I never thought you did, or would, and given the look of you, I believe you've been through the wringer. Can you tell me what's happened since we spoke last?"

Catherine nodded before she explained about the neighbors and Tom trying to beat her into a confession.

Detective Sheldon's jaw twitched. "Tell me you're filing assault charges."

"If you think I should, I will," she said softly. "Can I do that here?"

He sighed. "Technically, yes, but the report will have to go to Eldon for investigation. It's their jurisdiction."

Catherine sighed. "I'm not sure I trust them."

Sheldon nodded. "Okay, let's go on. How did you get away, and where does the fire come into it?"

"I don't know how the fire started. All I heard was breaking glass, and then the men all ran to see what happened. My body ached from the beatings, so it took me a while to get up off the floor where I'd fallen. The room was dim, only the table lamp was on, and the curtains were closed. I noticed smoke coming from under the door. It smelt horrible. That's when I realized the house was on fire. I pushed myself into the hallway to see what was going on. The fire was in the living room. The heat was unbearable, and I tried to stay focused, but I was panicking a bit and froze. I noticed Tom in the room. He was trying to get those people to stay and put out the fire."

"The house was on fire, and he wanted people to stay?"

She nodded. "That's when Tom noticed me. Donna, my friend, was arguing with him about letting me and everyone get out. He was refusing. Then her husband showed up and broke through the door. He dragged Donna out, and everyone else fled after him. Tom blocked me in the hallway. Luckily, Donna somehow ran back, shoved Tom, and grabbed my arm, pulling me out the door," she lied, keeping Jessica out of it.

After Detective Sheldon had taken down notes, he said gently, "Let's go back to what happened with the most recent accident. Start from the beginning again." His eyes were attentive, his demeanor one of compassionate readiness.

Catherine took another shaky breath, her gaze distant as she seemed to gather the strength to recount the horrors that had been inflicted upon her. "It all started when Eleanor, my nurse, deemed me well enough to be on my own," she began. "Tom had demanded I get dressed. He said we were going to visit friends, but I knew he was planning something. He was adamant that I was driving in that accident, and he was determined that I admit to it."

"And then what happened?" Detective Sheldon prompted.

Catherine explained about the second accident and how Tom had threatened her. She mentioned how she'd asked the deputies to take her into custody, but that they had refused. Then she took a breath before telling him again about the "therapy sessions."

"What the ever-loving hell?" he murmured. "You went through several days of that before the fire broke out?"

Catherine nodded. "Yes."

"Catherine," he began gently. "I need you to trust me. We will investigate this, find out the truth, and ensure your safety."

Catherine met his gaze, a glimmer of hope mingling with her fear. "Can you really help me?"

Detective Sheldon nodded. "I'll do everything in my power to see that you get justice. First, I need to have a paramedic take a look at you. I'll also need to get photos of your injuries."

"Okay," Catherine replied. She was glad to have a plan set before her.

"Just wait here, okay?"

Over the next hour, she was led to another room, a more

private one, where a paramedic looked her over, and a female detective came and took pictures of her injuries. She'd had to strip down to her undergarments for them to get the full scope of the bruises that had been inflicted upon her. Eventually, she was brought to a small office where Detective Sheldon joined her.

"I know that couldn't have been comfortable for you, but with this evidence, we should be able to move forward."

"So, what will you do now?" Catherine asked.

"Well, unfortunately, as I mentioned before, Eldon doesn't fall in our jurisdiction, so I'll have to talk to the sheriff there. I'm going to go call him right now. You can stay here. Do you want anything? Coffee? Soda?"

"No, I'm okay, but I don't know how cooperative the sheriff will be. Tom is pretty friendly with him."

"Well, let's hope he can be reasoned with."

She felt a fragile hope that maybe, just maybe, there was a way out of the darkness that had consumed her world. Catherine knew that the road ahead would be treacherous, fraught with dangers and uncertainties. But with the detective on her side, she was prepared to spread the truth about the horrors that had tormented her. The rain continued to fall outside. A symphony of cleansing and renewal.

Alan Sheldon walked out of his office; his mind heavy with the weight of the revelations Catherine had shared. He held his phone tightly in his hand, the number of the county sheriff's office glowing on the screen. He needed to hand over the assault case to the proper authorities, but he didn't have a good feeling about doing so. He'd dealt with Sheriff Mason before, and the man was rarely cooperative.

Standing in a closed-off room, Alan dialed the number, his heart pounding in anticipation. After a few rings, someone answered the call in a gruff voice. "Sheriff's office. How can I help you?"

"This is Detective Alan Sheldon over in Cincinnati," he stated professionally. "I'd like to speak with Sheriff Mason, please."

There was a brief pause before the voice responded, "Hold on a moment."

Alan tapped his fingers on the wall impatiently as he waited, his mind racing through the details he needed to share. The line crackled to life again, and this time, it was the sheriff himself.

"This is Sheriff Mason. What can I do for you, Detective?"

"Good evening, Sheriff," Alan began, his tone respectful but direct. "I'm on the case involving the car crash, the Tom and Catherine Morris case."

"And which crash would that be, Detective? The one where Catherine murdered some poor woman with her reckless drinking and driving, or the one less than a week ago where she attempted to murder her husband by grabbing the steering wheel and trying to force a head-on collision?"

Alan gritted his teeth. "Excuse me, Sheriff, but it seems you've not got your facts straight about either of those events; however, let me address the first. Tom Morris was the one behind the wheel, and we have video evidence of it, not to mention physical evidence of the bruising patterns on Catherine's body. As to the second, I'm sure you are aware that witness testimony contradicts what you've described. I've read all the reports, and I watched the bodycam evidence."

"Witnesses lie."

"Are you also aware that Tom encouraged several men in your community to beat the crap out of his wife after that incident?"

"What happens in a man's home behind closed doors is his own business, Detective."

"Not when it's assault, Sheriff!" Alan was frustrated and furious with the man's attitude.

There was a moment of silence on the other end before Sheriff Mason said, "Detective Sheldon, I appreciate your concern, but Tom Morris is a pillar of our community. He's well-respected, involved in various local organizations and charities, and he has a clean record."

Alan felt another pang of frustration at his response. "Sheriff, I understand the importance of community ties. However, I've gathered significant evidence that suggests there's more to this situation than meets the eye. Catherine Morris has shared disturbing information about her husband and his attempts to kill her."

"I've known Tom Morris for years," Sheriff Mason retorted firmly. "He's a responsible citizen, and I find it hard to believe that he would be involved in anything like that. As for Catherine, well, people make many claims for attention or other reasons."

Alan's jaw clenched, the tension in his body rising. "Sheriff, with all due respect, my duty is to pursue the truth, regardless of anyone's reputation. I've spoken to Catherine personally, and her fear is genuine. We can't ignore this based solely on the assumption that Tom Morris is a good community leader."

"Look, Detective, I have to prioritize my resources. If you believe there's a case here, gather more substantial evidence and come back to me. But for now, I can't investigate baseless claims that might tarnish the reputation of innocent individuals," the sheriff said harshly.

"I respect your position, but I implore you to consider the safety and well-being of Mrs. Morris. If what Catherine says is true, her life could be at stake."

"I hear your concern, Detective, but until you have concrete evidence, I can't justify taking action in this instance. If you uncover something significant, bring it to me, and we'll reevaluate the situation."

Alan sighed heavily; his disappointment clear. However, he would not back down just yet. He was prepared to push the boundaries of jurisdiction if it meant uncovering the truth. "Sheriff," Alan replied, "I have more than enough evidence to believe that Catherine is in a dire situation. I'm prepared to involve the state police if necessary."

There was a substantial pause on the other end of the line, and then Sheriff Mason spoke with an edge of warning in his voice. "Detective, I understand your dedication to this case, but I urge you to reconsider. Involving more outside authorities might complicate matters and disrupt the delicate balance of our community."

"Your concerns are noted, Sheriff," Alan countered. "However, I have a duty to ensure the safety and well-being of the citizens I've sworn to protect. If you won't take action, I'll have no choice but to escalate this to a higher level."

Sheriff Mason's voice grew colder. "Let me be clear, Detective. This is my jurisdiction, and I will deal with any outside law enforcement officers who come here as intruders. I won't allow this situation to spiral out of control."

Alan's frustration flared, his resolve solidifying. "I'm not seeking to undermine your authority. But I believe the safety of the community is at stake. If you won't take action, I'll be left with no alternative but to pursue other avenues."

The sheriff's voice remained firm. "Do what you must, Detective. But know that I will protect the integrity of my jurisdiction."

With that, the call ended, leaving Alan staring at his phone with a mix of determination and unease. There was a darkness lurking beneath that stability the sheriff alluded to, and Alan was committed to bringing it to light, no matter the consequences.

He stood outside the door to his office, his mind replaying the conversation he had just had with the sheriff. Taking a deep breath, he entered the office, his footsteps echoing in the quiet room. He found Catherine in the same chair; her bruised blue eyes red from crying.

"Catherine."

She looked up at him with apprehension. "What did the sheriff say?"

Taking a seat beside her, he sighed heavily. "He's refusing to pursue the case and plans to drive away any outside police forces if they investigate. He's taking his decision seriously, Catherine. However, I'm still willing to help you where I can. I just don't know where that is yet."

Catherine's gaze held a glimmer of despair as she took in his words. "Thank you, Detective. It means so much to know that at least you're taking this seriously."

He nodded, but he kept his expression solemn. "I won't rest until we've uncovered the truth, Catherine. But there's something else we need to discuss."

"What is it?"

Alan chose his words carefully. "When I spoke to Sheriff Mason, he clarified that investigating could complicate matters within the community. He's protective of his jurisdiction, and he even mentioned that anyone who investigates this case might be seen as an intruder."

"You mean... people from Eldon might see the state police as a threat?"

He nodded, his expression grave. "Yes, that's a possibility. And they may include you in that. While I'm doing everything to ensure your safety, I want you to know there might be those who view this situation differently. They might not understand the full scope of what's happening and come after you."

TWENTY-THREE

Alan strode purposefully out of his office an hour and a half later, leaving Catherine there to relax. He and Catherine had gone back over everything, filling in as many details as he could get her to recall. His mind churned with a mix of determination and frustration, a storm of emotions that matched the heavy clouds looming overhead. Catherine, the key witness in a case that had the potential to bring down Eldon's most powerful attorney, was in imminent danger of collapsing like a house of cards.

Alan's gut feeling told him that time was running out, and he had to get her into protective custody before it was too late. As he entered the bustling precinct, he scanned the sea of desks in the detective pool. The clatter of computer keyboards and the hum of hushed conversations filled the air. He spotted his partner, Detective Sarah Ramirez, leaning over a stack of case files.

Her face, usually a portrait of fierce determination, was etched with concern as she looked up at Alan's approach. "You look like you're about to go into a lion's den," she quipped.

"Sarah, you know me. I don't back down from a fight." His voice was resolute.

Ramirez nodded, obviously understanding the gravity of the situation. "So, what's the plan?"

Alan leaned in closer, lowering his voice. "I'm going to speak to the captain about getting Catherine Morris into protective custody. We can't afford to wait any longer. With the evidence she has against her husband, she's a ticking time bomb from his point of view."

Ramirez's brow furrowed. "But you know Sheriff Mason won't make this easy. He's got connections, and he's not afraid to use them."

Sheldon clenched his jaw, his frustration clear. "I know his cousin is Governor. But we can't let that stop us. We have to move quickly before Mason's influence can do any more damage."

As they spoke, the precinct's entrance swung open, and the imposing figure of Sheriff Mason strode in. His presence held the foreboding promise of destruction to Alan's case against Tom Morris.

Mason exchanged nods with a few officers, his cold, icy gaze eventually settling on Sheldon and Ramirez. "Detectives." His tone dripped with condescension.

Alan's grip on his resolve tightened. "Sheriff, we need to talk about Catherine Morris."

Mason raised an eyebrow, feigning ignorance. "And what importance does Catherine serve? Other than slander, of course."

"Don't play games, Mason."

Mason's lips curled into a faint smile, his eyes dancing with a mocking gleam. "She's the prime suspect in the car accident that killed that woman. It's been keeping you busy. But what does it have to do with me?"

Alan leaned forward in frustration, his voice low and

steady. "Catherine is a witness, not the one driving during the accident, as you are well aware. She's in danger, and we need to place her in protective custody."

Mason's amusement seemed to grow. "Protective custody? That's a rather tall order, isn't it? For a car accident witness? And what evidence do you have that would warrant protective custody?"

Alan's frustration simmered beneath his controlled exterior. "We have evidence of threats against her life. We can't afford to take any chances."

Mason's demeanor shifted again, his eyes narrowing ever so slightly. "Threats? You know, Alan, I'm not in the business of protecting every scared liar who walks through my door."

Alan's patience was wearing thin, but he held his ground. "This isn't just any witness, Mason. She holds the key to the entire case against Tom Morris. We can't let anyone silence her."

Mason's smile faded, replaced by a steely gaze that bore into Sheldon's soul. "You seem awfully invested in this case, Detective. One might think there's more to your determination than meets the eye."

Before Alan could respond, a voice interrupted their tense standoff.

"Is there a problem here, gentlemen?" Captain Davidson's arrival momentarily diffused the tension in the room.

Alan seized the opportunity. "Captain, I need your help. Catherine Morris is in danger. We have evidence of threats against her life. We need to get her into protective custody."

Davidson's brow wrinkled as he looked from Alan to Mason. "I'll need to see the evidence, Detective."

Mason's voice dripped with mockery. "Funny thing, Captain. I just received a call from a few friends in the Attorney General's Office. They seemed quite concerned about your department's involvement in this case."

Davidson's expression darkened. "What are you implying, Mason?"

Mason's smile was triumphant, a predator basking in the misery of its prey. "I'm implying that if you go forward with this protective custody plan, there might be consequences. For you, for your officers, and for this entire department. There's been an allegation that the evidence might have been tampered with."

The room seemed to constrict around Alan, a suffocating feeling of powerlessness settling in. He exchanged a tense look with Ramirez, who mirrored his frustration.

Davidson's gaze shifted between Alan and Mason, his decision hanging in the balance. After a lengthy pause, he finally spoke. "I'll review the evidence, Alan. But I won't decide without due diligence."

Alan nodded; his jaw clenched. He understood the tightrope Davidson was walking, but he couldn't shake the feeling that time was slipping through their fingers. As Mason left the room, his victory assured, Alan's shoulders slumped.

The battle had only just begun, and the shadows of deceit were growing deeper. Yet his mind was a tempest of frustration and doubt. The events of the past few minutes had left him feeling like a chess piece in a game he didn't fully understand. Protective custody for Catherine had been thwarted for the moment, and now he grappled with a unique challenge: A "he said, she said" case that threatened to unravel everything he had worked so hard to build against Tom Morris, not only for the death of Melissa Legrasse but also for the attempted murder of his wife. His conversation with Sheriff Mason had left a bitter taste in his mouth, the taste of powerlessness in the face of corruption. He knew he needed to regroup to navigate the treacherous waters ahead.

His thoughts were interrupted when he glanced up to see Ramirez standing there, a concerned look on her face. She had only been a small part of this case, yet Alan was grateful for her unwavering support.

"You okay?" Ramirez asked softly.

Alan sighed. "No, Sarah. I'm not okay. This whole situation is spiraling out of control, and I feel like I'm stuck in a maze with no way out."

Ramirez leaned against her desk; her expression sympathetic. "I know it's frustrating, but you can't lose sight of your goal. You need to protect Catherine and bring down Tom Morris."

Alan rubbed a hand over his close-cropped black hair, his exhaustion clear. "But how do I do that when the case has devolved into a 'he said, she said' situation? Mason's threats have thrown a wrench into everything."

Ramirez nodded, her gaze steady. "You regroup, Alan. Take a step back, re-examine the evidence, and clear Catherine's name. You can't let anyone control the narrative. And don't forget we do have physical evidence on our side."

Alan appreciated Ramirez's optimism, but his doubts lingered. "I wish it were that simple. I'm up against a powerful man who will stop at nothing to protect his interests."

Ramirez leaned in, her voice a quiet yet determined whisper, "You've faced tough cases before. Don't let fear and doubt cloud your judgment now. You owe it to Catherine to fight for her."

Alan met his partner's gaze, her unwavering conviction stirring a fire within him. He nodded slowly; his determination reignited. "You're right, Sarah. I can't back down. I'm going to review the evidence we have, piece by piece. Maybe there's something I missed. First, I've got to go tell Catherine about this."

· · ·

Alan's heart pounded as he stood outside his office, steeling himself for the conversation he was about to have with Catherine. He knew her life was still in danger, and he was determined to keep her safe, even if it meant stepping into the unknown. He swung open the door to his office. Catherine sat in her chair, her bruised eyes a mix of relief and uncertainty as she greeted him. The weak light in the room behind her seemed to enfold her in an atmosphere of secrecy and protection.

"Detective." Catherine's voice was soft. "What's going on?"

Alan offered her a small smile, his concern for her well-being apparent. "Catherine, I'm afraid I can't get you out of the woods just yet. Tom, it seems, is not giving up easily."

Catherine's shoulders sagged; her weariness clear. "I know. But thanks to you, I finally feel like I have a fighting chance."

"That's what I want to talk to you about. Regardless of the evidence we've accumulated, I can't keep you safe right now."

Catherine's brows furrowed and her expression fell. "What do you mean? I don't have to go back to Eldon, do I? I can't... I won't go back there."

Alan took a deep breath, the weight of his words settling on his shoulders. "No, you don't have to go back, but I can't get you into witness protection right now. Is there anyone you trust here in Cincinnati? Someone who can offer you protection outside of law enforcement? Someone who can keep you hidden from Tom?"

Catherine paused her gaze concentrated on her lap. "I don't trust anyone from Eldon, really, not since that first accident." She shook her head, still clearly thinking it over. She met Alan's gaze. "And I don't know anyone here in Cincinnati except you, Detective, and I certainly don't expect you to personally keep me hidden." She sighed.

"You don't have even one trusted friend who could help you?" he pushed.

She started to shake her head but then paused again as if

she suddenly remembered something, her expression brighten-
ing. "There's someone I think who might help me," she said
hesitantly.

The police station loomed behind Catherine. Its impressive
presence cast long shadows across the worn pavement in the
moonlight. She hadn't imagined when she first walked in that
she'd be leaving without police protection. However, fate had
dealt her a hand she couldn't avoid. She took a deep breath and
limped down the sidewalk to the edge of the parking lot. She
winced with each movement, the pain a constant reminder of
the recent torture. She sat down on the curb, the damp sensation of despair flowing through her body like a powerful
waterfall.

Catherine knew the risks of involving someone else in what
was going on, but she couldn't let Tom go unpunished. She felt
a mix of determination and anxiety, a blend that was becoming
all too familiar. She had the choice between calling two people.
They were the only ones she trusted. She reached into her
pocket and pulled out the phone Jessica had bought her, her
fingers trembling as she pushed the button to call Donna.

"Hello?" Donna answered hesitantly.

"Donna." Catherine's voice wavered. "It's me."

There was a moment of silence, then Donna's voice was
laced with worry. "Catherine! Are you okay? Where are you?"

Catherine took a deep breath, her voice shaky but determined. "Yes, I'm okay... well, as okay as I was when you saw me
last. But I need your help. Can you talk right now?"

"Of course, I can talk. What do you need?" Donna replied
quickly.

Catherine got up from the curb and moved to lean against a
nearby tree. The streets around the police station were calm
and quiet, giving her the peace that she craved to work through

her thoughts. She replayed the events of the past three and a half weeks, the accident that had changed everything, and the determination that had welled up inside her since.

"Hey, Cath, are you sure you're alright?" Donna sounded worried.

Catherine smiled weakly. "Yeah, I'm good. I just walked out of the police station in Cincinnati."

"The police station! What happened? Why are you outside the police station? They didn't arrest you, did they?"

Catherine took a deep breath, the weight of her emotions threatening to spill over. "No, no. I came here to talk to Detective Sheldon about everything that's been going on."

"You did? Catherine, that's... brave." Donna sounded shocked and slightly in awe.

Catherine was glad she'd managed to surprise her friend. "I couldn't just let it go, Donna. Tom deserves to face justice."

"I agree, but you need to be careful. You're not invincible. You don't know what Tom's planning."

Catherine knew she wasn't invincible. She was very much human and vulnerable, which she'd come to understand over the last several weeks. "I'm realizing that. What is he saying?"

"Cath, there's been a lot going on, and I haven't been able to talk to you about it because you haven't been answering your phone, and then Tom had you trapped in that house—"

"I know, I'm sorry. Tom kept taking my phone. He's had it since before that last accident."

"Whose phone have you called me from?" she asked, suddenly curious.

"Someone took pity on me and bought me a new phone."

"The person who got you out of the house?" Donna asked.

"Yes," Catherine replied hesitantly.

"Who was it? With that gas mask on I couldn't get a good look at them, and then all I could see through the windshield was bright red hair."

"The person who rescued me wants to stay anonymous, Donna. They asked me not to say who they were. At least not yet."

"I'm just glad they got you out. Are they from Eldon?"

"No, they aren't. She's... can you keep this secret?" Catherine had decided to tell a partial truth.

"To the grave," Donna replied.

"It was the woman who stopped Tom's car with her van the other day. That second accident. She's the one who rammed into us and pinned our car against the guardrail so Tom couldn't drive us into the back of that semi or force us into a head-on collision."

"Oh, wow. How did she even know what was going on?"

Catherine fretted for half a second and then came up with a small white lie to explain it. "She said she had come by to check on me because I'd looked so scared in the car. She saw the fire and rushed in to help."

"So, she's a real do-gooder," Donna said.

"Yeah, I guess so. Anyway, what has Tom been saying?"

"Oh. Are you sure you want to know?"

"I can handle it, Donna. What is he saying?"

Donna took a deep breath and murmured, "He's been spreading rumors about you. Blaming you for the fire, which everyone knows is baloney, but the men are all supporting him."

Catherine had expected that. "Of course they are," she said in frustration. "They don't want to admit they were busy beating the snot out of me."

"He's convinced nearly everyone in town that you're... well, he's saying that you're out of your mind on alcohol, and that's why you've been acting so erratically and why you crashed the car in the first place."

Catherine's hands trembled as anger filled her. Even though she knew that was what Tom had been doing, it hurt to hear that people believed him. "How did it come to this?" she murmured.

"Cath, you know Tom has been—" Donna broke off.

"Cheating?"

Donna sighed. "Well, yeah. But that wasn't what I was going to say."

"Controlling me since I met him?" she offered up her recent revelation.

"Yes. You were always way more outgoing than me, and then somehow, you became withdrawn and studious, and it was hard to connect with you. All our friends thought you'd turned into a snob, but... well, I knew there was something going on."

"I thought he cared about me. I thought it was so cool that this older guy was paying attention to me, encouraging me. I just wanted to make him proud in the beginning," Catherine whispered.

"I get it. You're the reason I'm studying law, you know. You used to talk about it all the time back in high school. How you were going to get into Harvard or Stanford and become a top lawyer like Tom Morris."

"Then Dad died."

"And you married Tom."

"I thought I loved him."

"I know. And for a while, I thought he was good for you, but then..."

"He started limiting my access to things."

"Not just that. I started seeing things."

"What things?" Catherine asked in confusion.

"First, it was just him flirting excessively with women at the firm. Clients and a few of the staffers. Then I started noticing after he made partner, he was buying expensive things, going to Cincinnati, New York, LA, San Francisco... there was the trip to London... and you weren't going with him, but he was booking two tickets."

Catherine frowned. "Wait... when did he go to those places?" She thought back over the past two years, but she couldn't recall Tom ever telling her he was going on any trips like that. There'd been several weeks where he'd said he was staying in Cincinnati, but she couldn't think of any trips.

Donna sighed. "That's what I'm saying. There's so much you don't know about what he's been up to."

Catherine sank into the tree, her head in her hand. "He's supposed to be my husband. I trusted him."

"I know this is hard to hear, but I thought you deserved to know the truth. Especially after everything he's done to you. I should have told you sooner, but you always defended him, and I didn't want to shatter the illusion for you. I'm sorry, Cath."

"It's okay. It's not your fault. But I'm not going to let him get away with this. I won't let him tarnish my reputation. I won't let him turn everyone against me."

"You don't have to do this alone, Cath. I'm here for you. I see through his lies. I always have."

Catherine felt raw and exposed. "Thank you, Donna. I don't know what I would do without you."

"We're best friends, remember? We'll face this together."

"I remember. Oh! I just remembered something else."

"What is it?" Donna asked.

"So I told Detective Sheldon everything that happened, except for the part about the woman who actually rescued me. Since she said she wanted to stay anonymous, well, I couldn't tell the detective it was her that helped me, so I said it was you."

"Is that all?" Donna laughed. "You had me worried. I don't care that you said it was me. I would have gone back in for you if you hadn't come out."

"That's good to know." Catherine smiled.

"So, the detective believes everything that's going on? He's not buying Tom's version of events?"

"Yes, and he's got the evidence to help prove it, except he's facing some resistance."

"What do you mean?"

Catherine swallowed hard. This was the part that worried her most. "Sheriff Mason, you know he's a close friend of Tom's, and I think he's related to him somehow, a second cousin, but I only recently found that out."

"Tom and Sheriff Mason are related? Well, that explains a lot, doesn't it?" Donna huffed.

"Yes, and he's refusing to cooperate and has threatened to call in favors from the Attorney General's Office."

"He should be impartial and focused on finding the truth. That's what we elected him to do, even if he is related to Tom," Donna replied, frustration clear in her tone.

Catherine grunted as she dug her toe into the grass. "I know, but he doesn't want to investigate at all. Detective Sheldon said he threatened to bring the state police into this if Mason wouldn't start cooperating, but the sheriff didn't change his mind and, instead, he doubled down with his Attorney General threat. It's like he's protecting Tom and trying to discredit me."

"You know his cousin is the Governor, right?" Donna murmured.

An air of unease settled over the line. She hadn't known that. No wonder the sheriff felt comfortable making threats against the police here in Cincinnati. And if he was related to the Governor, did that mean Tom was too? That was a scary thought.

"Catherine, what exactly do you know about the state police coming in?"

"Only that Detective Sheldon said he mentioned they might get involved if Sheriff Mason's bias continues to be an issue and mess up his case against Tom."

"I can't shake the feeling that Tom will find a way to use this situation to his advantage. He's always been good at manipulating people, especially the people in town."

"Tom's charm could easily sway them, and with rumors of the state police coming, he might convince them to take matters into their own hands." She gulped.

"Cath? Catherine? Are you okay?"

"I'm here," she whispered. "There has to be a way to stop him, to make him pay for everything he's done and is still doing."

"What if we can discredit him? Expose his lies and manipulation? Maybe then people would be more inclined to cooperate with the state police if they show up."

"Do you think it's possible to turn his family and friends against him?"

"Maybe. I've been thinking there might be something to all the money he's flashed around the firm. The trips and extravagant gifts."

"The only time I've ever seen him spend extravagantly was the night of our anniversary," Catherine whispered as she watched a car's taillights move down the street.

"What if he's been embezzling money?"

Catherine's breath caught in her throat. She considered the possibility. "Embezzling? Donna, that's a serious accusation. Do you think it's possible? Wouldn't the other partners realize that he was doing that?"

"I know it is, but I don't think I'm jumping to conclusions. There have been some odd things going on in the office. I think it's entirely probable that he's spending firm money instead of his own."

Catherine felt a wave of hope at Donna's words, but she remained cautious. "But how would we even find out if he's been embezzling?"

"I'll start by looking into the office paperwork and the

accounting books. If he's been misusing funds or funneling money for his own gain, there might be a trail we can follow."

"It's risky, Donna. If you poke around and you're wrong, it could backfire, and you could lose your job, or worse, end up arrested."

Donna's voice held conviction. "I know that's a possibility, but we can't ignore the signs and the doubts that are already there. It's better to know the truth, even if it costs me my job."

"If you're sure. I don't want you risking your neck for this. I already know he's been deceiving me, not just cheating on me, and controlling me, but I think... and I know this is going to sound absurd, but I think he groomed me."

"Looking back at things, yeah, I think you're right."

"I just can't figure out why."

"Maybe when this is all over, we can ask him."

The moon rose higher in the sky as Catherine gazed at the ground. She suddenly remembered she needed to find a place to stay. "Hey, do you think I could come and stay with you for a while? I can't go back to my house, not with Tom there."

"I don't think that's a good idea, Cath. You shouldn't be anywhere near Eldon right now."

Catherine's heart sank. "Oh, yeah, I guess you're right. It's just that I don't know what else to do. The cops can't put me in witness protection, and I don't have any mon—" She stopped and realized she did have one other recourse she could try.

"Did you think of something?" Donna asked hesitantly.

"Yeah, maybe."

"If whatever you're thinking doesn't work out, call me back. I'll be up for another hour or so. Maybe I can book you a room on my credit card or something."

"Thanks, Donna. I'll text you either way, so you won't worry."

"You'd better. Stay safe." Donna hung up.

The night was cool as Catherine leaned against the tree and

pulled up the three contacts in her new phone. With a sense of desperation, she pushed the button labeled 'medic.'

"Hello?"

"Jessica? It's Catherine."

"Catherine? Did you speak to the detective? Did he get you settled somewhere?" Jessica sounded a little surprised.

Catherine took a deep breath, her heart pounding. "Yes, I did, but no... they can't give me any kind of protection. I was sort of hoping..."

There was a brief pause, and then Jessica's voice came through, warm and reassuring. "I'm happy to help if you need me. I know we don't know each other well, but I promised to protect you, and I intend to keep that promise."

Gratitude and relief washed over her. "Thank you, Jessica. I can't tell you how much this means to me."

"Of course. Can you walk about two blocks up the street to the café on the corner? You should be able to see the sign from the front of the station on your right."

Catherine turned her head and looked down the street, catching sight of the sign lit up in the night sky. "Yes, I can do that. I see it."

"Go on in and order whatever you want. I'll be there as soon as I can. Hang in there," Jessica replied.

As the call ended, Catherine's heart felt lighter than it had in days. The kindness and compassion she had experienced from Jessica were beacons of hope amid her challenges. She made her way down the street to the café as though it was the last oasis of water in a desert, and she was dying of thirst.

TWENTY-FOUR

"I can't believe he would push me to this," Catherine murmured, her voice barely above a whisper. "Making me hide like a criminal in a seedy motel."

Jessica faced Catherine, her expression softening. "I know the accommodations aren't the best, but right now, this is the safest option you have. We need time to figure out our next move, and this place offers some anonymity."

Catherine's voice quivered with uncertainty. "What if someone recognizes me? What if—"

Jessica held up a hand to interrupt her. "I've taken every precaution, Catherine. I used a false name, paid in cash, and made sure your tracks were as obscure as possible. Nobody will connect you to this place unless you tell them you're here, which you aren't going to do."

Catherine nodded, a mixture of gratitude and fear in her wide eyes. She'd grown to trust Jessica, seeing as she had saved her more times than she could count since this nightmare began.

"You do need to tell Detective Sheldon that you're here, though," Jessica continued. "Only him, nobody else. I'm pretty sure you can trust him but don't trust any of the other cops. There may be too many even here in Cincinnati that are compromised when it comes to you."

Catherine glanced at her. "What do you mean? Why would they be compromised?"

"I'm not sure you're aware, but your husband has some pretty heavy connections in Ohio. Not just in Eldon. He's related to the Governor, did you know that?" she asked, looking exasperated.

Pressing her lips together firmly, Catherine gave a single nod. "I just found out recently. When we met, he told me he was an only child and had no living family, and I believed him. I never questioned it. Never questioned why no one ever said anything. I've been thinking about it, and I still don't understand it."

"He never called them aunt, or uncle, or sister in front of you?" Jessica asked.

Catherine thought about it for a moment. "No, never. He always used their names. I remember running into Mrs. Porter, she was my teacher in middle school, shortly after we were married. Tom called her Isabelle. I distinctly recall him saying, 'Isabelle, you know my wife, Catherine?' and she'd gone on to tell Tom that she'd been my teacher and how she'd always thought I'd go on to do more than I had. I'd been embarrassed that I hadn't, but Tom had told her that I wanted to be his wife and take care of him and our home. I'd thought he was defending me at the time, but now..." She frowned.

"Maybe he thought you knew?"

Again, Catherine thought about it. She'd lived in Eldon with her dad since she was a toddler, but she'd never cared, nor pretended to care who'd founded it. Nor had she paid any attention while growing up to who was related to who. It hadn't mattered to her, hadn't affected her life. And none of the people in town had the same last name as Tom and her, so she'd never even questioned his version of things. "No, he very clearly told me that he had no living family. It was something I thought we had in common after my dad died."

"Well, he obviously lied." Jessica sighed.

"I'm finding Tom is a consummate liar."

"He is. Anyway, because he's related to so many people in town, I think that's why they are willing to go along with him on things. It's not all charm, as I'd thought before."

Catherine pursed her lips and then decided to share what she and Donna had speculated. "Do you think that might be why he's kept things quiet from me? Because he's embezzling? Because he thinks I'll turn him in?"

Jessica gave her a considering look. "That's a possibility. This has been going on for longer than a few years. You've known him for what, five, six years?"

"Nine. I met him when I was fourteen."

"Right. Nine years, so at least that long, and most likely longer seeing as you've lived there practically your whole life and never knew he was related to half the town."

Catherine looked out the window at the rain-soaked streets, lost in thought. "Everything feels so surreal. Two months ago, I was living what I thought was a normal life, and now I'm here, in hiding from my lying, cheating, murderous husband, accused of a crime I didn't commit."

"I promise you, Catherine, you'll get through this," Jessica said firmly. "We'll clear your name and put Tom behind bars. But for now, you need to focus on staying safe."

When Catherine woke the next day, the clock on the nightstand read 2.30 p.m. She had slept longer than she intended, but the exhaustion that had been building up over the past few weeks seemed to have finally caught up with her. As she swung her legs over the edge of the mattress, the creak of the bedsprings filled the room. Her gaze settled on the small table by the window, where a plate of sandwiches and a bottle of water awaited her. A note lay next to the plate, written in Jessica's neat handwriting.

Hey, I figured you could use something to eat. I'll be running some errands today, but I'll be back to check in on you soon. Take your time and rest. – J

Catherine's stomach rumbled in response to the sight and scent of the food. She hadn't realized just how hungry she was until that moment. Picking up one of the sandwiches, she took a hesitant bite, savoring the taste of the turkey, Swiss cheese, and avocado with honey mustard. After finishing her meal and sipping the water, Catherine reached for her phone on the nightstand. She remembered that she needed to contact Detective Sheldon to let him know her whereabouts.

"Detective Sheldon speaking."

"Detective, it's Catherine Morris."

"Catherine? Are you alright?" Detective Sheldon's tone held a note of concern.

"I'm safe," Catherine replied, her gaze drifting out the window. "I wanted to tell you where I am. One of my friends got me a motel room under an assumed name. I'm at a place called The Willow Inn, in room 207."

There was a pause on the other end of the line for just a moment, then he replied, "Thank you for letting me know. I'll make sure your location remains confidential."

Catherine exhaled and felt herself relax. "Thank you, Detective. I trust you."

"I won't let anything happen to you, Catherine. We'll sort this out," Detective Sheldon reassured her.

After the call ended, Catherine pushed aside the covers, moved to the edge of the mattress and stood up, deciding it was time to face the day. Shuffling to the bathroom, Catherine splashed cold water on her face, trying to shake off the residual drowsiness. She stared at her reflection in the mirror, a woman who had been through more in the past few weeks than she had the rest of her entire life. Her face was a mass of blue, purple, green, and brown bruises, but the swelling was almost gone, and she could see more fully out of both her eyes. She tenderly pushed on the skin by her eye and sighed.

Emerging from the bathroom, Catherine found a shopping bag placed on the bed that hadn't been there ten minutes ago. Jessica had a key, so it wasn't worrying to her that someone had been in the room. Inside the bag were fresh clothes that she assumed were courtesy of Jessica. With gratitude, Catherine returned to the bathroom and turned on the shower. She hadn't had a proper one in so long that she wasn't sure she recalled what one felt like. She quickly undressed and removed the bandages around her ribs.

She stepped into the shower, and as the water cascaded over her, she sighed with pleasure. The warmth of the water soothed her aching muscles, and she stood there just basking in the feeling of the simple bliss of the moment. Shortly after, she dried off and changed into the clean attire, feeling a renewed sense of purpose as she slipped into a pair of jeans and a comfortable sweater. Just as she finished dressing, the sound of the motel room door unlocking caught her attention.

Jessica stepped inside, another shopping bag in her hand, her expression warm. "Hey there, I see you found the clothes," Jessica greeted, her eyes scanning Catherine's face. "How are you feeling?"

Catherine managed a small smile. "Better, I think. Sleeping helped."

Jessica nodded, stepped further into the room, and placed the shopping bag on the table. "I brought you some more essentials: toiletries, another change of clothes, and a few snacks. Figured you might need them."

Catherine gazed at her with gratitude. "You've done so much for me."

Jessica shrugged, a hint of a smile tugging at her lips. "We're in this together."

Catherine stirred, her body aching from the events of the past weeks, as the morning light streamed between the motel room curtains, casting a gentle glow across the worn-out carpet and onto the bed. She shifted on the mattress, wincing at the twinges of pain that radiated from various bruises and scrapes. Rolling onto her back, Catherine sighed, realizing that her body desperately needed more rest and healing.

Beside the bed, Jessica had left her a bottle of water and some pain pills. She smiled at her thoughtfulness. Catherine reached for the pills, downing them with a sip of water. She leaned back against the pillows, closing her eyes and focusing on her breathing, trying to relax her tense muscles.

As Catherine lay there, allowing herself to rest, she thought about her relationship with Tom, her dreams and aspirations, her sense of normalcy. That was all gone now. There was no putting her rose-colored glasses back on and returning to the life she once knew. Her life had been shattered, splintered into a million broken pieces that no longer fit together.

Hours passed as Catherine drifted in and out of sleep, the afternoon sun inching its way across the room. When she finally opened her eyes again, she felt a sense of calm and renewal wash over her. The painkillers had taken the edge off her discomfort, and the respite had allowed her body to heal more fully.

Slowly sitting up, Catherine swung her legs over the side of the bed and made her way to the bathroom. She glimpsed herself in the mirror—dark purple and green bruises surrounded her eyes, her face bearing the evidence of the struggles she had endured. But she also saw a reflection of strength, a woman who had weathered storms and was ready to rise again like a phoenix.

Splashing cold water on her face, Catherine felt a renewed sense of energy. She changed into the comfortable leggings and sweatshirt Jessica had bought her and glanced at her phone, realizing that she hadn't checked in with Jessica or Detective Sheldon since the previous evening. She hit the button to call Jessica first.

"Hey, how are you feeling? Everything okay?" Jessica's concern was clear in her tone.

Catherine felt a small smile lift her cheek. "I'm doing better, actually. I took the morning and early afternoon to rest, and it's made a difference."

"That's good to hear," Jessica replied. "Don't push yourself too hard, though, okay?"

"I know, I won't. But I need to be in top shape to tackle whatever comes next."

"You've got the right mindset," Jessica said. "I'm looking into some of the hinky things Tom's been doing. He's kept a pretty tight lid on it, but... it's not pretty."

Catherine frowned. "What kind of things? Can you tell me? Or do I not want to know?" she whispered.

"Look, you can't share this with the detective, what I'm doing isn't legal."

"Okay. What are you doing? You aren't going to get arrested, are you?"

Jessica snickered. "No. Not unless they catch me, and that's not going to happen. I've hacked into Tom's computer remotely. I can see everything he's been up to. He's got some pretty nasty stuff on there. Your neighbor Mark? Yeah, the guy's a rapist.

Tom has pictures and has been blackmailing him. That's not even the worst thing I've found."

Catherine gasped and covered her mouth with her hand. "Don't tell me anymore. I don't want to know."

"I don't blame you."

"What are you going to do with all that... that information?" she whispered.

"I'll make sure it finds its way to the proper authorities once the Tom situation is resolved."

That sounded reasonable. Catherine couldn't imagine allowing someone who'd committed crimes to go free because the information was somehow hidden. It didn't sit right with her. "Good."

"Do you need anything?" Jessica asked.

"No, I'm okay. I just wanted to check in."

"Okay, I'll see you later then."

After ending the call with Jessica, Catherine sent Detective Sheldon a text to check in. He replied quickly.

Good to hear, I should have news soon. Hang in there and stay safe.

Shoving her phone in her pocket, Catherine stepped outside the motel room for a breath of fresh air. The late afternoon sun felt warm against her skin. As she walked along the pathway that led to the parking lot, Catherine noticed a small park nearby, and she headed for it. She spent the remainder of the afternoon watching kids playing on the playground equipment and just relaxing.

As the sun descended, she made her way back to the room and noticed a note on the table. She picked it up and saw it was from Jessica.

Catherine, I'll be back soon. Taking a detour after my investigation to grab dinner for us. I know you were over at the park, but it would be safer if you stayed hidden, and remember that rest is just as important as action. ~ J.

Catherine smiled as she read Jessica's words. She settled back on the bed to wait for her to return when there was a knock on the door. Rising, she went to answer it. "Detective Sheldon," she greeted with a hint of surprise.

"Hello, Catherine," Detective Sheldon replied. "Mind if I come in?"

Catherine stepped aside, allowing him to enter the room.

He glanced around briefly, taking in the surroundings before settling on Catherine. "I wanted to check in with you personally." Detective Sheldon's expression was thoughtful. "I know you texted me, but I wanted to be sure you were actually safe here."

"I think I am. Nobody but you and a friend know that I'm here, and there's no way for anyone in Eldon to track me."

Detective Sheldon nodded. "Good to hear. Your safety is a priority, Catherine."

"Thank you, Detective. Your support means a lot."

The Detective's gaze met hers. "I'd like to go over a few details from the case with you if you don't mind?"

Catherine's heart raced as she nodded, her mind bracing for the questions that were sure to come.

"Can you walk me through the events that led up to the fire at your house again, starting with the second car crash?" Detective Sheldon asked. "I just want to make sure I've got everything I need and haven't missed anything important."

Catherine did what he asked. Recounting everything with every detail she could think of. From who was there beating her and who she noticed in the house at the time of the fire. They were all complicit, even if they hadn't laid a finger on her.

"Okay, I think I've got it all now. I also wanted to update you on my progress," he replied. "I've been in touch with the state police, and we've been working to gather enough evidence to get a warrant for Tom's arrest. It's a delicate situation because he's so well-connected, and we're being blocked by various judges and state officials."

Catherine's heart skipped a beat. "So, what's the plan then?" she asked.

"I've been collaborating with a couple of state investigators, ones I feel I can trust, and we're planning to head to Eldon. As soon as we secure the warrant, we'll pick him up for questioning regarding both road accidents, as well as you being held against your will and your assault."

"When will that happen?" Catherine inquired, her voice barely above a whisper. She'd been relying solely on her breathing exercises and countdowns to manage her mental health since the fire, as she had no access to her medication. With everything going on, she thought she was doing pretty well.

"We're working as quickly as possible," he assured her. "Our priority is to ensure your safety and gather as much evidence as we can when we issue him the arrest warrant and search warrants for the house and his office."

Catherine nodded. She sat on the edge of the bed, her thoughts racing as she processed the impending arrest of Tom. The culmination of weeks of investigation, hard work, and determination was almost at hand. But amidst the anticipation, a lingering sense of unease gnawed at Catherine's mind. "Thank you, Detective. I'm a bit worried, though."

"What's bothering you?" he asked.

"I can't shake this bad feeling I have," Catherine continued, her words earnest. "Tom's arrest, the state police—it's a big step, and I know you're doing everything you can to make sure justice is served. But I can't help but worry about what you might encounter in Eldon."

"I appreciate your concern. The situation is complex, and we're taking every precaution to ensure a smooth operation. The state investigators and I are well-prepared for whatever challenges might arise."

"I trust you, Detective. I know you're doing everything you can to protect me. I appreciate that."

"As I said, your safety remains my top priority."

Catherine smiled. "Please be careful of Sheriff Mason. He's not a nice man, and I know he'll do whatever he has to in order to protect himself and the people who keep him in office." She paused and then added, "I just recently found out that he's related to Tom. They're cousins. Apparently, half the town is related to him, and I never suspected because he never introduced them as such, and he told me when we met that he had no living family."

"I appreciate you telling me that, Catherine. I was aware that he had sisters and cousins in town, though I didn't know about the Sheriff being one of them. That does go a long way to explaining some of their motivations," Detective Sheldon replied. "We'll keep Sheriff Mason's warning in mind as we proceed. Our goal is to uncover the truth while minimizing risks to our people and the citizens of Eldon."

"Please be careful. I know you're capable, but I can't help but worry about your safety, too."

"Your concern means a lot to me, and I want you to know that I'm fully committed to getting justice for both you and Melissa Legrasse."

"Thank you."

"Don't worry. We'll navigate the challenges together, and we'll uncover the truth, no matter how intricate the web of deception going on in Eldon may be."

TWENTY-FIVE

Two months since the anniversary

Catherine awoke to the insistent ringing of her phone. As she fumbled for the device on her nightstand, her heart quickened at the sight of Donna's name flashing on the screen. It wasn't often that her best friend called at this hour, especially not with such a tone of urgency.

"Hello?" Catherine croaked out; her voice still thick with sleep.

"Catherine, you need to listen to me." Donna's voice crackled with an unusual mixture of anxiety and excitement. "I'm at the office, and I've found something... something big."

Catherine blinked her eyes, attempting to shake off the remnants of her dreams. She sat up in bed, clutching the phone closer to her ear. "Donna, what are you talking about? It's barely dawn."

"I know, I know." Donna's words rushed out, the sentences tumbling over each other. "But you won't believe what I've found. I've been digging through the financial records, the invoices, everything. And I think... I think we were right. Tom has been embezzling money from the company for years."

Catherine's mind snapped to attention. "Donna, are you sure? He's embezzling funds?"

"I wouldn't have called you if I wasn't certain," Donna replied firmly. "I've been cross-referencing records, tracing transactions, and there's a pattern. Someone has been siphoning enormous sums of money off through shell companies, off-book accounts, and it all leads back to Tom."

Catherine's pulse quickened. "Donna, I... thank you for doing all this. How will this sway everyone, though? How can we use this to make the people of Eldon believe Tom caused the accident I've been blamed for?"

"I have evidence—irrefutable evidence that will expose his criminal acts at work and show everyone what kind of person he really is. Once they doubt him, hopefully, it will free everyone from his hold, family or not. I think they'll believe me. I can prove what I'm saying. And if they start doubting everything about him, it might mean that they'll be more likely to listen to you. We can't let Tom's grip on them control their actions anymore."

The thought of Donna confronting Tom and unraveling the lies he had built around everyone on her own was terrifying. However, a part of Catherine recognized the necessity of the town facing the truth. Too many people had been in Tom's thrall for too long.

"Donna, what if they think you're wrong? What if they do to you what they did to me?" Catherine worried.

"As I said, I've combed through the records, cross-referencing every piece of information. The evidence is clear, and the pattern is consistent. I understand that you're worried about me, but we can't let this opportunity to show Tom's true colors go to waste."

Catherine was reluctant to endanger a friend, especially her best friend. But Donna's words resonated with Catherine—fear couldn't be an excuse for inaction any longer. The problem was Tom was involved in more than just embezzlement if what Jessica was uncovering was true. Only she couldn't share that with Donna. Doing so would reveal what Jessica had been doing.

She sighed but then asked, "Can I help in any way?" Her voice trembled slightly. "Confronting the whole town is going to be... unimaginable."

"We're in this together. And we won't be alone. If I can gather enough people that I trust to see the evidence on the sly, they'll understand the truth. We can all chip away at his power. His grip on everyone in town will wane."

A glimmer of hope mingled with Catherine's uncertainty. "You think if we bring more people into this, if they see what we've found, they'll stand with us?"

"Yes. Right now, Tom's strength comes from your isolation. He's relying on you feeling alone and powerless. But if we all unite, if we create a network of support, everyone can break free from his control."

The idea of enlisting others in their fight was both daunting and inspiring. Catherine had never imagined herself as a part of something so bold, so defiant. But the more she thought about it, the more she realized she couldn't continue to live under the shadow of Tom's lies. She had to take a stand, not just for herself but for everyone he had deceived.

"How are you going to do it? Who are you going to speak to?"

"I'll start small, with the people I trust the most. Jamie and a couple of people I know who aren't related to Tom, anyone who can vouch for my integrity and who won't dismiss me outright. I'll present the evidence, make them understand the gravity of the situation, and ask for their support."

Catherine's mind raced, imagining the conversations Donna would have to have, the vulnerability she would have to show. "What if they side with Tom?"

"All I can do is present the truth and let them make their own decisions. But I believe that when faced with undeniable evidence, most people will see through his lies."

"Okay, do it," Catherine said, feeling a spark of empowerment ignite within. "Expose Tom for who he really is."

Donna sat in the softly lit office, surrounded by stacks of documents and her laptop. The office was lifeless compared to the usual sounds of ringing phones, hushed conversations, and the clattering of keyboards. With each passing second, her resolve to help her best friend break free from the asshole she'd married deepened. Donna began capturing visual proof of the evidence on her phone so she could circulate it later.

Suddenly, Donna heard a "click," and her gaze flicked to the entrance as the glass doors swung open, and there he was— Tom, her best friend's husband. She knew he was a dangerous man to cross, but she was determined to take him down. He strode into the building with an air of confidence, his tailored suit and polished shoes commanding attention from the empty room. For a fleeting moment, Donna's mind wavered. Had he found her out? Would he make what happened to Catherine happen to her?

Donna, who had been taking pictures of a spreadsheet, took Catherine off speaker and ducked below her desk. She had to tread carefully. Her covert operation was at its most delicate stage.

As Tom's presence cast a shadow over the office, Donna tried to appear invisible. She knew that any hint of her presence could draw his attention. It was too early for her to be in the office. If he saw her, he would want to know why she was there.

The concerned sound of Catherine's voice in her ear became a distant drone as her mind raced with thoughts of strategy. Donna, ever the quick thinker, moved to the more well-hidden side of her desk.

The risk was enormous, and the stakes had never been higher. But the fire of determination burned within her—a fire fueled by the desire for justice and the need to break free from the shackles of deceit. She faced the emergency stairwell exit. However, Tom's presence in the center of the room was a stark reminder of the battle she was fighting.

As he looked around, Donna struggled to maintain her composure, her mind torn between her façade and the truth she held to her ear. Donna felt her phone vibrate. She subtly glanced at the screen to see Catherine had hung up and sent a message.

He's there, isn't he? Just play it cool and stay focused.

Donna's fingers tightened around her phone as she nodded almost imperceptibly in response. Catherine was right—she had to remain composed, even in the face of mounting tension. Tom remained in the center of the room, engaging in a conversation on his phone. Donna watched him from a distance, her heart heavy with conflicting emotions. She knew that the revelations she was on the cusp of making could shatter everyone's life as they knew it.

However, she couldn't allow the truth to remain buried any longer. As Tom's attention was momentarily diverted, Donna saw her opportunity. She made her way to the door on her knees, careful to keep her movements quiet. Her heart pounded as she navigated the maze of cubicles to the hallway. The adrenaline coursed through her veins, and with each movement, she felt the weight of the evidence on her phone, the power it held to change everyone's lives.

Just as Donna reached the stairwell, she heard footsteps in the hallway behind her. Her heart leaped, and she pushed to her feet, quickening her pace, the urgency of the situation propelling her forward. She reached the opening to the stairwell just in time, slipping down softly as the footsteps behind her grew louder. She exhaled a shaky breath, her pulse slowly beginning to steady when she heard the footsteps walk past the stairwell.

Outside, the cool breeze washed over her, and she pulled out her phone to send a message to Catherine. A sigh of relief escaped her lips as she sent a simple text.

He was there, but I made it out. I'll call you when I get home.

Donna knew that her covert operation had reached a critical juncture. The evidence on her phone was a powerful weapon, but it was also a fragile secret that needed to be protected at all costs. As she made her way home, she couldn't shake the feeling that she was on the cusp of something both monumental and perilous.

The evidence Donna had gathered was ready to be shared with the town to help bring Tom's deceit to light. Catherine knew their next steps were crucial, and the weight of the mission pressed heavily on her shoulders. As she thought, her phone buzzed softly, drawing her attention. She picked it up and saw a message from Donna.

I'm home. I'm going to transfer all this information to my old phone and lock it in the safe. I don't want to get caught with it on my main phone.

Catherine breathed a sigh of relief. She was glad Donna

was safe and had all the information they needed to take Tom down. A satisfied smile crossed her lips at the thought.

TWENTY-SIX

Two months and three days since the anniversary

A few days had passed since she'd spoken to Donna, and Catherine found herself at the small table next to the window, the soft glow of her phone screen casting a dim light in the room. Outside, the moon hung in the night sky, its pale light filtering through the curtains. She was engrossed in a game she'd downloaded out of boredom, tapping away on her screen, lost in a fantasy world of comfort. The soft chime of her phone and the switch of the display disrupted her concentration, and she glanced at the screen to see an incoming call from an unknown number. Frowning, she answered.

"Hello?" Her voice was tinged with curiosity.

"Catherine!" a voice on the other end of the line snapped.

It was a voice she recognized immediately—James, Donna's husband. But something was wrong; he sounded strained, agitated, and that instantly made her worry.

"James? How did you get my number?" Catherine's heart quickened. "Is everything alright?"

"No, everything is not alright!" James replied, his tone
sharp. "Have you done something to Donna?"

Catherine's brow furrowed in confusion over the threatening question. She hadn't spoken to Donna in a few days, but
it wasn't unusual for them to go awhile without chatting. Still,
there was an edge to James's voice that made her uneasy. "No, I
haven't heard from her," Catherine said cautiously. "Is something wrong?"

"She's gone, Catherine!" James said, his voice breaking
slightly. "She's disappeared!"

Catherine's heart skipped a beat. "What do you mean,
disappeared?"

"I mean, she's not answering her phone, and she hasn't been
home!" James spat out; his frustration clear in his tone. "I've
been trying to reach her for hours. I've been by the law office
and all over town, but there's no trace of her!"

Catherine's mind raced, her thoughts a jumble of confusion
and concern. Donna is her closest friend, and the idea of her
suddenly vanishing was unfathomable. "James, please calm
down." Her voice was as soothing as she could muster. "Maybe
she went somewhere and forgot to tell you." She knew that was
unlikely, but she was trying. "Do you know where she was last
seen?"

Catherine sat on the bed in the decrepit motel, her mind
racing as she tried to piece together the puzzle of Donna's disappearance. The room was quiet, the tension palpable, as she
waited for James to answer. The clock ticked away the minutes,
each one feeling like an eternity.

James's frustration was apparent in his voice. "She was in a
strange mood this morning and told me to call you at this
number if anything happened to her. She went to the office, and
no one has seen or heard from her since she left for the night.
You are the only lead I have."

Catherine's eyebrows raised. "The law office?" she questioned, just to be sure they were talking about the same place, even though she knew they were. What other office would Donna be going to?

James sighed, clearly annoyed by Catherine's questioning. "Yes. She's been working long hours lately, and she's been stressed about some project at work that she said she couldn't talk about but that you were aware of. When she didn't come home, I went to the office to look for her. I couldn't go into the building to check because there was a fire in the storage room, and they've closed the building for renovations."

"Wait, there was a fire at the firm?"

"Yes. I just can't believe this is happening. I'm living a nightmare!"

"I know it's overwhelming, James, and I'm sorry you have to go through this. I want to help you piece things together."

James's voice was filled with a mix of frustration and determination. "Tell me what's happening, Catherine. I need to find Donna and figure out what's going on, please. Please tell me."

Catherine took a deep breath, her mind racing as she debated how much information to share with James. She knew the photos on Donna's old phone were a significant piece of the puzzle. However, revealing their existence would likely lead to even more questions. However, she knew she had to tell him. "James," she began carefully. "Donna has been helping me gather evidence against Tom. She found some stuff at the office, and she took photos of it."

"Photos? What photos? Is this the project she said she was working on?"

Catherine took a deep breath. "Yes. She found incriminating documents that show Tom's been embezzling from the law office. They're on her old cell phone, which is locked in your safe."

James let out a heavy sigh, his emotions in turmoil. "If that's true, then... what do I do now? How do I get her back?"

Catherine's mind was already racing ahead, considering their next steps. She knew they needed to continue their investigation, but she was also aware of the dangers involved. Tom was clearly determined to keep his secrets hidden, and that made the situation even more precarious. The uncertainty of Donna's situation weighed heavily on her, but she was resolute in her determination to unveil the truth.

"James," Catherine said, her voice gentle but firm. "If something has happened to Donna, it's because of the evidence she found. We can't turn back now."

James hesitated. Catherine could hear him breathing hard over the phone, and she imagined him pacing in frustration.

"James. Are you still with me?"

James let out a sigh, his voice heavy with the weight of his worries. "Yeah, I'm okay. I just can't shake this feeling that I'm playing with fire, that whatever move I make will lead Donna deeper into danger."

"I'm right there with you, James, I promise. Find the phone. Once you have it, we can figure out our next step. I'll stay on the phone with you."

"Yeah, okay."

Though he said those words a moment ago, Catherine knew he was anything but okay. She just hoped he could hold it together long enough for them to figure out what to do next.

James felt a mix of emotions—frustration, doubt, and a deep longing to find Donna. He knew he couldn't let his fears control him, that he had to take action if he were to have any chance of finding her. With a deep breath, he decided. He got up from the couch and walked toward the bedroom door, his heart pounding with a mixture of determination and anxiety. He needed to find Donna's phone—the key to unlocking the truth behind her disappearance.

As he entered their bedroom, memories of her flooded his mind—her laughter, her presence, the way she had brightened his life. The ache of her absence was a constant reminder of the urgency of his mission. James moved to the closet where he kept the small safe full of their important documents. He pulled out the key and slid the lid open. His heart raced as he felt around inside for a familiar rectangular shape—Donna's old phone.

Relief flooded through him, and he carefully pulled the device out. The weight of the phone in his hand was both a comfort and a reminder of the gravity of Donna's situation. He knew that there might be evidence on this device that could hold the key to finding Donna and unraveling the mystery that had consumed his life. With the phone in hand, James headed back to the living room.

He sat down on the couch and stared at the device, his mind racing with the possibilities.

Catherine's voice echoed in his mind as he stared down at the small handheld device. As he contemplated the phone in his hands, he knew he needed to see the evidence for himself before he could fully believe that he was on the right path.

"James, are you there? Are you okay?"

James hesitated for a moment, then spoke slowly. "Catherine, I need to see what's on the phone before I send it. I need to know that it's worth the risk."

"From what she said, Donna got everything."

As they spoke, James powered on the phone, his heart racing with a mix of anticipation and anxiety. The device came to life, and he navigated to the gallery app, where he found a folder labelled *Funny Money*.

He clicked on the folder, and a series of photos and documents appeared on the screen. Images showed documents, notes, and photographs—all of which seemed to point to a trail of corruption and deception. The screen illuminated James's face as he scrolled through the photos of the evidence Donna had discovered. The weight of the information before him was heavy, and his mind raced as he tried to make sense of it all. He looked at the photos of documents—spreadsheets, invoices, and financial records. While he had never been adept at deciphering complex financial data, there was something about these documents that caught his attention. The numbers, names, and transactions seemed to form a pattern, a puzzle that begged to be solved.

James's fingers tapped on the screen, zooming in on one spreadsheet. The columns and rows of numbers seemed to dance before his cornflower blue eyes, but he focused on a specific section. His heart quickened as he realized the numbers showed large amounts of money. Law firm payments that were being funneled into accounts that didn't belong to the firm.

His mind raced as he connected the dots. The realization hit him like a jolt of electricity. The money was being redirected into personal accounts, and one name stood out among the recipients: Tom Morris, Donna's boss.

Without a doubt, James knew that Donna had stumbled upon something big, something that had put her in grave danger.

TWENTY-SEVEN

James had finally realized that Tom's wealth—at least not all of it—wasn't the result of hard work or through legitimate means. He'd stolen the money, embezzled funds, and maybe something far darker—Tom had to be the one who'd caused Donna's disappearance.

Donna was a beacon of warmth and kindness for him. She loved James with an open heart and open arms, and her absence was profound. When he'd called the law office and not gotten an answer, he'd then started calling the partners at the firm to look for her. Their official story was that she had worked that day and left shortly before the fire broke out. But James no longer believed that. Tom's odd behavior, the secrecy that shrouded the investigation, and the sudden windfalls of money he'd flashed around town played through his mind.

James couldn't shake the feeling that the path he was about to tread would have far-reaching consequences. He realized Catherine had been a fountain of truth throughout this ordeal. Her unwavering determination was a lifeline amid uncertainty. What had they all done to her?

"James? Have you found it?"

"Catherine, I've decided," James began, his voice resolute. "I can't let this darkness fester any longer. It's time to bring everything to light."

Catherine gasped. "What are you saying, James?"

Taking a deep breath, James sent all the photos from Donna's phone to Catherine. "You were right. Donna gathered evidence—documents, financial records, emails—that shed light on Tom's criminal activities. I believe you. About everything."

"James, this is... thank you."

"No, thank you," James replied, his voice unwavering. "Send all this stuff to that detective, okay?"

"I will," she assured him.

"You've shown me the truth, Catherine. And I've decided that the best way to reveal the truth and maybe bring Donna out of hiding is to distribute the information on the town's website. I want everyone to see what's been happening behind closed doors." He sighed. "Maybe then I'll find out what's happened to Donna."

Catherine leaned back in her chair, her fingers tapping nervously on her knee. "James, this is a big step. Once you put this information out there, there's no turning back. Are you sure you're ready for the consequences?"

"I've thought about this, Catherine. I can't stand by and watch injustice continue. Tom can't get away with what he's done, and I need to do this to find Donna."

Catherine let out a sigh, her gaze fixed on the documents. "Okay, James. I trust your judgment. If you believe this is the right course of action, then I'll stand by you. Just please be careful. It's what Donna would want."

"Thanks, I know she would. You be careful too." He sounded relieved.

"I will."

"Catherine, do you think Tom..." He stopped and then began again. "You don't think he's killed Donna, do you? It's just... the more I think about it, the more something feels off with the story the partners at the firm have been telling me."

Catherine's brows furrowed, her concern deepening. "What do you mean?"

"Maybe the fire... maybe he killed her or got rid of her body in the fire. I hate to say it, but Donna's disappearance is just too convenient."

Catherine considered his words, before saying softly, "You think there's a possibility she might be dead?"

"I don't know," James replied, his frustration clear. "But the idea keeps gnawing at me. If he has... so help me God, he will pay for it."

Catherine let out a slow breath. "James, I understand your concerns, but it's just a theory. I know as well as the next person what Tom's capable of, he's tried to kill me a couple of times, but maybe Donna agreed to disappear because he threatened her. Or maybe she disappeared on her own to keep you safe. We don't know what's happened yet."

"You're right. I'll stick to my plan and get it out on the town website. I'll call you if I hear anything. You'll do the same, right?"

"Of course. You'll be the first one I call."

Catherine sat at the motel table, her fingers dancing over her phone screen. The events of the past few weeks were taking their toll on her. The evidence that Donna had compiled, the documents that laid bare Tom's illicit activities, were ready to be sent to Detective Sheldon, but she also wanted to let him know Donna was missing, so she prepared a text letting him know what was going on and that she was going to be sending everything.

Catherine hesitated for a moment, her hand hovering over

the *send* button. A sense of both responsibility and anticipation welled up within her. Taking a deep breath, Catherine pressed the button, watching as the text message disappeared into the digital abyss. Once it was sent, she started sending all the documents, one after another. It wasn't long before a response came through, Detective Sheldon's familiar name lighting up across her screen.

> *Thank you for sending this, Catherine. I'll review the documents immediately, and I'll keep an eye out for your friend.*

Catherine leaned back in her chair, relief washing over her. She knew this was the right thing to do, that the evidence Donna had gathered needed to be in the hands of the authorities. But the implications of what this could mean for Tom and for the town were profound, considering so many of the townspeople were related to him and possibly just as corrupt.

As the afternoon sun cast long shadows through the window, Catherine's phone buzzed with an incoming call. It was Detective Sheldon. She answered, her voice steady despite the anxiety she felt.

"Catherine, I've gone through the documents you sent," Detective Sheldon began, his tone serious. "The evidence is substantial, and it confirms our suspicions about Tom's activities."

Catherine's heart raced as she listened, her hope mingling with a sense of trepidation. "What about Donna?"

"We've got a missing person alert out for her, and the state police have her image and details. We'll do our best to find her."

"Thank you. What happens now?"

"We're preparing to move forward with the state police," Detective Sheldon replied. "We'll need to interview Tom."

Catherine nodded. "And what about my suspicions that

Tom is involved in Donna's disappearance?" She knew he'd already said they would look for her, but she was very worried that Tom had done something to her.

"We'll be revisiting the circumstances of the office fire and ensure there were no victims. Don't worry, if Tom is holding her somewhere, we'll find her," Detective Sheldon assured her. "The additional evidence you've provided will be crucial in our efforts to uncover the truth."

After ending the call, Catherine sat back in her chair, her mind worried. She had set in motion a series of events that would inevitably change the course of many lives—Tom's, James's, Detective Sheldon's, the townspeople's, and hers.

Hours had passed since the call with Detective Sheldon. Catherine stared out the window. The fog shrouded the streets, and a mix of tension and uncertainty charged the atmosphere. Catherine's role in the events had left her with a growing anxiety that gnawed at the edges of her consciousness. Her fingers tapped restlessly against her phone screen. The silence from James and Detective Sheldon had become deafening. She had sent a text message to both, but they hadn't replied, which left her feeling even more anxious.

The frustration of not knowing what was happening, of being left in the dark, weighed heavily on Catherine's shoulders. She glanced at her phone, the urge to call the detective once again almost overwhelming. But something held her back —the fear of bad news, of more questions than answers, of facing a reality she might not be ready for. With a sigh, she picked up her phone again and hit the button labeled "medic."

"Hey, Catherine, is everything okay?" Jessica's voice came through warm and familiar.

"Hey, Jessica. I... I need to talk," Catherine replied.

There was a pause on the other end of the line before Jessica's tone turned serious. "What's wrong? Has something happened? Has he found you?"

Catherine hesitated for a moment; her words caught in her throat. "No, he hasn't found me, but yes, something's happened. My friend Donna is missing. Remember I told you she was looking into Tom's embezzling? Well, she found stuff, but now she's missing. And Detective Sheldon said that he and the state police were going into Eldon, and I just don't know what's going on. I'm worried."

"That's a lot to unpack. Yes, I recall you telling me about Donna looking into Tom's embezzling. I had a look at her social media and looked into her."

"What? Why?"

"Because I'm trying to keep you safe, and I wanted to make sure she was actually an ally."

"Oh, and what did you find?"

"Nothing to say she wasn't being a real friend. I couldn't find any ties to Tom other than the fact she worked at the law firm. Either way, I haven't seen your friend since before I brought you to Cincinnati."

"Oh."

"What did the detective say?" Jessica asked.

"He said he'd keep an eye out for her."

"Well, that's good. I'll keep a look out for her too. I did see that the detective and state police have entered the edge of town, but it's not looking pretty. Tensions are rising between the townspeople and the state troopers."

"That doesn't sound good. What are they doing? What's going on?"

"So, the ones on Tom's side have put up barricades and are blocking main roads in and out of town and are in a standoff with them," Jessica explained. "From what I gather, they feel that outsiders are meddling in their affairs, that their town and its people are under threat. That's coming from the local social media page where they've called for more people in town to stand up against this tyranny."

Catherine's mind raced as she processed Jessica's words. She knew that Eldon had always been very close-knit, but she hadn't realized how much of the town was related to one another until recently. She'd never been on the town's social media page, mostly because she hadn't been very active within the town. Looking back now, Tom had kept her pretty sheltered and isolated from everything and everyone, it seemed.

"What are the police and Detective Sheldon doing?"

Jessica answered, "They've called in some more state troopers. No shots have been fired, and they're trying to get a negotiator in to help. I'm on the ground, trying to keep out of sight of both groups, keeping an eye on the situation. Detective Sheldon has told them they have an arrest warrant for Tom Morris, but that seems to have the townspeople angry. Sheriff Mason and his deputies are backing them, saying the state is overstepping their jurisdiction."

Catherine's anxiety deepened. This was turning into some sort of crazy event like the ones she'd read about in school. Waco, Texas, came to mind, and she suddenly feared that this would turn into the same kind of event all because they wouldn't give up Tom. It was wild and nerve-wracking. "Do you think it's going to turn out like that?" she asked after voicing her fear to Jessica.

Jessica's reply was measured. "It's hard to say. Emotions are running high, and there's a sense of unease in the air. The last thing anyone wants is for this to escalate into something uncontrollable. However, it does look like both sides are ready to go to war..."

The sound of shots rang out over Jessica's end of the line.

"What was that? What's going on?" Catherine exclaimed, as more blasts sounded across the line.

"Crap. I need to hang up and find a safer place to keep an eye on this and not get shot. I'll call you back as soon as I can, but please, Catherine, be careful."

Catherine's mind raced. "Jessica, wait! Are you okay?"

But the line had already gone dead.

TWENTY-EIGHT

Catherine paced, clutching her phone tightly, glancing at it every few minutes as if the act itself could make it ring. But hours had passed since she'd last heard from any of them—Jessica, James, or Detective Sheldon.

The shooting she'd heard going on in Eldon had her terrified that one of them was injured or killed. She knew that the detective and the state troopers wanted to bring Tom to justice, and from what Jessica had said, the town had planned to fight against giving him up. Catherine had hoped that one of them would call to shed some light on the situation and calm her nerves. But as the hours wore on and the sun went down, her optimism waned.

She paced back and forth on the carpet, her footsteps echoing in the silence. The motel room was eerily quiet. It was as if the world had paused, leaving Catherine alone with her thoughts. She couldn't shake the feeling that something was wrong. Catherine had tried calling Jessica, James and Detective Sheldon, however all her calls went unanswered or straight to voicemail.

As the minutes stretched into hours, Catherine's worry grew into full-blown anxiety, though she had thus far avoided having any kind of panic attack, for which she was grateful. Maybe with everything that had happened to her, she'd finally grown out of them? *Or had them beaten out of me,* she thought darkly.

She sat down on the bed, her fingers tapping anxiously on her knee. The room was now bathed in the soft glow of lamplight, casting long shadows that seemed to dance around her. Her mind raced through various scenarios that could be playing out in Eldon. She knew Jessica had been an army medic, so she had to be used to this kind of thing, right? Maybe she was helping anyone who had been injured by those gunshots she had heard over the phone. Had anyone been injured? Had the shots come from the cops or from the townspeople?

Catherine shook her head. There was no way to know for sure, sitting in this motel room almost two hours away. Maybe she was overthinking things, and there was a logical explanation for their unresponsiveness—a dead battery, a faulty cell tower, anything other than being injured or worse. But her intuition nagged at her, telling her that something was amiss. She gazed up at the moon, its pale light washing over her. It felt like a lonely sentinel, watching over the uncertainty that had settled in her heart.

As the night deepened, Catherine felt powerless, sitting on that bed with no answers and no one to turn to. She dialed Detective Sheldon's number once more, her fingers trembling slightly. The call went unanswered again, and Catherine felt a surge of frustration. She left a worried message, urging him to call her back as soon as he received it. The thought of something happening to him or one of her friends sent a shiver down her spine.

She glanced at her phone, willing it to ring, hoping for some sign of life from her friends. But the screen remained stubbornly blank, devoid of any new messages or missed calls. The silence was deafening, and Catherine's struggle to keep her composure was becoming increasingly difficult. She took a deep breath; she knew she needed to stay calm, to think rationally, but the knot of anxiety in her chest was tightening with every passing minute.

To distract herself, Catherine stood up and paced the room again. The worn carpet underfoot muffled her footsteps, but it did little to ease her restlessness. She looked around the dingy space, taking in the faded curtains and peeling paint. This place felt like a world apart from the chaos that was unfolding in her hometown, a temporary refuge from the storm that raged within her.

Sitting back down, Catherine pulled up the state and local news, scanning for any updates on the ongoing situation in Eldon. Her heart pounded in her chest as she caught snippets of information—gunshots fired and officers down. She wished she were there with her friends, offering her support, anything to help them navigate this dangerous terrain.

She shifted on the edge of the bed, her fingers gripping the edge of the mattress to ground herself. She closed her eyes, took slow, deep breaths, letting the rhythm of her breathing anchor her in the present moment. Calmer, she went back to the news on her phone. As she sifted through articles, the sound of her phone ringing cut through the room's silence. Catherine's heart leaped with a mix of hope and apprehension.

The caller ID displayed an unknown number, and for a moment, she hesitated. But then, with a determined breath, she swiped to answer the call.

"Hello?" Her voice was steady, masking the anticipation that churned within her.

"Catherine Morris?" The voice on the other end was deep, authoritative.

"Yes, speaking."

"This is Detective Mitchell Adams."

She had never heard of Detective Mitchell Adams, nor had anyone mentioned him in any discussion.

"I apologize if I've startled you," Detective Adams continued, his voice tinged with concern.

"It's okay, I just wasn't expecting anyone except Detective Sheldon to call me. Is he alright?"

"That is why I am calling. Detective Sheldon was injured earlier this evening, and your name and number have been continuously popping up on his phone. I understand you are related to the case he was working on in Eldon?"

"Yes, yes, I am, but is he okay? You said he was injured. What happened?"

"All I can say is he is receiving medical attention, and the situation is still volatile in Eldon."

"Does that mean that they didn't arrest Tom?"

There was a pause on the other side of the phone, then he said, "No, ma'am. No arrest has been made at this time." Detective Adams took a deep breath before adding, "I wanted to let you know that Detective Sheldon's cases have been temporarily transferred to me. With his injuries and the ongoing investigation, he's been placed on medical leave. So, I will be your point of contact."

Catherine fell silent, the weight of Detective Adams's words sinking in. "Why you?"

"Are you asking why your case has been transferred specifically to me?"

"Yes."

"I see. Well, I am a seasoned detective, and the captain felt this case could use fresh eyes given the... tension that is taking place between our department and that of the sheriff's department in Eldon."

"But—"

"Catherine," Detective Adams cut her off, his voice measured, "I've been reviewing the evidence, the leads, and the connections Detective Sheldon has uncovered."

Catherine had a sinking feeling in her gut. Something wasn't right. Still, she whispered, "And?"

Detective Adams's voice was unwavering. "And I've come to the conclusion that there is not a case against Tom Morris for any of your allegations."

Catherine's heart plummeted to her feet. Tom had been the mastermind behind everything, a person of interest whose actions had raised suspicions. He'd gotten nearly the entire town to fight against the state police just to keep him from being arrested. To hear this man say there was no case left her in disbelief. "What do you mean there's no case?" she said.

Detective Adams spoke firmly, his voice harsh. "The entire case is built on toothpicks. The accident was nothing but that. An accident. There is nothing to say he was drinking and driving, no blood test or breathalyzer was given at the time of the accident, the other driver has disappeared and hasn't given any evidence. As to your allegations of assault, it's your word against his. And the second car accident isn't even in our jurisdiction. It's in Sheriff Mason's, and my understanding is that it was ruled an accident due to wet road conditions. As for your murder allegations in the missing person case, there is nothing substantial to link Tom Morris to that."

Catherine's mind raced as she processed Detective Adams's words. "How can you say that? There are pictures and video evidence. Tom is involved," Catherine said, her voice cautious. "He was driving the car when that woman was killed, he has been threatening me, he had me beaten, and he has been committing financial fraud—"

"I have looked at everything, and I don't believe any of that to be the case. Detective Sheldon's pursuit of the truth has led him down a biased path, and the evidence doesn't support the conclusions he's drawn."

Catherine considered the implications of Detective Adams's assessment. Detective Sheldon's investigation had been driven by his commitment to uncovering the truth. It was clear Detective Adams's commitment to doing so was questionable.

"What are you going to do now?" Catherine asked, her voice tinged with disappointment.

Detective Adams's voice was grave. "I need to re-evaluate his approach. My priority is finding the real culprit, the one responsible for the events Detective Sheldon has been investigating."

Catherine's mind raced as she considered what the detective was suggesting. It led to raised questions about the detective's validity. "Where are you going from there?" Catherine's voice held a note of frustration.

"Simple. I don't need to gather any more evidence, but shift the focus of the investigation," Detective Adams replied. "I have re-examined the leads and reassessed the information Detective Sheldon has collected. I've even called Sheriff Mason."

Catherine's heart skipped a beat at the mention of Sheriff Mason. "What did he say?" she asked cautiously.

"He's willing to forgive the state police's misinformed actions."

Catherine's brows furrowed. Forgive? The idea Sheriff Mason would be open to forgiving the state police was unexpected. "How did you manage that?" she asked skeptically.

"He agreed to do so if you return to Eldon and surrender to him—"

Catherine quickly ended the call. The threat before her was frightening; she was at a crossroads that could alter the course of her life. Her throat felt dry, and her palms were clammy as she struggled to find a way out. The idea of returning to Eldon and surrendering to Sheriff Mason was a daunting prospect, one that stirred up a tangle of fears and uncertainties. The thought of potentially being sent to jail terrified her. Catherine's eyes welled with tears. She didn't know how she could get out of this mess without Detective Sheldon's help.

TWENTY-NINE

Catherine paced back and forth across the motel room, her heart pounding like a drum in her chest. The clock on the wall ticked away each second, mocking her growing anxiety. She clutched her phone tightly in her trembling hands, her fingers hovering over the screen. It was late, the parking lot and city streets beyond were cloaked in darkness, and the silence in her room was deafening. She glanced at the phone's screen once again, her eyes pleading with the universe for a miracle.

"Come on, Jessica," Catherine whispered under her breath, her voice a mix of desperation and longing.

She had nobody else to turn to, nobody who could understand the tangled mess her life had become. Jessica was her last hope, her lifeline in a sea of uncertainty. Catherine's mind raced back to the last time they had spoken, the gunshots filling the air as she hung up. However, she knew if anyone could make it out of that situation unscathed, it would be Jessica. She had training in the military, it had to benefit her in that situation, right?

With a deep breath, Catherine pressed her trembling finger against the screen, starting the call. The phone rang, each chime echoing like a gunshot in the room's stillness. Her heart raced faster with every passing ring, her hopes riding on each fleeting sound. And then, just as Catherine felt her spirit beginning to sink, a voice broke through the tension like a beam of light.

"Hello?"

Jessica's voice, warm and familiar, flowed into Catherine's ears like a balm for her wounded soul. Tears welled up in her wide eyes as relief washed over her.

"Jessica." Catherine's voice wavered, the weight of her emotions threatening to spill over. "Oh, Jessica, you're alright."

There was a pause on the other end, a pregnant silence that seemed to stretch for an eternity. Catherine held her breath, waiting for Jessica's response, praying that she wouldn't hang up.

"I'm fine. I managed to get back to my van and get out of town via a back road and, well, going slowly through a field to get to the main road." Jessica's voice held a mixture of determination and concern. "I'm sorry I worried you. That wasn't my intention."

Catherine let out a shaky breath, her voice quivering as she spoke. "I'm so glad you're okay... I didn't know who else to call."

"What's wrong?" Jessica's tone shifted, infused with a deep empathy that only genuine friends possessed. "You sound really upset, and not just because I was MIA for a few hours."

The words came tumbling out in a rush, Catherine's voice cracking with raw emotion. "Jessica, I'm in trouble. I'm in so much trouble, and I don't know what to do. I thought... I thought maybe you could help me, or at least listen."

"Of course. I told you I would always help you. Take a deep breath and tell me what's going on."

Catherine closed her eyes, willing herself to find the strength to articulate the mess that had become her life. A moment later, she launched into her tale, recounting the conversation she had had with Detective Adams. Jessica listened in silence, her quiet attention a lifeline as Catherine bared her soul. When the tale was finally told, there was a pause on the other end, an extensive silence that stretched between them like an invisible thread.

"Jessica, I don't know what to do." Catherine heard the desperation in her own voice. "Part of me thinks that maybe I should just do what he said and hand myself in, even though I didn't do anything wrong. But another part of me is terrified that Sheriff Mason will use it as an excuse to fabricate evidence against me and lock me up forever."

Jessica's voice was gentle but firm. "I can't make this decision for you, but I can offer you my perspective. Turning yourself in might put an end to the standoff in Eldon, but you have to consider the other consequences of doing such a thing. Those people believe you are guilty of driving drunk and killing Melissa, of trying to kill yourself and Tom in that second accident. You won't get a fair trial, and—you're right—Sheriff Mason will make sure you are locked up for the rest of your life. Are you really prepared to go through that? To allow Tom to get away with everything?"

Catherine's heart ached with the truth in Jessica's words. "But what's the alternative?" She was filled with frustration. "If I don't turn myself in, I might have to run from Tom forever. I'll always be looking over my shoulder, wondering when he'll catch up to me."

"Running isn't the only option," Jessica replied, her tone measured. "There's another aspect you need to consider— Eldon. The attack on the state police has put the entire town on edge. If you turn yourself in, they'll come down on you with everything they've got. But if you let things play out... well, that detective isn't going to get away with just brushing the case under the rug. The state police are a separate entity, they aren't going to just drop this."

Catherine's mind whirled as she absorbed Jessica's words. The attack on the state police had shattered the façade of tranquility in Eldon, revealing the underbelly of anger and resentment toward the state's tyranny that simmered beneath the surface.

"But what do I do, then?" Catherine's voice was a whisper, as if speaking too loudly might shatter the fragile threads of her understanding. "If I don't turn myself in, if I don't run, what's left?"

Jessica's voice held a steely resolve as she answered, "You need to distance yourself from Eldon, Catherine. Stay away from there until this all blows over. Lie low, keep a low profile, and focus on something else for a while. If you go to Eldon, you'll be putting yourself in the crosshairs of their anger."

Tears welled in Catherine's wide eyes as she contemplated the gravity of the choice before her. She knew Jessica was right, that going to Eldon would be a dangerous gamble. Her voice trembled as she said, "I don't know if I can do this anymore. It's not just about me—it's about my town, my friends, my neighbors, people I've known my whole life. They aren't all corrupt, but they are all paying the price for this."

"I understand, Catherine," Jessica said softly. "But you have to weigh the risks. If you go, you're choosing to face the wrath of an angry town full of Tom's relatives and supporters. If you run, you're choosing to protect yourself and the people you care about."

As the conversation continued, Catherine's mind swirled with conflicting emotions. The choices before her felt like a tangle of threads, each one leading down a different path, each path uncertain and fraught with challenges. In the end, Jessica's words provided a glimmer of clarity amidst the confusion. As the call drew to a close, Catherine knew she had a tough decision to make—one that would shape the course of her future in ways she couldn't yet comprehend.

"Thank you, Jessica. I needed someone to tell me that what I was doing was right, to help me see things from a different perspective."

"Anytime, Catherine." Jessica's voice was unwavering. "Remember, I'm here for you no matter what. I want the truth about Melissa's death to come out, just like you do. All you have to do is hang tight. I'll be at the motel soon. I want to take you somewhere else so that detective can't find you."

"You think he'll come here and try to force me to go back to Eldon?" Catherine fretted.

"It's a possibility. If he doesn't know where you're at, he will find you from that call. He can look at what cell tower it pinged from. In fact, as soon as we hang up, I want you to turn your phone off and take the battery out. Okay?"

"Okay," Catherine replied.

"I'll see you soon."

With those words echoing in Catherine's mind, Jessica hung up. The moon had risen higher in the sky, casting a cool light across the room as she did what Jessica had told her. And as she stared out the window through the small slit between the curtains, she knew that the choices before her were like the dawn—uncertain, but full of possibility. She was standing at a crossroads, her next steps undefined, but she had the strength of Jessica's advice to guide her. And in that moment, Catherine knew that whatever she chose, she wouldn't be facing it alone.

The neon lights of the motel sign flickered erratically, casting an eerie glow across the cracked pavement. It was early in the morning; the sky was still dark as the sun had barely crossed the horizon, and the world seemed to hold its breath as Jessica parked her van outside Catherine's seedy motel room. The decision to take action had been swift, driven by the urgency of the situation. With a determined exhale, Jessica stepped out of her van and headed for the room.

As she reached the door, her heart hammered in her chest, a mix of worry and determination coursing through her veins. She raised her hand and knocked gently, the sound echoing across the parking lot. After a moment, the door creaked open, revealing Catherine's tired and anxious face.

"Catherine," Jessica greeted her softly, a reassuring smile tugging at her lips. "Do you have everything packed up?"

Catherine stepped aside to let Jessica in. The room was poorly lit, the faded wallpaper peeling at the edges, and the air carried a faint odor of mildew. It was a far cry from the comfort of Catherine's home, a stark reminder of the choices she had been forced to make.

"Thank you for thinking of all this. Yes, I've got everything." Catherine's voice was thick with gratitude as she closed the door behind Jessica.

"No need to thank me," Jessica replied gently. "I want to make sure you're safe and taken care of. I've arranged another hotel room for you. It's safer, and it should be a more comfortable place to stay."

Catherine's eyes widened with surprise, gratitude shining in her gaze. "You didn't have to do that. I can't ask you to—"

"You're not asking, Catherine," Jessica interrupted kindly. "I'm offering because I care about you, and I want to make sure you're in a better environment. Plus, I've brought some food and essentials. You shouldn't have to worry about anything right now."

Tears welled in Catherine's wide eyes as she took the bag Jessica offered her. "Thank you," she murmured and then let out a small laugh as her watery gaze met Jessica's.

Jessica smiled and laughed a little too. "I know it's not much, just another new phone with the same numbers in it, some toiletries, snacks, and another change of clothes. It should help you get by for a while. The new hotel is just a few blocks away. You can leave that other phone here."

"Okay." Catherine pulled the first phone Jessica had bought her out of the bag sitting on the bed, pulled up James's number, added it to the new phone, and then put the old one on the table. "I'm glad we don't have to go far, but I can tell you I am so happy to get out of this place. It's kind of depressing."

"It really is. Come on, let's go." Jessica picked up the other bags and opened the door.

As they left the motel room behind, stepping out into the cool night air, Catherine took a deep breath. They climbed into the van, and Jessica made sure Catherine was buckled before starting the van and pulling out from the parking lot. She looked over at Jessica. It was obvious Catherine wanted to ask her something, but was hesitant.

"What is it?"

"Can I ask you something about what that detective said when he called?"

Jessica's gaze flicked to her and back to the road. "Sure. I don't know if I will answer or not, but you can ask."

"He said you'd disappeared and hadn't given any evidence of the crash. Why?"

Jessica sighed. She'd wondered when Catherine might start questioning her about herself. "Because, technically, I'm not alive."

Catherine seemed taken aback. "What do you mean?"

Jessica pulled over on the shoulder of the road and put the van in park with the hazards on so she could turn to speak to her. She needed to make Catherine understand that there were reasons she couldn't mention to the cops or anyone, without going into too much detail. "You know I'm ex-military. What you don't know is that I'm currently listed as MIA, and I prefer it that way."

"MIA? You mentioned it before, but I don't know what that means."

"Missing in Action. My unit was hit in Iraq by an RPG. I was blown clear, but all of my unit was killed. I was found unconscious by a... we'll call her an innocent bystander. She brought me home and ended up smuggling me out of the country. My sister hadn't even known I was alive until I showed up at her place about two months before the... before she died."

"Is your name even Jessica?"

Jessica smiled. "Yes. My ID is fake, but I kept my first name. So, you can see why I don't want to be mixed up in legal things, right? And that... if I were to be, I'd have to come clean about who I am and how I'm alive. Do you understand? I would be in a lot of trouble because the military doesn't look kindly on those who desert. Trust me, I would be in more trouble than you can imagine."

Catherine nodded. "I understand. I wouldn't want to see you get into trouble just for helping me."

Jessica put the van in drive and pulled back onto the street. As they arrived at the new hotel, the difference was stark. The lobby was well-lit and clean; the receptionist welcoming and professional. Jessica helped Catherine with her belongings, making sure she had everything she'd need.

"Hey," Jessica began. She was still really concerned about Catherine's well-being, especially knowing she struggled with her mental health. The funny thing was, though, that she seemed much stronger now mentally than she had been back when their paths first crossed. "You need to continue lying low for a while. I know it's difficult, but it's the safest option right now. Don't go anywhere that Tom and his friends might think to look for you. Stay off the radar."

Catherine nodded, and Jessica could see that she understood the gravity of the situation she was in.

"It's not just about avoiding the authorities; it's about

steering clear of the danger that lurks within Eldon's shadows. There is so much going on in that town, and if you get caught, you're going to end up in the middle of it, and I'm afraid of what that might mean for you."

"I'm scared," Catherine admitted, her voice barely above a whisper. "I don't know how long I can keep this up, how long I can hide."

Jessica placed a comforting hand on Catherine's shoulder, her gaze steady. "You're stronger than you think, Catherine. I've watched you grow so much over these last couple of months. You've been through a lot. And besides, you're not alone in this." Jessica smiled at her. "I'll be here to support you every step of the way. Just take things one day at a time and don't lose hope."

Catherine nodded, her wide eyes filling with tears. "What should I do if I feel I'm in trouble, or if I think I'm being followed?"

Jessica thought about this for a moment. When she spoke, her words were measured and reassuring. "If you ever find yourself in a situation where you feel unsafe or think you're being followed, I want you to turn on the location service on the phone. That will ping me immediately. Don't hesitate—your safety is the priority."

Catherine's eyes widened. "You mean just make the location available on the phone?"

"No, I installed a family location app on your phone. I can show you, here, hand it to me." Jessica went into the apps and tapped on it. "Okay, see this? Just turn it on. It will ping my phone with your location and show me your movements. I'll be able to track you wherever you are."

Catherine took back the phone. "I hope it never comes to that, but I appreciate you setting this up. I'll use it if I have to."

"I don't want you to feel like I'm going to track you all the time. I just wanted a way to be able to if you got into trouble."

She nodded. "It's a good idea. I'm just worried."

"You're strong, Catherine," Jessica said, wanting to encourage her. "But it's okay to ask for help when you need it. I'm here to support you, and I'll do whatever it takes to keep you safe."

"Thank you. I feel like I'm armed with a plan now," Catherine said, her eyes bright and alive now that the bruising was fading away. "I don't know what I would have done without you. You've been my rock through all of this, and I can't believe how generous you've been considering how we met. You could have easily hated me because of what happened."

"What happened linked us in a way, and you're right, I could have hated you; in fact, I did for a bit when I thought you were driving the car. That night I came to your room... I was mad with grief over what happened. You were strong even then, but you didn't see it though. The way you fought me off... it was impressive," Jessica replied.

Catherine's brow furrowed. "Why didn't you go after Tom like you did me?" she whispered.

Sighing, Jessica took a moment to think about that before answering, "I wanted to. I really wanted to, but you changed my mind. I didn't want to become something I hated, and I would have if I'd killed someone in cold blood like that, so I decided I would get my revenge another way. I told myself I would find a way to make sure he faced justice, not just for what he'd done to Melissa, but for what he was and still is doing to you."

A beautiful smile crossed Catherine's lips, which lit up her whole face. "You have no idea how much I appreciate you."

Jessica returned her smile with warmth as she replied, "We're in this together, Catherine. We look out for each other. Just promise me you'll stay cautious and take care of yourself."

"I promise," Catherine whispered, still smiling. "I'll do whatever it takes to stay safe."

. . .

As the morning arrived, Catherine felt a sense of purpose descend over her as Jessica helped her settle into her new surroundings. The world beyond her hotel room might be filled with uncertainty, but Catherine knew she wasn't facing it alone. She had Jessica as a guiding light—a thread of trust connecting her to a person who would go to great lengths to ensure her safety. For now, they sat by the window talking and laughing about the things they had in common, which was quite a bit considering how different their lives had been prior to meeting.

Catherine took a deep breath, drawing strength from the knowledge that she had allies in her corner. She had people who believed in her and would stand by her side, no matter what the challenges that lay ahead were. With Jessica's advice echoing in her mind, Catherine allowed herself to hope—hope for a future where the shadows of fear would be replaced by the steady light of resilience and the unwavering bonds of friendship.

Eventually, as the morning grew brighter, Jessica rose from her seat. "I need to get going, I've got some things to take care of," she said, her voice tinged with reluctance. "But remember, if you need anything—anything at all—call me." She paused and then pulled something from her pocket. "Also, take this. Just in case you need to get some food or any essentials."

Catherine nodded and took the cash Jessica offered, the gratitude in her eyes saying more than words ever could. "Thank you. I don't know what I would do without you."

Jessica's smile was warm and reassuring. "You're not alone in this. Lean on me when you need to. We'll get through this together."

As Jessica left the hotel room, Catherine felt a renewed sense of determination. She knew the days ahead would be a test of her resilience, her strength, and the bonds that held her life together. But with Jessica's words echoing in her heart, she took a deep breath and embraced the shadows of solace that enveloped her. She was ready to face whatever challenges lay ahead.

THIRTY

Two months and one week since the anniversary

The afternoon sun filtered through the sheer curtains, casting a warm and gentle glow across the beautiful hotel room. Catherine stirred in her sleep, slowly rousing from the depths of slumber. The room exuded an air of calm, with its tastefully decorated interiors and a soothing color palette that invited relaxation. A faint scent of freshly bloomed flowers lingered in the air, further enhancing the tranquil ambiance. With a yawn that betrayed the depth of her sleep, Catherine moved to the side of the comfortable queen-sized bed and sat up. She glanced around the room, taking in the fine details that adorned every corner. The plush armchair by the window seemed to beckon her for a leisurely afternoon read. As her eyes adjusted, she realized there was a neatly folded note between the door and doorframe. Curiosity piqued, she stood up and walked over to the door. She reached out and pulled it free. The paper was of a high quality, the words elegantly scripted in ink. The note read:

Good afternoon, Jodi. We hope you had a restful sleep. Break-fast will be sent up for you whenever you're ready. Take your time and enjoy the amenities the hotel offers. Should you need anything, our staff is available 24/7. We wish you a delightful stay.

A small smile tugged at the corners of Catherine's lips. The personal touch of the note made her feel welcome and valued despite them being unable to know her real name. She folded the note and placed it on the table before standing up once again. With a languid stretch, she padded over to the window, drawn by the inviting view that awaited her.

The sight that greeted her was nothing short of breathtaking. The hotel was nestled amidst a picturesque landscape—lush gardens, gently swaying trees, and a pristine pool that shimmered under the sun's caress. It was a view that seemed to transport her to a tranquil paradise. Lost in the moment, Catherine found herself drawn toward the balcony. She slid open the glass door, stepping out into the warm embrace of the sun. The gentle breeze played with her hair as she leaned against the railing, letting her gaze wander across the horizon.

She was extremely grateful to Jessica, not only for keeping her safe but also for paying for this wonderful hotel room. She'd been paying for the motel as well, which hadn't been as pricy as this place had to be, and Catherine knew it all had to be eating into her savings. She'd have to find a way to pay her back somehow.

Time seemed to stand still as Catherine immersed herself in the moment's serenity. With a contented sigh, she turned and strode over to the edge of the bed. She glanced at the clock on the bedside table, noting that it was well into the afternoon. She'd missed the offered breakfast, but maybe they could send up lunch. Once dressed, Catherine called room service and was happy to find she could order food. While she waited, she caught up on the latest news before she embarked on her day's activities, not that they consisted of much more than hanging out in her hotel room. She picked up the remote control from the nightstand and turned on the sleek flat-screen television that adorned the wall.

The screen blinked to life, and the hotel logo dissolved into the familiar sight of a news anchor seated at a desk. However, today was not like any other day. The screen transitioned to a live feed from a scene that sent a jolt of surprise through Catherine's veins. The caption at the bottom of the screen read: *Eldon Standoff: Tensions Escalate Between Towns-people and State Police.*

The camera panned over a chaotic scene in the small town of Eldon. Crowds of people, their faces etched with anger and anxiety, stood clustered together along the main street. Many held signs with warnings, advocating for their rights and decrying what they saw as government overreach. In contrast, a line of stern-faced state police officers clad in riot gear formed a barrier, attempting to maintain order in the face of mounting tension.

The news anchor's voice narrated the unfolding events, explaining that the standoff had been sparked by an attempted arrest of one of the town's community members. The towns-people were protesting against the recent attempt to arrest the criminal within the town limits. Eldon, once known for its idyllic atmosphere, had now become the stage for a fierce clash of ideologies.

The camera shifted to a familiar face. Christina Bitterman, a seasoned reporter known for her incisive coverage, appeared on screen. Dressed in a field reporter's outfit and a protective vest, Christina stood at the forefront of the scene, her micro-phone in hand.

"Good morning." Christina's voice rang out from the televi-sion. "We are here in Eldon, where tensions have reached a boiling point between the townspeople and state authorities. The residents are demanding answers from the state about why they have come in to harass one of their town leaders, and they are expressing their deep-seated concerns over what they see as an erosion of their rights to govern themselves."

Catherine's brow furrowed as she watched the scenes of turmoil unfold before her. She knew about the brewing conflict, but seeing it unfold on the screen gave it an entirely different weight.

Christina's voice continued, carrying with it a sense of urgency. "The situation remains tense as both sides stand their ground. The state police have issued a statement urging calm and cooperation, but the townspeople remain resolute in their demand for a repeal of the curfew ordinance and for the removal of the state troopers from the town. It's a volatile situation, and the outcome remains uncertain."

Catherine's fingers tightened around the remote control, a mixture of emotions swirling within her. The stark contrast between the tranquility of her hotel room and the chaos on the screen was jarring. She felt a deep sense of concern for the people caught amid this conflict, their lives and livelihoods disrupted by a clash of beliefs.

As the news segment continued, Christina interviewed several townspeople and state officials, attempting to capture the complexity of the situation. Voices of frustration, fear, and determination penetrated through the television speakers. The emotions were palpable, the divide between the two sides seemingly insurmountable.

Catherine's thoughts raced, grappling with the implications of what she was witnessing. She wondered if the townspeople knew about the underlying factors yet. To everyone else, it was just a stark reminder of the simmering tensions that could boil over in any community, given the right circumstances. But of course, Catherine knew about the hidden factors that fueled the standoff in Eldon.

Christina's voice resonated through the room. "There is a lot of speculation about what has been going down here. However, one thing is clear—the residents of Eldon are determined to stand their ground and protect what they believe to be their rights."

Catherine's attention was captured as Christina continued her report. The camera panned to show the line of state police officers, their presence a stark reminder of the power dynamics at play. But then Christina's expression turned somber, and her tone grew more serious.

"Behind the scenes, there are reports of heightened surveillance in the town," Christina said, her emerald-green eyes fixed on the camera with unwavering intensity. "Sources have shown that the state police have been closely monitoring the townspeople, gathering information and intelligence about the backgrounds of many of the residents. The exact extent of this surveillance is unclear, but it has added a layer of complexity to an already charged situation."

The idea of the community under surveillance, their every move scrutinized, eased Catherine's fears about them coming after her. She sat on the edge of the bed, her mind a whirlwind of thoughts and emotions. The events unfolding in Eldon had captured her attention and stirred a sense of responsibility within her. As she understood the claims of surveillance and hidden truths, her gaze continued to drift to the television. It was a window into the world beyond her sanctuary.

Christina's timbre was steady and professional as she spoke. "Before we go, the state police have requested the help of anyone who might have information on this event. Anyone who may have knowledge about the town of Eldon and its residents who will come forward willingly will be most appreciated. We would be interested in this information as well. Please contact the state police, and then email us so that we can bring you, the viewers, updated reports on the unfolding situation in Eldon. You can find the email on our website. Our promise to all of you is that we *will* get the truth out."

Catherine sat on the edge of the bed, her smartphone cradled in her hands. Now, as the momentum built and voices were raised, she grappled with a decision that weighed heavily on her conscience.

Christina Bitterman's hotline seemed like a lifeline. It could be a way for Catherine to get word out about what was really going on in Eldon. The stories she had heard were a mosaic of perspectives, each contributing to the picture of what was happening in the town she'd grown up in. Catherine's personal knowledge about the situation tugged at her heart and stirred a maelstrom of emotions. She stared at the number displayed on her smartphone, Christina's name etched beside it. The temptation to call was strong; she had a desire to contribute to the unfolding narrative, to uncover the truth. But as she contemplated the decision, a chorus of doubts echoed in her mind. *What if my involvement leads to unintended consequences? What if I accidentally talk about Jessica? I wouldn't want her to be found out...* Catherine wondered, her fingers tapping against the phone's surface. She had experienced firsthand the weight of information that could disrupt lives, which could change the course of events in unexpected ways. The line between truth and consequences felt blurry, and she grappled with the uncertainty of the path ahead.

The memory of her fight against Tom resurfaced; the conversations over the past two months replaying in her mind. His words had carried veiled threats, a suggestion that he would kill her for what she knew about him. The fear that had gripped her then still lingered, a shadow that whispered of danger and potential harm.

The revelation that there was surveillance going on in

Eldon and knowing there were hidden motives among the townspeople had the potential to unravel the fabric of Catherine's community. She would be exposing vulnerabilities and sowing further discord in the town. She questioned whether the truth, even if unveiled, would lead to a just resolution or further turmoil, not just for the town but for her.

Her doubts urged her to remain quiet for fear that Tom or his friends would find her if she started revealing things to the press.

THIRTY-ONE

Catherine's steps were heavy as she paced the room, each one laden with the weight of the past week's events. She had discovered that Detective Sheldon had been brought to the same hospital she'd been in, Ohio Valley Medical Center. She'd been calling the hospital every day, desperate for any morsel of information about him and his recovery. However, the staff had remained frustratingly tight-lipped because she wasn't a relative.

Her footsteps reverberated off the stark white walls, a constant reminder of her solitude in this race against time. Catherine had only known Detective Sheldon for a couple of months, but ever since he had helped her search for the truth in the car crash case, he had left an indelible mark on her. They had forged a bond amidst the chaos, a connection that went beyond the confines of their search for the truth. And now, knowing he was lying in a hospital bed, possibly battling for his life, Catherine felt an urgency unlike any she had experienced before.

As she called the nursing station once again, her jaw set with determination, she could hear the annoyed voice of the staff. She imagined the bored exchange as the phone rang with that practiced tone that hinted at secrets being kept behind the facade of professionalism. Once the ringing was about to stop, Catherine took a deep breath, mustering the strength to ask the question that had been gnawing at her for days.

"Excuse me," she said, her voice steady. "I've been calling every day to check on Detective Alan Sheldon. Can you please tell me how he's doing?"

The nurse on the other end of the line sounded like a middle-aged woman with a tired tone. Catherine could hear her fingers tapping the keyboard she pictured in front of the woman, her gaze probably fixed on the computer screen. Catherine could sense the hesitation in the call, the unspoken reluctance to share the truth.

"And who might I ask is calling?"

Catherine sighed. "My name is Catherine Morris."

"I'm sorry, ma'am," the nurse replied, her tone practiced but not unkind. "I can't provide any information about patients without proper authorization, and your name is not on the list."

Catherine's frustration bubbled up, threatening to spill over. She had expected this response, yet it still stung. She had expected to be met with a wall of silence, but her determination remained unshaken.

"I understand the protocol," Catherine said, her voice unwavering. "But Detective Sheldon is not just a patient to me. He's a friend, and I've been deeply concerned about his well-being. I've been calling every day, hoping for some news, some update. Please, can't you at least tell me if he's stable?"

The nurse's voice softened, and for a moment, Catherine thought she heard a flicker of empathy in her voice. But that fleeting connection vanished as quickly as it had appeared. "I'm truly sorry," the nurse said, her voice tinged with regret. "I wish I could help, but I can't provide any information without proper authorization from the family or the patient themselves."

Despite her irritation, Catherine's tone was gentle because it wasn't this nurse's fault; she was just doing her job. "Can you at least tell Detective Sheldon that Catherine Morris has been calling about him when you see him?"

"Of course. I'm so sorry it has to be this way. It's a legal issue though. I'll personally be sure to let him know. I am sure he will be happy to know that you have been asking after him."

"Thank you. When you do talk to him, can you give him my new phone number?"

"Of course, dear. What is it?"

Catherine rattled off the new number, thanked her again, and hung up.

The nurse's voice echoed in Catherine's mind. The weight of guilt hung heavy on her shoulders as she sat in the mostly dark hotel room, her fingers tracing absent patterns on the sheet. Her mind was consumed by a single, relentless refrain. Detective Sheldon. He had been injured because of her, because he had been drawn into taking her side in the car crash investigation, into the swirling currents of danger that she had failed to expect.

She stared down at the table, her thoughts a tempest of regret, guilt, and self-blame. Their connection had deepened since they cleared Catherine's name. Their shared search for the truth forging a bond that seemed to defy the boundaries of time. However, beneath the surface of their blossoming relationship, there was a shadow. It was a shadow that now loomed over her heart, reminding her of the pain she had inadvertently caused.

Catherine remembered hearing the gunshots vividly, the thought of Detective Sheldon getting hit by one etched into her mind like a scar.

Darkness swallowed her soul as she blamed herself for his injuries.

. . .

Alan's eyelids fluttered, fighting against the weight of darkness that had consumed him for what felt like an eternity. Slowly, like a fog clearing, the world seeped back into his consciousness. He was aware of a dull ache that radiated from his chest, and each inhale felt like a struggle. The surrounding room was quiet, sterile, and unfamiliar. White walls, soft beeping sounds, and the faint scent of antiseptic filled his senses.

As his awareness sharpened, memories filtered in. The shooting in Eldon. Agonizing pain that had seared through his body as he fell. The overwhelming darkness that had swallowed him whole. The fact he was even alive defied the odds, and he could only assume that he was somewhere in a hospital. Struggling to regain control of his body, Alan tried to shift his focus to his surroundings. He attempted to move his fingers, but they felt heavy, as if encased in lead. Gradually, he twitched them, and a surge of triumph shot through him.

A sense of determination ignited within him, propelling him to overcome the lethargy that gripped his body. Time lost its meaning as Alan continued his battle against the remnants of unconsciousness. Minutes blurred into hours as he gradually regained the ability to move more parts of his body. Each minor victory brought him closer to the surface, to a world he was eager to reconnect with.

Finally, as if breaking through a barrier, Alan's eyes fluttered open fully. The harsh brightness of the hospital room's lights made him wince, and he blinked several times to adjust. It took a moment for his eyes to focus on his surroundings, but when they did, he stared at the white ceiling tiles above him.

As he attempted to process his situation, a wave of relief washed over him. He was alive. He had survived the shooting, despite the odds stacked against him. But the victory was bittersweet, for he couldn't shake off the memory of the pain that had nearly consumed him. As his gaze shifted around the room, he noticed the various medical equipment that surrounded him. An IV stand loomed beside his bed, and wires connected him to monitors that beeped and pulsed with a rhythmic cadence.

Alan knew he was lucky to be alive. However, he couldn't suppress the feeling that he had crossed over to a realm between life and death, a place where shadows danced at the edge of his vision. His thoughts were interrupted by a soft knock at the door. Turning his head with a newfound effort, he saw a nurse entering the room. She was a middle-aged woman with kind, honey-brown eyes, her demeanor radiating a sense of care that he found oddly comforting.

"Good to see you awake, Detective Sheldon," she said with a warm smile as she approached his bedside. "You've given us all quite a scare."

Alan cleared his throat, his voice raspy as he spoke. "How... how long have I been out?"

"Three days," the nurse replied, her tone gentle. "You've been through quite the ordeal. But you're a fighter, and your progress has been remarkable."

Memories of the shooting flooded back to him. The chaos, the gunfire, the searing pain in his chest from the armor-piercing bullet that had gone through his Kevlar vest. Alan's jaw tightened as he fought back the emotions that threatened to overwhelm him. He had questions, so many questions. About the arrest, about the shooter, about how close they were to closing the case. "Where am I?" Alan asked, his voice a whisper.

"You're at Ohio Valley Medical Center," the nurse answered. "You're in stable condition now, but it's going to take some time for you to fully recover."

Alan nodded, absorbing the information. He shifted his gaze back to the nurse, his curiosity getting the better of him. "Has... anyone called me?"

The nurse's eyes softened. "A woman, Catherine Morris, has been calling here. She's been worried about you. And several officers have stopped by the desk to see how you were doing."

Catherine. The thought of her brought a surge of concern that Alan struggled to put into words. She had been one victim in his car crash investigation, unwavering in her determination to bring justice to Eldon. Luckily, she was protected and far away from Eldon's aggressive reign. "Do you think..." Alan hesitated, his throat tightening. "Am I allowed to have visitors? Could she come and visit?"

The nurse's smile was warm, her expression compassionate. "Mrs. Morris left her number with us. She asked that we give you her number, but we couldn't give her any information about your condition without your consent. If you agree, I could give her a call and let her know you're awake and tell her that you'd like to see her. Would you like me to call her?"

A mix of anticipation and anxiety churned within Alan's chest. He wanted to see Catherine, to reassure himself that she was safe, and, if he were honest with himself, to find solace in her presence. But he also feared how he might appear to her in his current state—weak, vulnerable, far from the capable detective she needed to be on her side.

Swallowing his doubts, he nodded at the nurse. "Yes, please. I'd appreciate that."

The nurse left the room to make the call, leaving Alan alone with his thoughts. He closed his eyes, took a deep breath, and let the reality of his situation sink in. He had survived, and he had a second chance to continue his fight for justice.

Catherine's phone vibrated on the hotel nightstand, breaking the early morning silence. She reached for the device, a slight frown forming as she read the caller ID: Ohio Valley Medical Center. Her heart quickened in a mix of worry and anticipation. It had been three days since Detective Sheldon had been admitted for his gunshot wound, and she had been keeping vigil by her phone, hoping for news.

"Hello?" she answered, her voice a mix of urgency and concern.

"Good morning, is this Mrs. Catherine Morris?" a gentle voice inquired.

"Yes, it's me. Is everything okay with Detective Sheldon?"

"I'm Nurse Anderson from Ohio Valley Medical Center. I'm calling to inform you that Detective Sheldon has woken up and is asking about you. He expressed a desire for you to visit him."

A wave of relief washed over Catherine, but it was chased by a surge of uncertainty. Jessica had warned her to lie low, to avoid drawing attention to herself. The danger that had followed her from Eldon still loomed, and Jessica's warnings echoed in her mind like a haunting refrain. "Thank you for letting me know," Catherine replied, her voice steady despite the turmoil within her. "I'll be there as soon as I can."

"Very well. We'll be expecting you," Nurse Anderson said before ending the call.

Catherine stared at her phone for a moment, torn between her concern for Detective Sheldon and the shadow of caution that had settled over her. She had promised Jessica that she would avoid anything that could put her in danger, and visiting Detective Sheldon in the hospital seemed like a risky move. Yet, she felt obligated to the detective, and her need to be there for him warred against her better judgment.

As she mulled over her options, memories of them working together flooded her mind. Detective Sheldon had been her anchor, her mentor, and her friend. Their bond had grown, and the thought of not being there for him when he needed her tugged at her conscience.

Catherine's phone buzzed again, and she saw a text message from Jessica.

Hey, just wanted to check in. Everything okay? Do you need anything?

Catherine sighed, typing out a response.

I just got a call from the hospital. Detective Sheldon woke up, and he's asking for me.

Almost immediately, a reply popped up.

Be careful. You know the risks of going out. If you do, remember to turn on that app if you get into trouble.

Catherine clenched her phone, her fingers trembling. She knew Jessica was right. She knew she should heed the warnings and stay away. But the thought of leaving Detective Sheldon to face his recovery alone was unbearable. She typed out a response.

I'll be cautious. But he's done a lot for me, Jessica. I can't just abandon him.

The reply was swift.

I get it. Just don't let your guard down. Keep your eyes open.

Catherine slipped her phone into her pocket and paced the hotel room, torn between her duty as a friend and the instincts that had kept her alive. She knew Eldon held secrets that could get her killed, that the danger was real and insidious. But she also knew that Detective Sheldon needed her, that the two of them working together were her lifeline.

With a determined exhale, Catherine decided. She would visit Detective Sheldon, but she would do so cautiously. She would take every precaution to ensure her safety while not compromising his recovery. Gathering her thoughts, Catherine left the hotel and got a taxi to the medical center using some of the cash that Jessica had given her. The early morning sun painted the sky in shades of gold, and the city seemed to hold its breath as she navigated the familiar streets. Her heart raced with a mixture of trepidation and determination.

Arriving at the hospital, Catherine found herself in the same sterile environment where she had spent countless hours. The memories of the investigation, the shared desire to uncover the truth, and investigative conversations, surged to the forefront of her mind. She knew that her presence was needed now more than ever, but the specter of danger loomed, casting a shadow over her purpose.

As she approached Detective Sheldon's room, her steps slowed. She took a moment to steady her nerves, reminding herself of the need to be cautious. She knocked softly before entering, and her heart skipped a beat as she saw him propped up in bed, his gaze turning toward her.

"Hey," Detective Sheldon greeted with a faint smile, his voice weaker than she remembered.

"Hey," Catherine replied, her own smile tinged with a mix of relief and concern. She approached the bed, her wide eyes studying his face for any signs of distress.

"I'm glad you're here," Detective Sheldon said, his gaze steady on hers.

Catherine pulled up a chair beside his bed and sat down, her fingers tapping nervously on the armrest. "I'm glad you're awake. How are you feeling?"

"Like I've been hit by a truck," Detective Sheldon replied with a weak chuckle. "But I've been worse."

Catherine couldn't help but smile, her worries momentarily eased by his humor. "You had me worried, you know. From what I was able to gather, the doctors weren't sure if you were going to pull through."

Detective Sheldon's expression grew more serious, his gaze fastened on hers. "Thank you for the concern, Mrs. Morris. The nurse said you'd been calling daily. Is there something you need to tell me?"

The hospital room seemed to shrink as Catherine took a deep breath, steeling herself for a conversation she knew would be difficult. She watched as Detective Sheldon, propped up on pillows in his hospital bed, regarded her with a mix of curiosity and concern. "Actually, yes." Catherine's fingers twisted nervously in her lap as she gathered her thoughts. "While you were... unconscious, Detective Adams took over your cases. He's been investigating everything, including the car crash."

Detective Sheldon's expression shifted, a flicker of surprise and apprehension crossing his features. "Adams? Why would he take over my cases?"

Catherine hesitated, choosing her words carefully. "I don't know all the details, but he seemed convinced that you were wrong about the conclusion in the car crash case. He said Tom's guilt was being blown out of proportion. He believes I'm responsible."

Detective Sheldon's eyes widened in disbelief, his body tensing as he processed her words. "He thinks you're guilty? After reading all the evidence I've gathered?"

Catherine nodded; her gaze unwavering. "I tried to question him about it. He told me I should hand myself in, that he's working to bring justice to the victim's family. But I hung up. He said the evidence points to me."

A mixture of anger and frustration flashed across Detective Sheldon's face, his knuckles lighter as he clenched the sheets beneath his fingers. "Evidence? This is ridiculous! I've laid out every piece of evidence against Tom for the crash. And now he's accusing you of being a drunk driver?"

"I know it's infuriating, Detective Sheldon. I couldn't believe it either. But I've been lying low for the time being and hoping the state police can handle this."

Catherine sat by his bedside, her fingers absently tracing patterns on the edge of the sheet. The weight of the recent revelations hung in the air, a palpable tension that both united and unsettled them. His gaze was fixed on the window, his expression contemplative. After a moment of silence, he turned his attention to Catherine, his eyes serious and determined.

"Catherine, I've been thinking," he began, his voice measured, "about the danger that might still follow you."

Catherine nodded, and her heart tightened as she met his gaze, her fingers stilling on the edge of the sheet. She had expected this conversation, but was unsure how to navigate it. The truth had a way of exposing vulnerabilities, of forcing them to confront the darker aspects of their reality.

"I don't want you to put yourself in harm's way," Detective Sheldon said. "You've already faced enough danger, and now, with Adams accusing you and the threats looming... I'm afraid something could happen to you."

Catherine's throat tightened, and she swallowed hard, her gaze dropping to her hands. "Detective, I understand your concerns, and I promise I'll be careful."

His lips twitched into a half-smile, his eyes softening as he regarded her. "Thank you for understanding. I can't look out for you from a hospital bed. Also, I need you to promise me something."

Catherine's brow furrowed in anticipation, her heart quickening. She could sense the seriousness of his request, and she knew that his concern for her safety was genuine.

"Promise me that, after this, after you leave here, you'll lie low until the state troopers have Tom and the others in custody," he said, his voice gentle but firm. "Stay out of public areas, avoid unnecessary risks, and keep yourself safe."

Catherine's gaze met his, her heart aching at the weight of his words. The thought of distancing herself from everything... of stepping back from the challenges they faced, was difficult to swallow. But she also knew that Detective Sheldon's request came from a place of genuine concern, a desire to shield her from the danger that had surrounded her in Eldon.

"Isn't there something I can do to help?" Catherine asked, her voice tinged with frustration.

"I'm not asking you to hide. I'm asking you to protect yourself. This situation is dangerous, and I'm sure you don't want something to happen to you again because I certainly don't."

Tears pricked at the corners of Catherine's wide eyes, and she swallowed the lump in her throat. She had faced danger head-on countless times now, so the thought of leaving the detective to face the challenges alone, of allowing him to shoulder the burden of both his health and her safety, was a tough pill to swallow.

"I promise I'll be cautious," Catherine finally said, her voice soft but resolute. "I'll avoid unnecessary risks, and I'll stay out of public areas. But I won't abandon you, Detective."

His expression softened. "I don't expect you to, Catherine. I just want you to take care of yourself. You're a civilian, and that means there's a greater risk for you than there is for me. I'm trained to deal with this kind of thing."

Catherine nodded. "I understand. I'll take your advice, and I'll do everything I can to stay safe."

His lips curved into a faint smile; his gaze unwavering on hers. "Thank you, Catherine. You're a strong woman, and I have faith in you."

THIRTY-TWO

Catherine had spent the last hour visiting Detective Sheldon in the Ohio Valley Medical Center and getting him up to speed on the events of the last few days. Now, she stood in front of the hospital parking lot in the dim, brisk evening. She felt an unexpected mixture of excitement and trepidation since she'd seen the detective. She felt as though things were looking better, that everything was going to turn out right now she knew he was on the mend.

But now she needed to return to the hotel. As she looked around the parking lot, the familiar surroundings took on a different hue. The rows of cars, the bustling medical staff walking back and forth, even the towering hospital building itself. They were all a small part of a life she had left behind. She took a deep breath, trying to steady her nerves, and paused for a moment. She glanced at the hospital building. The place had been both a sanctuary and a battlefield for her. Soon, it would be nothing more than a memory.

Catherine's thoughts drifted to Jessica while she waited for the taxi she'd called. She wondered what her new friend was doing, if she was back in Eldon watching the happenings there, or if she was somewhere nearby in Cincinnati. Catherine's attention was abruptly drawn to a familiar sight. A white van was idling at the curb just a few feet away from her. Her heart skipped a beat as she recognized its make and model—it looked like Jessica's van.

She couldn't see the driver from where she was standing, but she thought if she could just catch a glimpse, she'd know whether it was Jessica. Catherine's grip tightened on her phone as she contemplated the van. Could it be her? She had told Jessica that she was coming to the hospital to see Detective Sheldon, so maybe it was. Maybe she'd come to take her back to the hotel or have dinner with her.

Catherine's heart raced with anticipation as she walked toward the idling van. As she got closer, her intuition whispered that there might be more to this encounter than mere chance and that she needed to be cautious, so she slowed down, taking a wary step forward, her thoughts swirling.

The side door of the van slid open just as Catherine called, "Jes—"

Her words caught in her throat as a group of men emerged from within. Her eyes widened in recognition and alarm; they were unmistakably Tom's friends, the same men who had beaten her. She froze, a deer caught in the headlights. Before she could react, firm hands closed around her arms, gripping her with a force that stole her breath. Panic surged through Catherine as she struggled against their hold, her screams echoing in the open air.

"Let go of me! What are you doing? Help!" she shouted, but she was too far from the hospital building for anyone to hear her.

How did these men know she was here? And what were they going to do to her? The shock and fear were overwhelming, threatening to paralyze her. As Catherine fought against her captors, her wide eyes darted toward another figure in the back, who sat, seemingly waiting for them to finish. A chill ran down Catherine's spine—this was far from a chance encounter.

"Let me go!" Catherine's voice cracked with desperation as the men forcibly propelled her toward the open van. She kicked and thrashed, summoning every ounce of strength she could muster, but their grip was unrelenting. Panic and anger intertwined within her, fueling her determination to break free.

Just as Catherine's struggling and screaming reached fever pitch, the figure emerged from the van's shadowy interior. Tom's face, twisted into a malicious grin, was a horrifying confirmation of her worst fears. The same man who had once claimed to love her now radiated malevolence. The electric blue eyes she had once loved were now gleaming with a vindictive satisfaction that sent shivers down her spine.

Catherine's heart pounded in her chest as she fought against the hands that held her. The van's interior was dark and stifling, punctuated by her labored breaths and the scuffling of feet. Her mind raced with a single, determined thought: escape. Just as she was making progress toward the open side door, a sharp blow landed against the side of her face, sending a shockwave of pain through her skull. The force of the impact sent her reeling, and her vision swam with a blur of colors and disorientation.

Catherine's scream of pain and surprise was cut short by the backhanded strike from Tom, silencing her cries in an instant because she was too in shock to make any noise. The van's interior fell into a tense silence, broken only by the sound of Catherine's ragged breathing. She clung to the remnants of her strength, her fingers gripping the cold metal floor beneath her. Tom's presence loomed over her like a sinister shadow, his eyes flashing with a chilling mix of anger and satisfaction.

"I suggest you keep your mouth shut, Catherine." Tom's voice was low and threatening.

Catherine's cheek throbbed with pain, and her head swam

as she struggled to gather her wits. Defiant, the instinct to survive battled against the weight of her captors' power. She met Tom's gaze with fury, her voice trembling but resilient. "You won't get away with this."

Tom's chilling laughter echoed within the confines of the van. "Oh, my dear, I believe I already have. And don't think about trying to garner sympathy from anyone here. They would never betray me. Family doesn't, you know."

The reality of her situation hit Catherine like a physical blow. She was trapped, surrounded by men who were more than willing to use violence to achieve Tom's goals, whatever they were. As the van rumbled along the back roads, the sounds of the outside world grew distant, muffled by the walls of her makeshift prison. The darkness outside was punctuated by the occasional glow of passing streetlights, casting fleeting shadows across her vision. Catherine's thoughts raced as she desperately sought a way out of her predicament.

The opportunity presented itself when the van slowed slightly, approaching a junction in the road. Catherine's eyes darted around the interior for something, anything, that she could use as a weapon. Her fingers brushed against a small, sharp object, and a plan formed in her mind. Gathering her strength, she lunged forward, using the element of surprise to her advantage. She wielded the makeshift weapon with all her might, slashing it across the arm of the one man who held her. The man's startled cry mingled with the scent of blood as he released his grip, allowing Catherine to scramble to her feet. Adrenaline surged through her veins as she rushed toward the rear doors of the van, her breath coming in short, desperate gasps as she pushed it open. The night air rushed against her face as she neared the exit, a tantalizing promise of freedom within reach. But just as she was about to make her escape, a powerful hand closed around her wrist, yanking her back into the van's interior.

Catherine's cry of frustration was drowned out by the van's engine as it roared, the acceleration sending her sprawling on the floor once more. Her breath was ragged as she pushed herself onto her hands and knees, her head spinning with a mixture of pain and determination.

Tom's face contorted with fury as he glared down at her. "You're making this much more difficult than it needs to be, Catherine."

Catherine met his gaze with defiance her voice hoarse but resolute. "You won't get away with this. The state troopers will find you."

Tom's laughter was a derisive snarl, a stark contrast to the concern that flickered in his friends' eyes. "You think they'll be able to catch us on these back roads? That's not going to happen. Besides, by the time we reach Eldon, those state troopers will be gone. It pays to have family in high places."

Despite her fear, Catherine refused to back down. "Hospital security will have seen you kidnapping me. You're not going to win, Tom. I don't care if you're related to the president. You're not going to get away with any of this."

Tom's laughter pierced the night air, a chilling tension that hung over the scene. His narrow eyes gleamed with a twisted amusement, a delusion of invincibility that defied the reality unfolding around him. "You don't understand, Catherine. I'm above the law. The state police can't touch me." Tom's voice was laced with arrogance. He had become a prisoner of his lies and deceit, all because he was convinced that he was untouchable.

The reality of her situation was grim, but Catherine refused to succumb to despair. As the van's occupants remained distracted by their delusions, a spark of hope ignited within Catherine. Her fingers fumbled in her pocket, finding her phone. With trembling hands, she extracted it, her fingers racing to unlock the device.

The van's interior was filled with conversations and laughter; they clearly thought they'd gotten away with kidnapping her. Their distraction provided Catherine with the perfect cover for her furtive movements. She took a deep breath, her heart racing, as she turned on the tracking app. Her fingers danced across the screen, tapping with a sense of urgency.

As she hit the button for the app, a cop car passed the van on the opposite side of the road, its lights flashing in a blaze of blue and red. The sudden burst of sirens and lights momentarily distracted Tom and his friends, their attention focused on the police vehicle.

Catherine's heart raced as she looked at the app, hoping that Jessica was somewhere paying attention. The chance to reach out to her was a glimmer of hope in the darkness. She slipped the phone back into her pocket to hide it. As the police car sped past and faded into the distance, the tension within the van eased, replaced by an air of relief and false bravado.

Tom's laughter echoed once more, his claims of invincibility taking on a desperate edge. Catherine's heart ached for the man she'd thought he was, but she knew that man couldn't ever have existed. She wondered why he'd ever married her in the first place. Looking at him now, she decided to ask.

"Why did you marry me?"

Tom looked back at her over his shoulder, a sneer on his face. "Because you were so eager to do what I wanted. So eager to please me. I liked that you did whatever I said, even ignoring your father's worries about being around me. You were like a cute little puppy I could train to do tricks. I thought you'd be easy to mold into the perfect, dutiful wife."

Catherine stared at him with horror. How had she been so blind? How had she not seen this side of him? But something he'd just said piqued her curiosity. "What do you mean I ignored my dad's worries?"

"Don't you recall your father telling you I wasn't the man

you thought I was?" He laughed. "Maybe not. You probably blocked it out after I killed him."

The world stopped. Catherine felt as though her heart had been ripped out of her chest.

Tom had murdered her father? How?

THIRTY-THREE

Catherine gasped as if in physical pain. Tom's words had blown her world apart. "I... I... you... you said he... he had a... heart attack," she gasped between the words.

"A few eye drops in his soda, and he did. It was easy." Tom stared at her with a malevolent grin. "It had to happen. He was trying to get you to go away to college. Trying to send you away from me. I couldn't have that. Who knew what kind of thoughts would enter your head if you had."

Her entire life, or the last nine years of it, had been a lie. Everything had been a lie.

Catherine sat in the back of the van, her mind reeling. She'd had no idea the depths of his depravity. He'd hidden everything from her. Nothing had been real. The van sped along dirt roads, kicking up dust and debris, but she hardly noticed. She was too dumbstruck to make any sense of what was going on.

The van came to a stop, and Tom got out, going around to the back to open the door. He gripped Catherine's arm, his fingers digging into her flesh as he pulled her out forcefully and marched her through the entrance of his law firm. Catherine stumbled, her sneakers pounding against the marble floor. Her eyes darted around the unfamiliar surroundings. She'd rarely been allowed at his office.

Realizing she was most probably in imminent danger, she knew she had to try to get him to see reason. At the very least, it would stall for time, and Jessica would be able to find her. She had to do something. She couldn't just let him kill her. She had to see this through, she had to make sure he faced justice. Not only for Melissa but also for her dad and for herself.

"Tom, you don't need to do all this," she hissed, attempting to wrench her arm free from his grasp. Her voice trembled, much to her disgust. She needed to be more forceful, more confident.

Without a word, Tom tightened his grip and continued to drag her through the empty reception area. She could tell he was a man consumed by a mission—his face was set in a determined grimace—and that scared her.

He opened the door to one of the private meeting rooms, a sliver of light cutting through the dimness of the hallway, and pushed Catherine inside. She stumbled into the room, her back hitting the edge of the table. Within moments, Catherine noticed James slumped on the floor, his body covering something in the corner. His fingers absentmindedly petting frayed fabric.

The room felt like a prison, a pit of solitude they couldn't escape. Catherine blinked, her wide eyes adjusting to the dim light, and that's when she saw it. It wasn't just James. The figure he was slumped over was Donna.

The room was suffocating, the walls closing in on Catherine as a sense of dread settled over her. The unfamiliar law office felt like a labyrinth of secrets and uncertainties, a place where reality and nightmare collided. And the sight of Donna unconscious beside James turned the situation into something even more sinister. It wasn't just her life on the line now; it was also her friends' lives. Catherine's gaze shifted to

Tom, her eyes narrowing as they met his. He was leaning casually against the door, his demeanor infuriatingly calm, his lips curling into a mocking smile that sent shivers down her spine.

"Tom, what the hell have you done?" Catherine asked, clenching her fists at her sides as anger filled her.

Tom's laughter was like a knife to her nerves. "Oh, Catherine. I will admit, you've been amusing over the last few months, more than you have been in the entirety of our marriage. So, I'll let you in on the narrative I will propose to everyone. You see, you've always been quite the liar. And I'll have to admit when questioned that even I didn't expect your lies to escalate quite like this."

Catherine's jaw tightened as she took a step closer, her voice sharper now. "Cut the crap, Tom. Tell me what you've done to Donna and James." She wasn't going to play his game.

Tom's eyes sparkled. "What have *I* done? Sweetheart, I've done nothing. As I will be telling Sheriff Mason later, I'm merely an observer in this little drama."

Catherine's patience was wearing thin, her frustration boiling over. She lunged toward Tom, her fingers uncurling from her fists as she glared at him and struck out with her nails, hoping to scratch the hell out of his face, but he caught her wrist.

"Don't play games with me, Tom," she hissed. "I can see Donna and James slumped over in the corner. What did you do to them?"

Tom's laughter echoed through the room as he dropped her hand. "Oh, sweetheart, you have quite the imagination. Donna and James are merely sleeping."

Catherine stared at him. Did he really believe that? "Sleeping? What are you talking about?"

Tom's smile turned predatory, his narrow eyes settling on her. "You always thought you were so clever, Catherine. But you were only as clever as I allowed you to be. Now, look who's trapped in the end."

Catherine's heart pounded. The room continued to close in on her, the walls becoming a prison of her own making. She took a step back, her gaze darting around, searching for an escape route.

"Tom, stop this. Whatever you're planning, it won't end well." Catherine's voice wavered; it was a plea for reason.

Tom laughed once more, his narrow eyes darkening. "Oh, it's far too late for that. The wheels are already in motion."

Catherine knew she needed to find a way out, to escape the trap that Tom had set. But as she turned toward the door, her heart sank as she realized he was already steps ahead of her.

With a sinister smile, Tom stepped forward, his hand reaching for the doorknob. "I think it's time our little chat ends, Catherine. This conversation is moving in useless circles."

The door clicked shut, the sound a final verdict.

She turned back to face the door, her voice sharp and unyielding. "You can't keep us here, Tom. Someone will notice we're missing."

Tom's laughter was like nails on a chalkboard, the sound grating against her nerves. "Oh, sweetheart, you underestimate my family and the power of manipulation. By the time anyone important realizes you're gone, it'll be far too late."

Catherine's mind raced between desperation and strategy. She needed to break free from his capture, to unravel the threads of deception that he had woven around everyone. "Tom, listen to me. You don't have to do this." Her voice was a mixture of pleading and defiance as she kept her gaze locked on the door, her fists clenched at her sides, her determination fueling her resistance. "I won't let you kill us, Tom. We're not your puppets."

Tom's laughter echoed through the halls like a discordant off-key tune. Catherine knew she and the others were trapped in a web of deceit that they might not escape from unscathed. She had no idea what Tom was planning. She half wondered if he was going to set fire to the building. It was the only thing that she could think he might try with them locked inside this room.

Catherine was desperate, frightened. She had to find a way out. With a clenched jaw, she stepped toward the door, her fingers curling into fists as she pounded on the wood, each thud a testament to her resolve.

"Let us out! Tom, you can't keep us here!" Catherine shouted angrily. She desperately needed to get out before her body decided it needed to go into panic attack mode. She hated that feeling, and she'd do anything to avoid having them come back.

But the door remained unmoved, its surface unyielding to her efforts. Catherine's frustration grew. She couldn't give up, not now, not when the stakes were this high. With a deep breath, she propelled herself forward, her shoulder colliding with the door in a burst of raw energy. The impact sent shockwaves through her body, the force jarring her bones. But the door remained steadfast, a silent barrier. Catherine staggered back, her breath coming in ragged gasps as pain radiated from her shoulder. She glared at the door, her resolve unwavering. She couldn't let fear and frustration consume her. She had to keep fighting.

"Dammit, Tom! Open this door!" Catherine's voice was a fierce, defiant shout, her words a battle cry.

But her demands fell on deaf ears, and the room was enveloped in an eerie silence that seemed to mock her efforts.

Catherine's frustration boiled over. "You won't get away with this! We'll find a way out!"

A groan came from the far side of the room, and Catherine's attention snapped to the corner where James was stirring. His eyes fluttered open; his gaze unfocused for a moment before recognition set in. He pushed himself into a sitting position, his movements slow and cautious.

"Catherine?" He sounded confused and in shock, his brows furrowing as he took in their surroundings.

Catherine's heart ached as she looked at him, the relief of seeing him awake tempered by the grim reality of their predicament. She moved closer to him, her voice soft and reassuring as she didn't want to wake Donna. She was lying in James's lap and seemed to be sleeping. "James, are you okay?"

James's gaze met hers; he seemed tired. "I'm fine, I think. But there's no use. The door is solid, Catherine. We're not getting out."

Catherine's heart sank. The weight of their dilemma was ever-present, but so was the glimmer of determination that burned within Catherine. Her gaze shifted between James and the closed door. Her mind raced with possibilities, with strategies to break free.

"James," Catherine's voice was steady, her eyes linking with his, "we will get out of this and reveal to the world everything Tom is hiding. I promise you."

James stared at her with despair. "No, Catherine. We're up against something bigger than us. Tom is calculated, manipulative. He's got his entire family helping him, working with him. That's more than half the town. We need more than just defiance to get out of here."

Catherine nodded, considering their options. The door remained an immovable barrier, and Tom's manipulation was like a shadow threatening to suffocate them. But Catherine was unwilling to let fear dictate their actions.

She smiled suddenly, recalling she had her phone. Tom hadn't known about it to take it from her.

She pulled it from her pocket. Quickly pulling up Jessica's messages, she sent her a text.

Hey, I'm in Eldon, trapped in a room at Tom's law office with my friend Donna and her husband James. Please hurry!

"Who did you text? And how do you still have your phone? Didn't Tom take it from you?" James blinked; confusion heavy in his gaze.

"I messaged someone on the outside. Someone who will get the state troopers to save us. All we have to do is hold out and wait for them to arrive." Catherine grinned. "And Tom did take my phone a while back, but I'm going to bet that he arrogantly thought I wouldn't have gotten a hold of a new one, so he didn't bother to check."

James attempted to smile, but his eyes were bleak, a look of utter despair and dismay. Catherine couldn't understand why he wasn't happier about this. They were going to be free shortly.

"James, what is it?"

James's sigh was heavy, his shoulders slumping. "Catherine, you have to know what Tom and his family are capable of."

A sense of foreboding settled over her as she waited for James to continue.

His voice was low, laced with a mixture of desperation and resignation. "Tom and the others will resort to extreme measures to ensure that we won't be able to testify against any of them."

"But—"

James's gaze remained fixed firmly on hers, his expression a mixture of sorrow and regret as he interrupted her. "He's going to silence us, Catherine. Permanently. Your friend won't be able to reach us in time."

Terror washed over her. She looked around the room, her eyes finally landing on Donna's still form, slumped over James's lap. Catherine shifted her gaze back to James's face. Worry for her friend had her asking, "James, what happened to Donna? Is she okay?"

Pain filled his eyes as he, too, looked at Donna. He took a deep breath, his voice heavy as he murmured, "I think... Donna's dying."

Catherine's heart seemed to stop, the words hanging in the air like a heavy cloud. Her mind raced to process the information, to grapple with the reality of the situation. Donna, her best friend she had been so desperate to protect, was somehow dying. "No," Catherine whispered, her voice a fragile thread of disbelief. "No, I don't believe it. That can't be true."

"I wish it weren't true. I broke into the building and found Donna here, locked in this room. Tom, or someone, had knocked her out. When we were trying to escape, Tom found us. There was a struggle. Tom had a gun, and he fired a shot at us. And... Donna was hit."

Catherine's gaze was fixed on her friend's still form. The sight of Donna's pale face and James's hand covering her wound was a painful reminder of the fragility of life, of the consequences of the battle she had waged against the shadows. Catherine's body trembled as she sobbed. Despair gripped her heart. She turned to James, her eyes pleading with him to make sense of the devastation that surrounded them.

"James, I'm so sorry this happened." Catherine's voice wavered, a fragile thread of disbelief and grief.

"I've been keeping pressure on her wound for so long. I don't think she's going to make it. She's slowly bleeding to death. I'm trying, Catherine, but... I don't know how much longer I can keep this up."

Catherine's heart ached as she watched James, the frayed threads of his strength threatening to unravel.

Suddenly, a new sound emerged, one that sent a shiver down their spines. Outside the door, they heard the unmistakable echoes of chaos—shouting, running footsteps, and the sound of heavy objects crashing to the ground. Catherine's heart raced as she exchanged a worried glance with James. The unmistakable sound of gunfire shattered the uneasy calm in their makeshift prison, and soon, more gunshots echoed through the hallways. The reverberations sent shockwaves of fear through her veins. She exchanged a wide-eyed glance with James.

"What's happening?" Catherine's voice was a breathless whisper.

James's expression was tense. "I don't know. Maybe it's the state troopers you called up."

If that was the case, armed resistance could only mean one thing—someone was violently opposing the state troopers who were coming to apprehend Tom. The threat of danger was more tangible than ever. The law office had become a battleground.

Amidst the echoes of gunfire and shouts, a somber realization took hold—a realization that cut through the chaos like a blade of clarity. Catherine's gaze was distant, her expression contemplative. The sound of the distant rumble of the ongoing conflict surrounded them, but her mind was consumed by something much darker. Tom's family and friends, the ones who were fighting to protect him from facing justice, their loyalty to him, their blind support, it was insane to her. Their allegiance to Tom went beyond reason. She just prayed that, in the end, they all would have to face justice for what they were doing.

THIRTY-FOUR

As Catherine stood near James and Donna, she heard determined footsteps beating a loud rhythm on the floor beyond the door. The sound was growing closer, and then, just as she thought they might continue to move past and carry on down the hallway, they stopped.

The door swung open, revealing Tom breathing heavily, a menacing look on his face. She watched his eyes narrow as he stepped into the room. His focus went from James and Donna on the floor to Catherine, and he raised his hand, pointing a gun at her.

Catherine's heart pounded as she faced the barrel of Tom's gun. The weight of their shared history hung heavily in the air, a reminder of the secrets Tom had kept hidden for so long.

"Tom, please..." Catherine's voice trembled, like a scared child.

When she first started dating Tom, she'd thought he was the most incredible person she could ever have met. He was smart and funny, he treated her like an adult, encouraged her to study and work hard for her dreams. She had loved everything about him. She hadn't cared that he was so much older than her. In her eyes, he'd been perfection.

But it had all been a lie.

He'd played her from the first moment they'd met.

Now when she looked at him all she could see was the disgusting monster he really was.

Tom's eyes bore into her, his expression full of anger and betrayal. "Catherine, do you even understand what you've done to me?" His voice was bitter, each word dripping with disdain.

She took a shaky breath, her palms clammy with nerves. "I did nothing. This is all because of the choices you've made, Tom. The things you've done. Not me."

A humorless laugh escaped Tom's lips. "Oh, of course. You caused none of it. Just like you didn't kill that innocent woman, and don't have a drinking problem, or listen to me. If you went to therapy and believed me, you wouldn't need to die now."

Catherine's hands trembled as she held her phone in a tight grip, the device's camera trained on Tom's uneasy expression. The room felt stifling, the weight of his secrets pressing down on them like a heavy fog. She had reached a breaking point, a moment where she could no longer afford to stay silent.

"Tom," Catherine's voice quivered, "you can't keep deflecting this. You can't keep blaming me for your actions."

Tom's narrow eyes flickered with unease and frustration. He shifted from one foot to the other, as if he was uncomfortable with what he was doing, but Catherine doubted he actually was. "I've told you, it's your fault. It's that simple. I have to do this because of you."

Catherine's jaw tightened as her resolve hardened. She had spent countless nights replaying the events that had led them here, dissecting every decision and every consequence. She took a steadying breath and pressed record on her phone's camera.

"I need you to answer some hard questions," she declared,

her voice shaking but determined. Catherine held the phone steady, her gaze unwavering.

"You can film me all you want, that video is going nowhere." He smirked.

Catherine pressed on. "I need to know, Tom. How do you plan to escape the consequences of what you've done? You murdered my father, embezzled money from the law firm, killed Melissa Legrasse, tried to murder me, shot Donna, and you've kidnapped me and James. Have you no conscience? How on earth do you think you're going to get away with all this? You must know the cops are aware of it."

Tom's face paled, but his eyes continued to bore holes into Catherine.

Catherine's voice remained firm. "I've given you a chance to explain, to be honest. But you've escalated and pushed things to beyond your control, and you're going to lose."

Tom's fingers clenched around the gun, his knuckles turning white. "You don't understand the truth. Everything that's happened is because of you."

"Seriously? You're still going to blame me? Fine then, enlighten me, Tom!" Catherine's frustration bled into her words. "You've been lying to me from the start, and I won't carry your burdens while you dance around accountability."

A conflicted expression crossed Tom's face. Catherine knew her persistence was forcing him into a corner, a place he clearly didn't want to be. Her grip on the phone tightened as her anger flared.

"You've destroyed lives, Tom. You've destroyed people who didn't deserve any of this."

Tom's head snapped up. "None of this was supposed to happen this way! If you had just died in that accident, then none of this would be happening! This is your fault!"

Catherine shook her head, her voice tinged with bitterness.

"I knew you were trying to kill me in that accident! I told Detective Sheldon I thought that might have been your intent."

Tom's lips pressed into a thin line. Without a word, he left the room.

Catherine watched him go, her heart heavy with a mixture of emotions. She had hoped that this confrontation would lead to a breakthrough, that Tom would finally take ownership of his actions, but he was still blaming her. But as the moments ticked by, doubt crept into her mind. Had she pushed him too far?

Minutes stretched into an agonizing silence before Tom returned. In his gloved hands, he held a new gun. The room was heavy with tension as Catherine and Tom faced each other, their gazes locked in a silent battle of wills. The weight of the past loomed large.

Catherine's voice was steady, her determination unwavering. "Tom, you can't deny the truth any longer. The evidence is right here. You can't escape the consequences of your actions."

Tom's lips curled into a bitter smile, his electric blue eyes flickering. "Oh, Catherine. You always were the optimist, weren't you? But let's be realistic here. There is no evidence to prove anything against me."

Catherine's resolve strengthened. "That's not true, Tom. With the information the police have, every prosecutor worth a grain of salt would be able to build a strong case that will expose all your crimes, not to mention those of your family."

Tom laughed sharply. "You really believe that, don't you? You think you can take down everything I've built with a handful of photographs and some dashcam footage? I'll just say you used Photoshop, and my friend is already working on making sure that footage gets corrupted. The paperwork proving everything is gone. Up in smoke."

"Tom, you can't keep avoiding this."

Tom's jaw clenched as he stared back at her, angry and

desperate. "Catherine, this is not the time or place. We aren't discussing this anymore. I'm done."

Catherine's eyes flashed with a spark of defiance. "No, Tom, we aren't done. You need to face the consequences of your actions."

Tom lunged forward and grabbed Catherine's arm. She winced as his fingers dug into her soft skin, the force of his grip sending a jolt of pain through her. "We're leaving." Tom's voice was low, a dangerous edge lacing his words.

Panic surged through her veins. She struggled against his grip, trying to free herself from his hold. "Let go of me, Tom! You can't control me like this!"

Tom's grip only tightened, his fingers digging into her arm with a renewed intensity. Catherine's senses were on high alert as Tom dragged her past the large windows. Her gaze was drawn to the street below. She could see state troopers positioned behind cars, facing off with various townspeople. It was an unwelcome reminder of the choices that had led them down this treacherous path. As Catherine strained to listen for any signs of what was happening outside, a sudden burst of gunfire shattered the air.

She turned toward Tom with alarm, knowing it was his men, his family, who were fighting.

Another round of shots rang out, closer this time. Catherine knew that the time for Tom to face justice was coming soon. What that would look like and whether she would survive to see it were the questions she couldn't wrap her head around. She couldn't see him just giving up and surrendering now.

In front of her, Tom's presence was a heavy reminder of the choices he had made, the paths he had taken that had led them here. There was a weight of inevitability in the air, a sense that Tom had reached a point where the truth could no longer be evaded. Now that he was dragging her off to her potential death, the weight of the truth felt almost unbearable. Catherine's determination was wearing thin, her fear simmering beneath the surface. Yet her resolve was unyielding, her mind steady despite the turmoil within her.

As the seconds ticked by, the tension between them seemed to stretch and warp, the air growing thicker with each passing moment. The halls of the law office seemed to taunt Catherine, a portal to a reality she didn't want to experience. She took a deep breath, her heart aching with a mixture of fear and sorrow as they took steps toward the back exit. As they approached the door, Catherine's feet grew heavier than before, as if wanting to root her to the spot. Her gaze flickered toward the path to her death, then back to Tom. But Tom dragged her toward the door, nonetheless.

The sound of sirens continued to wail in the distance. Tom's fingers tightened around the door handle as he pushed it open. Catherine was dragged close behind him, her eyes darting from shadow to shadow for any other threats she would have to face. The events of the past weeks had led them to this point, a point of disaster.

Just as Tom stepped outside, a sudden impact smashed into his face. His grip on the door handle loosened, and he staggered backward.

Catherine's gasp of shock was drowned out by the sound of the impact, her eyes widening as she watched Tom stumble and fall to the ground. A person emerged from the shadows, seeming to materialize out of the darkness. Catherine's heart leaped into her throat, her instincts screaming at her to be cautious. As the figure came closer, the dim light revealed a familiar face.

"Jessica?" Catherine's voice was a mixture of surprise and relief.

Jessica's eyes were wide with concern as she rushed toward Catherine, a brick in her hand, her expression a mix of urgency and fear. "Catherine, are you okay? Did he hurt you?"

Catherine's voice trembled as she recounted the events, the kidnapping, the danger she had faced.

Jessica weighed up their options. "We need to get you out of here. It's not safe."

Catherine's voice was resolute despite the fear that still lingered. "Jessica, the others. James and Donna are trapped in the meeting room."

"What? They're still alive? Are they okay?"

Catherine described Donna's injuries. She also revealed what Tom had said about her father's death.

Jessica's face paled as she listened, her eyes wide with disbelief. "I didn't know that about your dad... I can't believe all this."

Catherine's voice was steady as she continued, "We need to go back. We need to help Donna and James."

"It's too dangerous. We don't know how long Tom will be unconscious or if he's planned for people to find him if he doesn't return."

But Catherine's resolve was unwavering. "I can't leave them there, Jessica. They're in danger because they wanted to help me. It's my time to return the favor."

The surrounding street was still and quiet, the danger lurking far away in the office's front.

Jessica hesitated. "Okay. But we need to move quickly and quietly. We'll get them out safely."

Minutes stretched into an agonizing march as they retraced Tom and Catherine's steps. Their senses were on high alert as they approached the meeting room. The large door loomed before them. Catherine's hand hesitated on the doorknob, wondering what they would find inside. With a deep breath, she pushed open the door.

Jessica followed closely behind her. Inside, James was still slumped over Donna, his hand pressed over her wound. His expression was a mixture of fear and relief as he looked up at Catherine and Jessica.

Precious seconds ticked by, then James's voice cut through the tense silence. "You two need to go. Don't wait for us."

Catherine's brows furrowed. "What do you mean, James? We can't leave you here."

James's expression was resolute, his cornflower blue eyes landed on Donna's face as he spoke. "I won't leave Donna. We'll find a way out, but you need to go. It's too dangerous."

"But we're in this together. We'll find a way out for all of us," Catherine said.

"No, Catherine. I won't put any of you in danger because of us. You can get out. So do it."

Catherine's heart ached as she met James's gaze, the depth of his resolve clear in his eyes. The bond between him and Donna was unbreakable, despite the danger they were facing.

Jessica's voice was strained when she said, "He's right, Catherine. We need to find a way out, and we can't risk James and Donna's safety."

Catherine was torn between her loyalty to her friends and the urgency of the situation. "But we can't just leave them here."

As she moved toward the doorway, Jessica's voice was a hushed whisper as she spoke to James. "I'm calling for an ambulance. We won't leave you here without help. Hopefully, the state police will be able to help them get to you."

James gave Jessica a small smile. "Thank you. Just make sure you both stay safe."

Catherine's voice wavered with emotion as she looked back at James and Donna. "We won't stop until we bring this to an end. We promise."

THIRTY-FIVE

Catherine and Jessica walked toward the back door of the law office; their breath visible in the cool evening air. The events of the past few hours had left them rattled and their nerves frayed by the unexpected turn of events. Their eyes met, a silent understanding passing between them. They needed to leave discreetly and regroup somewhere safer. Catherine glanced back into the office. She couldn't shake off the feeling that something was amiss—that the danger they thought they had left behind might still linger, hidden in the shadows.

"Come on, let's go," Jessica whispered, her voice tense with unease. She grabbed the handle of the door, pushing it open enough to peer out, scanning the area.

The alleyway behind the law office was narrow and deserted. Jessica stepped out cautiously, her eyes darting around, while Catherine followed suit, her senses on high alert. Where was Tom?

As they hurried down the alley, their footsteps echoed off the walls, creating an eerie rhythm. The soft patter of raindrops was the only other sound that accompanied them. The street-lights cast long shadows, each one harboring a secret of its own.

Catherine muttered to Jessica, "I thought Tom would come find us if he woke up... Where is he?"

"My bet is he knew you went back in for Donna and James. He's probably around here somewhere. We need to get you out of here."

"What's the plan?" Catherine's voice trembled slightly; her eyes fixed on the shadowy alley before them.

Jessica's lips curled into a grim smile. "First, we'll need to get to my van—past the gunfire. It's how we get to safety."

"Where is it?"

"At the end of this alley on the other side of the street," she replied. "But it won't be easy to get there. The townspeople, Tom's family in particular, have turned fanatical, and the state troopers are trying to quell the uprising. They could be anywhere across the path."

Catherine exchanged a tense look with Jessica. "How are we supposed to make it through that? We'll be caught in the crossfire."

Jessica's eyes gleamed with urgency. "That's where my military training comes in. I'll lead us through the shadows. Just stay close to me. Time is of the essence."

Without another word, she turned and crept along the alley, disappearing into the darkness as if she were a part of it. Catherine followed suit; her senses heightened by the adrenaline coursing through her veins. Puddles sloshed beneath their steps, a rhythm that underscored the gravity of their mission.

As they approached the street, they saw a narrow path leading to the van through a couple of off-hand fights. Jessica paused, her hand raised to signal Catherine to stop. In a low whisper, she outlined the route they would take—a convoluted path that wound through the fights, below the prying eyes of the townspeople and the state troopers. With each step, Catherine felt her heart race in synchrony with the sound of her footsteps. They slinked through the battle, Catherine's senses on high alert. The town that had once been a peaceful haven had transformed into a battleground, with gunfire ringing through the air.

Jessica's guidance was their lifeline, steering them clear of danger and closer to the van. But their journey was far from uneventful. The rain had transformed the town into a desolate landscape, its streets glistening and slippery. They were halfway there. The atmosphere was heavy with tension as the fight waged on. Catherine's heart raced as they crawled along the winding path, her fingers dirtied by the gravel.

"We're almost there." Jessica's voice cut through the silence; her gaze fixed on the road ahead.

The van was a few steps away, under a dim streetlamp that seemed both familiar and foreign. Memories of Catherine's childhood flashed before her eyes—playing in these streets, attending local events, and growing up alongside friends who had become like family.

As they crouched for cover, Catherine peered up, her heart skipping a beat. The scene before her was one of chaos and defiance. The town's familiar faces had transformed into a ragtag militia, guns in hand, standing their ground against the state troopers who advanced with calculated brutality. Catherine's eyes widened as she recognized several figures she had known since she was a child. Jeffery, one of her neighbors, stood at the forefront, his face a mask of fierce determination. Beside him was his son Marcus, who had played football back when she'd been in high school with him and his brother. She wondered where Michael was, and as she scanned the area, she saw him farther down the line.

"They're defending him," Catherine whispered, her voice catching in her throat.

Jessica's gaze followed Catherine's, her expression one of concern. "They're risking everything for Tom."

As if on cue, a barrage of gunfire erupted, echoing through the rain-soaked streets. Bullets whizzed through the air.

"We have to help them," Catherine said, feeling protective of the people she'd once called friends and neighbors. She glanced at Jessica with determination before she tried to move forward to head into the fight. She had no plan, other than the need to save them from themselves.

The tenacity of those she used to call friends took Catherine by surprise. Jeffery wielded a shotgun like a machine gun, his eyes blazing as he faced off against the cops. Marcus was a force to be reckoned with, his determination clear as he deflected bullets with a metal sheet, each impact resonating with a chorus of defiance. But amidst the chaos, Catherine's attention was drawn to Michael, who was barking orders and coordinating the defense with a precision that spoke of strategic brilliance. He had always been nice to her when they were in school. He had been one of the smart guys and the head of the debate team, and now he was the pillar of strength upon which the town's defense relied.

Suddenly, a chilling cry cut through the air as a group of troopers advanced with an onslaught of firepower. Catherine's heart raced as she watched in horror as two figures fell, Jeffery and Marcus, their bodies crumpling to the ground. Time seemed to slow as the rain mixed with her tears, her voice lost in a scream of despair.

Jessica dragged her back with the help of the slippery, rain-soaked streets. "We have to keep moving. You can't save them."

Jessica's voice snapped Catherine back to reality, her grip on Catherine's arm firm as they navigated through the chaos. Catherine wiped her tears. Her gaze fixated on Michael, who continued to lead the defense despite the loss of his father and brother. She felt a renewed surge of determination to help in some way, a fire ignited by the knowledge that these were people she had known since childhood. Time seemed to freeze as her eyes met Michael's. His expression was a mixture of surprise, recognition, and what looked like a plea for help.

Catherine's feet wanted to move forward, but Jessica held her back. A single shot echoed through the air. Michael's eyes widened in shock, his body swaying before collapsing on the ground.

Catherine fell to her knees. "No," she whispered, her voice breaking, "Michael, no."

Jessica tugged on Catherine's sleeve; her pale blue eyes filled with empathy. "Catherine, you can't save him. We have to go. We can't stay here."

The rain continued its relentless assault. The weight of loss pressed down on Catherine like an unyielding force. The path to survival felt like a burden, a reminder of the lives that had been shattered because Tom wouldn't face the consequences of his actions. Catherine's chest tightened, her feet refusing to move forward.

The image of Michael's lifeless eyes haunted her thoughts; his sacrifice for Tom etched into her mind like an indelible mark. She had known him since she was a little girl. And now he was gone. The emotions that had been building within Catherine threatened to spill over, overwhelming her like a tidal wave. But Jessica's presence beside her was a silent anchor, a reminder that she wasn't alone in all this.

As if sensing Catherine's turmoil, Jessica reached out, her hand finding Catherine's. The touch was gentle, a lifeline amid despair. "It's okay to grieve, Catherine. I get it. These people were your friends and neighbors, but just remember, they're doing all this for Tom, because of Tom."

Catherine's voice cracked as she struggled to speak. "I should have done something... I should have stopped him before it could come to this..."

Jessica's grip on Catherine's hand tightened, her voice firm but filled with empathy. "You did everything you could, Catherine. We're up against forces beyond our control. These people made a choice, just like the others, to defend Tom. They knew the risks, and they stood by Tom's side."

Catherine's tears spilled over; her vision blurred by a torrent of emotions. She wiped her cheeks with the back of her hand, her voice barely audible as she choked out her words.

"Some of them were my friends at one time, Jessica. I've known many of them since I was little. I never thought... I never thought it would come to this."

Jessica's gaze held a mixture of understanding and unwavering support. "I know it's painful, Catherine. But we can't stay. The van's not much farther."

The weight of Catherine's grief threatened to consume her. But within the depths of her pain, she found a glimmer of resolve, a thread of determination that refused to be extinguished. She turned to Jessica, her eyes filled with sadness and strength.

"Okay, I know you're right, it's just hard to let go of that grief," she whispered.

Jessica's grip on Catherine's hand never wavered, her pale blue eyes remaining locked on Catherine's with a steadfast intensity. "Trust me, you can't let despair consume you. You've got a lot to live for. Come on, let's get going."

As they approached the back of the van, Catherine's gaze flickered to Jessica, who was focused on finding her keys. The camaraderie between them was unspoken, a connection forged through trials and challenges. Their journey had been marked by danger and loss, but it had also illuminated the strength that existed within them.

"We're almost there." Jessica's voice cut through the silence, her words carrying a note of reassurance.

Catherine nodded, her gaze drifting to the battle once more. The state troopers held a beacon of hope, a potential triumph over Tom and the unraveling of the conspiracy that had engulfed her life. But as they rounded the corner of the van, Catherine's heart skipped a beat. A figure stood by the door.

Catherine's eyes widened, shock and fear flooding her senses. Her mind struggled to process what she was seeing. The figure turned, revealing himself. Tom stood there, armed and manic in the steady rain, his gaze meeting Catherine's with a sick determination.

THIRTY-SIX

Time slowed down as Jessica's heart raced. She could feel Catherine trembling beside her, her wide eyes reflecting the fear that she had to be feeling. Tom had them blocked from the van, and Jessica knew it was their only way out of Eldon. But as the seconds ticked by, Jessica searched for a way for them to escape.

As Tom's finger squeezed the trigger, Jessica's instincts kicked in. Adrenaline surged through her veins, sharpening her senses. In a split-second decision, she lunged forward, her movements fueled by fear and determination. The sound of the gunshot echoed through the alley as the bullet whizzed past, a hair's breadth away from its intended target.

Jessica's outstretched hand closed around Tom's gun hand, her fingers digging into his flesh. She knew she was stronger than the average woman, having trained hard in the Army, and she had kept up that training. She used that strength now to force Tom's hand to drop the gun. A silent battle of wills played out. Jessica's heart pounded in her chest as she faced off against the man who seemed determined to destroy everything in his path. She knew she had to get the gun out of his grasp at all costs, but the desperation in Tom's narrow eyes told her he would stop at nothing to regain control. With every passing second, her fingers tightened around the weapon, her knuckles turning white. Tom's crazed grin widened, revealing his teeth, which seemed to glint in the dim light.

"You think I'm just some random lunatic?" he taunted, his words dripping with bitter sarcasm. "I've got the law on my side, you know."

"The law? What law would that be?" said Jessica. "Your cousin, the sheriff? Because from the looks of things, I'd say you're both going down."

Tom's eyes gleamed with a manic light as he stepped closer to Jessica, his body tense and unpredictable. "I've been watching her." He nodded toward Catherine, his voice low and conspiratorial. "She's the one who's been causing all the trouble in this town."

Catherine gasped; her voice full of disbelief. "That's not true!"

Tom's laughter echoed once more, the sound grating. "Oh, but it is, sweetheart. I've got evidence of your drinking problem. I've got witnesses. The law is on my side, and this is a citizen's arrest."

Jessica frowned in irritation. "You are insane. You have no authority, what are you even talking about?"

Tom took a step closer. "She thinks she can get away with this, don't you see?" His voice was a venomous whisper.

"You're either delusional or a liar," Jessica replied.

"So, she's got you indoctrinated too. She's the villain here!"

"Just tell me what you want," Jessica said, her voice edged with frustration.

Tom's smile faded, replaced by a cold, calculating gaze. "I want you to admit it," he hissed, his words cutting through the night air like a blade. "I want you to admit that you know the truth about what happened. That Catherine was driving the car that killed Melissa! That she was drinking and driving!"

Jessica took a step back, her eyes narrowing as she studied Tom's face. "You want to hear the truth?"

"Yes, tell me the truth. You know she's hiding the truth from you, from everyone," he taunted, his words dripping with bitterness.

"The car accident wasn't an accident at all, was it?" Jessica taunted.

Tom's face contorted into a sneer, his eyes glittering with a deranged intensity. "Don't lie to me," he spat, his voice rising in a crescendo of madness. "You think I don't know? You think I don't know what she did to Melissa?"

"Let's talk about Melissa," Jessica warned, her voice edged with sorrow and anger.

"Melissa's not a part of this anymore, you know that," he hissed. "This is about Catherine. She can't escape what she's done."

His words were poison, a reminder of the lies that had refused to let her sister rest in peace. Melissa—the sister whose life had been lost in a car crash that had seemed like an accident. But now, the shadows were lifted, revealing a truth that was more sinister than she could have imagined. With a surge of anger, Jessica's grip on the gun in his hand tightened, her knuckles turning white.

"You rammed your car into us on purpose. You killed her because she ended the affair you two were having. The affair I told her wasn't good for her," she stated, her voice sharp and commanding. Tom needed to admit the truth, and Catherine needed to understand the screwed-up game he had been playing.

Tom's face twisted into a wicked smile, his narrow eyes dancing. "That's not the truth," he said in a taunting whisper.

"That's not the truth. She ended our affair, but I hold no ill will to her."

"I have the text messages you sent her to prove you weren't happy. That you threatened her. Not to mention, you also had a tracker on her phone. You knew where she was that night. I have proof that you checked that tracker," Jessica finally spat, her voice laced with anger and desperation. She couldn't let him break her, couldn't let his madness consume her sanity.

Tom's laughter echoed through the alley. "Did I?" he mused; his face twisted into a mask of derangement. "Or maybe Catherine had control over my phone."

With a sudden surge of determination, Jessica's voice grew steady and unwavering. "You planned this," she declared, her eyes meeting his with a resolute intensity. "You planned to kill both Melissa and Catherine that night."

Catherine's eyes widened with shock and disbelief as she stared at Jessica, her mind struggling to process the words that had just been spoken. The truth, a sinister tapestry of deception and madness, had unraveled before her eyes, leaving her reeling.

"Tom planned to kill me *and* your sister? From the beginning?"

Jessica's gaze was steady, her voice low as she recounted the coiled web of lies that Tom had woven. "Yes," she confirmed. "He didn't want Melissa telling you about the affair, which she was planning to do, and he was tired of being a married man. He was always going to crash the car and blame you, but he'd hoped you would die in the process, which was why your airbag never deployed. Imagine his shock when you lived through it. You surviving made things so much more difficult, right, Tom?"

The revelation of Tom's cruel intentions ignited a fire within Catherine, a fierce need for justice and retribution.

"Catherine, you need to run," Jessica cautioned, her voice

low and measured. "Tom is dangerous, and he's proven that he's willing to do anything to achieve his goals."

Catherine's hands clenched into fists, her nails digging into her palms. "I can't just do nothing," she spat, her voice tinged with bitterness. "He killed my dad, he shot Donna, he planned to kill me, and he killed your sister, Jessica. He took everything from us."

Jessica's expression softened as she glanced at her, but she kept her grip tight on Tom's hand. "I agree with you," she grunted. "But I told you before, that kind of revenge won't bring anything back, and it won't undo the past. You need to run to safety so that the truth can get out. That is the only thing that will change your future."

Catherine's eyes filled with tears... grief and anger threatening to overwhelm her. "I know that," she whispered, her voice a fragile murmur. "But I can't just leave you to die."

She watched Jessica's gaze shift back to Tom. His face, his perverse intentions—they were all consumed by the darkness that had enveloped their lives. The cold metal of a gun was in a tug of war between them. Jessica's grip on Tom's gun hand tightened and twisted his wrist. Catherine could see her fingers were white with tension as she faced off against the man who had orchestrated so much pain and chaos.

"It ends now," Jessica hissed, her voice dripping with anger and defiance.

With a swift movement, her knee connected with Tom's groin in a forceful blow. The impact was enough to knock the wind out of him, the gun slipping from his fingers and skittering across the pavement. Tom's face warped into a mask of pain and surprise, and he stumbled backward. Without hesitation, Jessica's fist shot forward, her knuckles connecting with Tom's sharp jaw in a satisfying impact that even Catherine heard. Tom stumbled back further. But before Jessica could react, his fist shot out in retaliation, striking her squarely in the chest. The impact knocked the wind out of her and sent her sprawling backward.

Catherine's eyes landed on the discarded gun that lay on the ground between them. Without hesitation, she moved forward, her fingers closing around its cold metal. She turned her back to Tom and Jessica, her body positioned protectively as she faced away from the scene.

She held the gun in her trembling hand. Tom was inches away from her, his eyes burning with a manic intensity into her back. The rain-soaked ground beneath her feet seemed to shift and sway as Catherine crouched there, caught between her fear and the determination she felt to end this once and for all. Suddenly, a faint sound cut through the air, the soft flick of metal against metal.

"Catherine!" Jessica's voice broke through the silence. "Watch out!"

Catherine's grip on the gun tightened as she turned and faced her husband. The man who had manipulated her, lied to her, and stolen everything from her. Catherine's heart skipped a beat, her eyes widening as she saw Tom's hand. A switchblade gleamed in the dim light, flipping open with deadly precision.

Her instincts kicked in, a surge of adrenaline coursing through her veins as she realized danger was inches away from her. The streets around her blurred as her focus narrowed on the gleaming knife. Without a second thought, Catherine's body moved on pure instinct. She shifted her weight, her hand tightening its grip on the gun as she lunged to the side, narrowly avoiding the path of the deadly blade. The ground slipped beneath her feet, her body stumbling as she fought to regain her balance. Tom's face contorted in frustration as his attack missed its mark. The switchblade glinted in the dim light and falling rain as he repositioned himself.

Catherine's breath came in ragged gasps as she gripped the gun, her wide eyes moving to Tom's face with fear, but she was resolved to see this through. She aimed the weapon at Tom's advancing form. Her hands trembled; the weapon heavy in her grasp. She'd never shot a gun before, but that wasn't going to stop her.

"Stay back!" she shouted at her husband.

Tom remained defiant. "Go ahead, pull the trigger," he taunted. "You couldn't hit me even if you tried."

She knew she wouldn't be able to hit him if she aimed for his face, but if she aimed for his center mass, she might just be able to stop him, especially if she fired more than once.

"You won't do it." Tom stepped closer. "You don't have it in you."

Catherine felt nothing but determination as she stared at him. She looked into Tom's eyes, searching for any hint of vulnerability, any sign that he might back down.

"You're just like all the rest," he sneered. "Too weak to do what needs to be done."

Catherine's finger stayed poised over the trigger as she prepared to make a choice that would define their future.

The rain was a quiet echo of the choices that had led them to this moment. Catherine's grip on the gun was steady, her eyes fixed on Tom's face as she made her final decision. And in that moment, as the rain fell around them and Tom lunged forward, the bullets exploded through the center of Tom's chest, forever altering their journey.

THIRTY-SEVEN

Two months, one week, and two days since the anniversary

The fluorescent lights overhead hummed softly, casting an otherworldly glow on the sterile white walls of the interrogation room. Catherine sat on the edge of her chair, her heart like a drumbeat as she anxiously awaited the police officer's verdict. She glanced at the clock on the wall, its hands moving at an agonizingly slow pace, marking the passing minutes that seemed to stretch into eternity.

Detective Marcus Rivers leaned against the table; his piercing green-gray eyes fixed on Catherine. His expression was somber, betraying none of his thoughts as he studied her intently.

"Catherine, I understand that this has been a harrowing experience for you," Detective Rivers began, his voice carrying a warmth that was unexpected, given the circumstances. "I want you to know that we've investigated the events that transpired in Eldon over the course of the last week and last night. Our priority is to ensure that justice is served, and that means evaluating all the evidence at hand."

Catherine's fingers tightened around the edge of the table, her knuckles turning white as she braced herself for what might come next. She had spent the previous night replaying the events over and over in her mind, trying to make sense of the chaos that had unfolded.

"We've spoken to witnesses, gathered forensic evidence, and reviewed the security camera footage from the law office," Detective Rivers continued. "Based on our findings, it's clear you were acting in self-defense when you shot your husband."

A wave of relief surged through Catherine, almost overwhelming her with its intensity. She had feared the worst, that her life would be forever altered by the split-second decisions she had been forced to make. The tears that had been threatening to spill over now welled up in her eyes, and she blinked them away, her voice trembling as she responded.

"So... does that mean I'm free to go?" she asked.

Detective Rivers nodded, his expression softening. "Yes. You're free to leave. The evidence supports your claim that you were in immediate danger and acted to protect yourself. I also wanted to share with you that, given the evidence, we've also determined that you are clear of any involvement in the accident that took the life of Melissa Legrasse. And that there will be charges filed against the men who assaulted you at your husband's behest."

Catherine's hands shook as she reached for the Styrofoam cup of water, the weight of the ordeal finally beginning to lift from her shoulders. She stood, her legs feeling weak beneath her, and faced Detective Rivers. "Thank you. I appreciate you letting me know," she said, her voice thick with emotion.

Detective Rivers gave her a reassuring smile. His eyes filled with empathy. "It's my duty to uphold the law, ma'am. No thanks are needed."

As Catherine walked out of the interrogation room, she felt a strange mixture of emotions swirling within her. Relief, but also a lingering sense of unease. She couldn't shake the memories of last night—Tom's chilling gaze, and the instinctive surge of fear that had propelled her into action. As she walked through the station to leave, she overheard several officers discussing what had taken place over the last week in Eldon, but she didn't stay to listen.

Outside the police station, the midday sun bathed the city streets in a warm glow, a stark contrast to the cold confines of the interrogation room. Catherine took a deep breath, the air filling her lungs with a newfound sense of freedom. She reached into her pocket and pulled out her phone, her fingers trembling as she pushed the button on a familiar number.

"Hello? Catherine?" came the voice on the other end of the line.

"Yeah, it's me," Catherine said, her voice still shaky. "I'm okay. They let me go."

Jessica let out a sigh of relief. "Thank God for good police officers. What did you tell them about me?"

Catherine took a deep breath. "I told them I hired you as a bodyguard. I think they accepted that answer. He told me they're making a case against the men who assaulted me, and I heard a couple of officers discussing the stuff that happened in Eldon. They've arrested the sheriff and his deputies, as well as half the town."

"That's good to hear."

"And I've officially been cleared of any wrongdoing in the accident that killed Melissa." She breathed out in relief.

"I fully expected that," Jessica replied.

"Any word about Donna and James? I haven't had time to call anyone else."

Jessica let out a sigh, and Catherine knew it wasn't good news. "I received a call from a contact at the hospital that I'd asked to keep me updated. Donna... Donna didn't make it. She passed away before the paramedics could get her to the hospital. I'm so sorry."

Catherine gasped in shock, her heart immediately filling with sorrow. "Oh no, please say that's not true. I can't believe it. Poor Donna... and James."

"I'm so sorry. I know she was your best friend, and after everything that's already happened, you're probably feeling so grief-stricken. I wish I could help. This must be a lot to take in, considering everything you've been through."

Catherine's voice wavered. "It's just... it's so much."

"I know it's overwhelming, Catherine. If you need to talk, I'm here for you," Jessica said, her voice gentle and comforting.

Catherine's voice grew quiet. "What about James? How is he holding up with all this?"

"I talked to James after I heard about Donna. He's grief-stricken too. Completely devastated. It's clear he really loved her."

"He did. He was crazy about her, and Donna was just as crazy about him," Catherine replied.

"He did want me to tell you that he's going to testify against the sheriff and all the rest of the people who were involved in the standoff and that he looked at that paperwork again, the stuff that Donna had found. It wasn't just Tom who was embezzling. Durbin and Banks were also doing some weird things. He said they were defrauding clients and basically embezzling from them."

Catherine's eyes widened. "Oh, wow, that's unexpected."

"I know," Jessica said. She exhaled in what sounded like relief. "Well, I guess we got what we wanted in the end."

"Justice for Melissa."

"And for your father, and Donna," Jessica added. "Hey, do you want me to come pick you up?"

Catherine glanced around the bustling streets, feeling strangely disconnected from the world around her. "Yeah, if you wouldn't mind? I think I need some time to rest. I'll be waiting outside the police station."

"Alright, I'll be there as soon as I can," Jessica said.

After ending the call, Catherine sat down by the tree she'd leaned on before and wondered what came next.

Catherine gathered her belongings from the home she had shared with Tom and sought the shelter of the hotel room while her previous cage of torment underwent repairs. She'd grappled with deciding whether to put the house on the market. She was torn between the comfort of her familiar surroundings and the reality that her house was no longer the haven it used to be. In the end, she decided it was best to leave her past and Eldon behind her.

She had barely settled into her hotel room when her phone rang, an unfamiliar number flashing on the screen.

Curiosity piqued, she answered the call, her voice tentative as she said, "Hello?"

"Good afternoon. Is this Catherine Morris?"

"Yes," Catherine replied. The voice on the line sounded vaguely familiar, but she couldn't place it. "May I ask who is calling?"

"This is Christina Bitterman from Channel 7 News."

Catherine's heart skipped a beat. "Hello, Ms. Bitterman. How can I help you?" Catherine replied, trying to keep her surprise from seeping into her voice.

"I hope I'm not catching you at a bad time. I wanted to reach out to you because we've been following the story of the recent conflict in Eldon and its impact on the victims. It's quite an interesting tale, and I believe our viewers would be fascinated to hear about your experience," Christina explained.

Catherine had expected the battle between Tom and his family and the police to be a big story. However, she hadn't expected her personal story to attract the attention of a news anchor. She felt a mix of excitement and nervousness, torn between the desire to share her journey and the vulnerability of putting her story out for the world to see.

"I appreciate your interest, Ms. Bitterman. It has been quite an unexpected journey," Catherine replied.

"We would be honored to have you share your story on our news program. It's not just about what happened in the town that week, but also the emotional journey you've been through —being groomed from a young age, married to the man who murdered your father, wrongly accused, framed by your husband, in fact, having to live in hiding and fighting for your life. It's a story of resilience and adaptability, something our viewers can certainly connect with," Christina explained with sincerity.

Catherine considered the offer. She thought of all the people who might go through their own challenges and how her experience could prevent something like what Tom put her through from ever happening again.

"I'm honored by your offer, Ms. Bitterman. If sharing my story can protect even one person, it's worth it," Catherine replied.

As the days stretched into weeks following the broadcast of Catherine's interview, the impact of her story continued to ripple through Cincinnati and across the nation. Catherine received messages of support from all corners of the country, reminding her that vulnerability had a way of forging powerful connections. Amidst the newfound contacts, a lingering feeling of safety settled within Catherine.

Now she sat in a comfy armchair, on the phone with Jessica. The air was filled with the aroma of freshly brewed coffee, and the sounds of cheerful birds provided a backdrop to their conversation. "You won't believe how crazy my life has become since the interview, Jessica," Catherine began, excitement in her voice.

"I can guess." Jessica laughed. "I've been watching you on TV."

Catherine took a deep breath, her eyes shining with a blend of emotions. "It's incredible, really. The interview resonated with so many people, and now I've been approached with offers for a book and even a movie deal."

Jessica's voice sounded excited. "A book and a movie? That's amazing, Catherine. You're going to be a household name."

"At least that way, I'll be able to pay you back all the money I owe you," Catherine said.

"I've told you before there's no need. But there is something I need you to do for me," said Jessica.

Catherine frowned, sensing the shift in Jessica's tone. "What is it?"

Jessica hesitated for a moment. "I know you kept my name out of things during the interviews and all, and I really appreciate it. The thing is, those offers for the book and movie—they always want to delve into every aspect of the events. They'll want more details about the people who supported you, the challenges you faced, and the emotions you went through."

Catherine's voice remained neutral, though she felt a flicker of concern. She didn't want to put Jessica in a bind of any kind. "That's probably true."

Jessica sighed. "They'll want to include me in the narrative, Catherine. They will want to portray our relationship and the role I played in supporting you during everything that happened."

A shadow crossed Catherine's face, her eyes momentarily clouded with uncertainty. "Oh, yeah, I can see that they might."

Jessica's voice softened. "I wanted to talk to you about this before you decided. You know there's been a lot of attention surrounding you and Tom, and Melissa. I just wanted to ask that you continue to keep my part in things quiet."

Catherine's fingers curled around her coffee cup as she smiled. She knew Jessica had to stay under the radar, and from everything she'd shared, Catherine knew that Jessica had always been a very private person, even before joining the military, and had never liked the spotlight. "Of course. I wouldn't dream of outing you now. I will continue to use a fake name when I describe what you did for me. You've been my guardian angel through this whole thing. I can't ever repay you for what you've done for me."

Jessica's voice was full of gratitude and respect. "Thank you for understanding, Catherine. It's not that I don't support you—you know I always will. I just can't be in the public eye, and I need to protect myself and my peace of mind."

"You and your peace of mind matter to me, Jessica. What you've done for me means more to me than any book or movie deal. I would never dream of going behind your back."

"I knew you'd get it. And I appreciate that."

Three months passed, and Catherine continued to navigate the offers that had come her way, along with the end of the court trial for the kidnapping and assault charges. The men had all pleaded not guilty but had been sentenced to ten years each. The remaining trials were still pending.

Detective Sheldon had been by quite often. They'd become good friends, and often visited each other when he wasn't busy with work. Catherine enjoyed his company, and she trusted him more than anyone else in her life these days, aside from Jessica.

One evening, as Catherine sat by her window, watching the sun dip below the horizon, her phone buzzed with a message. It was from Jessica, a text that held the weight of finality.

I wish I could tell you this in person, but they're keeping you under police supervision until the trials are over. I'm going away for a while, out of the country, and I don't know when I'll be able to get in touch with you again. I don't think you'll be needing me anymore, but if you ever do, just shoot me an email and I'll be there.

You're going to be in the spotlight and become famous. I wish you all the best in the world. You deserve it. Take care. ~ J

Catherine stood on the balcony, gazing out at the city lights. The wind rustled through her hair as Catherine whispered to the night, "Thank you, Jessica, for being a part of my journey, even if it was just for a while. I hope you find the peace and solitude you're seeking."

As Catherine looked ahead, she carried with her the lessons learned from her terrifying and unexpected journey—a journey that had not only reshaped her life but had also touched the lives of countless others who had seen themselves in her story.

She looked forward to the next step. She was finally going to college to become a therapist. She had applied to Ohio State and had gotten her admission acceptance earlier that day. Life was looking up, and she couldn't wait to face it head-on.

A LETTER FROM COLE

Dear Reader,

Thank you so much for taking the time to read *The Anniversary*. If you enjoyed it, do sign up to the following link to stay up to date with all of my future releases. Your email address will never be shared and you can unsubscribe at any time.

www.bookouture.com/cole-baxter

This story was based off an idea I had a few years ago, and a big "what-if" scenario. I hope you liked it!

If you loved *The Anniversary*, I would be very grateful if you could write a review. I'd love to hear what you think, and it makes such a difference helping new readers to discover one of my books for the first time.

I love hearing from my readers – you can get in touch with me through social media.

Thanks,

Cole Baxter

facebook.com/ColeBaxterAuthor
tiktok.com/@colebaxterauthor

PUBLISHING TEAM

Turning a manuscript into a book requires the efforts of many people. The publishing team at Bookouture would like to acknowledge everyone who contributed to this publication.

Audio
Alba Proko
Sinead O'Connor
Melissa Tran

Commercial
Lauren Morrissette
Jil Thielen
Imogen Allport

Cover design
Toby Clarke

Data and analysis
Mark Alder
Mohamed Bussuri

Editorial
Ruth Jones
Melissa Tran

Copyeditor
Laura Gerrard

Proofreader
Lynne Walker

Marketing
Alex Crow
Melanie Price
Occy Carr
Cíara Rosney

Operations and distribution
Marina Valles
Stephanie Straub

Production
Hannah Snetsinger
Mandy Kullar
Jen Shannon

Publicity
Kim Nash
Noelle Holten
Myrto Kalavrezou
Jess Readett
Sarah Hardy

Rights and contracts
Peta Nightingale
Richard King
Saidah Graham